"What is it about me that is so heartily distasteful?"

Her speech was one of hurt, but her tone was without feeling.

Perhaps there was more to his enemy's daughter than Charles had wagered. For all her steady pace and dispassionate voice, her hand trembled.

"You want my honesty," he surmised.

"Yes."

Charles hesitated. "While Lady Alice is indeed lovely, so too are you."

Lady Eleanor looked sharply up at him, her eyes wide. For all her careful hiding behind her emotionless mask, the shock on her face was a surprise.

"I do not find your hair awful." In truth, its color was vibrant and beautiful. "It is your demeanor that is unwelcome."

Lady Eleanor did not react.

"Are you sure you wish me to continue?" he asked.

She nodded. "Yes. I believe I need you to."

She was right. She did need to hear what he had to say. For her own good.

He went on. "You are cold. Polite? Yes, but you have no joie de vivre. Your delivery is without feeling. You have no...passion."

"Passion is vulgar."

"Passion is necessary."

Author Note

Thank you so much for reading *How to Tempt a Duke*. I wanted to briefly reflect on the strange marriage portrayed at Gretna Green. I've always been a fan of truth being stranger than fiction—this is one of those cases. When I researched who officiated weddings at Gretna Green in 1814, when *How to Tempt a Duke* is set, I discovered it to be Joseph Paisley. He died in 1814 and allegedly performed ceremonies while very drunk, and toward the end of his life, he even performed them from his bed. Given the time period I was writing, I had to write this into my story. I hope you enjoy this slice of strange historical fact as much as I did.

MADELINE MARTIN

—

How to Tempt a Duke

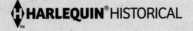

Recycling programs for this product may not exist in your area.

ISBN-13: 978-1-335-63556-3

How to Tempt a Duke

Printed in U.S.A.

Madeline Martin is a *USA TODAY* bestselling author of historical romance novels filled with twists and turns, steamy romance, empowered heroines and the men who are strong enough to love them. She lives a glitter-filled life in Jacksonville, Florida, with her two daughters (known collectively as the minions) and a man so wonderful he's been dubbed Mr. Awesome. Find out more about Madeline at her website, madelinemartin.com.

***How to Tempt a Duke* is Madeline Martin's gripping debut for Harlequin Historical!**

Visit the Author Profile page
at Harlequin.com.

To Tracy: thank you for your guidance, your encouragement and your friendship— you helped make this incredible dream come true for me.

Prologue

As reported in the *Lady Observer*, from the evening of April the fifth, 1814, the below *on-dits*—following a very detailed account of lobster patties, chilled oysters and a decadent lemon syllabub.

What is a sumptuous affair without a bit of scandal?

It all began when a certain Belle of the Season danced not only a second set with a blue-eyed earl with whom we are all acquainted, but a third. As if that were not enough for the rapacious attendees to feast upon, the Earl then took the lady's face in his hands and kissed her.

Mercy me!

Following this salacious display of affection came their official announcement of engagement, which produced a collective look of relief from the attendees. And disappointment from some, I'd wager, as there are always those who love a taste of scandal to season their tongues.

Suffice it to say the entire scene was quite riveting. Some might even say romantic.

And perhaps this Lady Observer *might agree, were it not for the other person in this tale who warrants consideration. After all, before the Belle of the Season emerged in mid-March and blossomed with the enviable beauty of a summer bloom, there was another who caught the cerulean gaze of the Earl.*

There was no mention of an engagement, this is true, but all believed there would be in time. Including the lady, no doubt.

While one cannot blame the Belle of the Season, to whom the burgeoning relationship was unknown, neither can one blame love, which strikes fast and without warning.

Regardless of where the blame lies, the tale has not ended happily for a lady who masks it so well she's earned the unfortunate moniker of Ice Queen.

She has watched the entire heartbreaking scene unfold before her dry eyes with a composure tightly reined, as if she were bored. While this only perpetuates rumors of her cold nature, one cannot help but wonder at her ability to maintain such stoicism after everything she's been through in recent years.

If her heart is truly ice, as some claim, it stands to reason that it would shatter more easily when broken...

In other observations, Lady Norrick's gown was quite the thing. So many beads adorned her dress she had to keep sitting to alleviate its pressing weight...

And on went the article, further educating those who had been unable to attend on how very fine Lady Norrick's gown was...

Chapter One

April 1814

There it was—between a cataloged detail of the lobster patties and a thorough description of Lady Norrick's ball gown lay the entire tale of Lady Eleanor Murray's most humiliating moment.

And a perpetual reminder of that blasted moniker.

Ice Queen, indeed.

Inside she was anything but ice, with untethered emotion lashing and writhing until an aching knot settled in the back of her throat.

But ladies were not to show emotion—and she was, after all, a Murray. Murrays were strong. They did not show fear. And they certainly did not concede to hurt, no matter how it twisted within one's soul.

She stared down at the crinkled page in her hands. The corners of the paper fluttered and called to attention the way she trembled.

She wanted to read the story again and wished for the usual: a detailed account of dinner, as always very thorough, told through the eyes of the *Lady Observer*, and trifling little *on-dits* that did not include her. Simple, in-effectual tales—like pointing out someone who had had two glasses of champagne instead of one, or whose reticule might have been left behind after the guests departed, followed by speculation as to why it had been left with such haste.

But the words of the story had not changed. Lady Alice had swept late into the Season, bright and beautiful and devoid of the desperation clawing at Eleanor. Every man had been drawn to her—including Hugh.

Eleanor's heart gave an ugly twinge.

Not Hugh. Lord Ledsey. She no longer held the right to address him or even think of him so informally. That right belonged to Lady Alice now. To make matters worse, Lady Alice was such a kind soul, and so lovely a person, it rendered her impossible to dislike. How very vexing.

The life Eleanor had envisioned with Hugh—summers at Ledsey Manor, the Season spent at Ledsey Place, freedom from having to plod along in the dreaded search for a suitable husband—all of it now belonged to Alice.

Eleanor's throat went tight. Dash it—she was about to cry.

A delicate knock sounded at her closed door.

She quickly shoved the paper under the pillow of her bed, blinked her eyes clear and grabbed up a book. "Enter."

The Countess of Westix swept into the room, followed by a footman carrying a large boxed parcel. Eleanor's mother indicated the dressing table with a wave of her hand and then addressed her daughter. "I'd like a word with you."

The footman obediently placed the parcel on the seat before Eleanor's dressing table and left the room, closing the door behind him.

Eleanor eyed the curious package first, and then her mother. The Countess wore a lavender evening gown sparkling with beadwork over a net of black lace. She was lovely, despite the silver in her golden hair, which had been coiffured to its usual state of perfection. There was not a wrinkle of worry or anger on her smooth face, but still Eleanor's stomach gave a familiar wrench—as it did any time her mother entered her room.

A lecture was forthcoming.

But what of the curious gift?

Her mother regarded the book Eleanor held. "What are you reading?"

"The Festival of St. Jago," Eleanor replied slowly.

Surely her mother had not come into her room to discuss her selection of literature?

The Countess tilted her head dramatically to the side. "Upside down?"

Eleanor focused on the page for the first time. It stared up at her from its flipped position. Exactly upside down.

Drat.

"Perhaps you were reading something else?"

The Countess of Westix lifted her brow in the way she always did when it was obvious she'd spotted a lie. That look had plagued Eleanor through the course of her very rigid childhood. Or at least after Evander had been sent to school, following the incident with their father, since when life had become impossibly strict.

Eleanor set the book aside with careful measure. The *Lady Observer* gave an incriminating crackle from beneath her pillow.

The Countess sat on the bed beside her daughter. "I read it, too. And I've heard the rumors—what they say about you."

Eleanor pressed a fingernail into the pad of her thumb until it hurt more than her mortification. It was a trick she'd used as a girl, when emotion threatened to overwhelm her, as though she could pinch the feeling out of herself with the sharp sensation.

She did not want to be having this abysmal conversation

with her mother, having to relive the awful moment *ad nauseam*. Hadn't the experience itself been torment enough?

"I'm proud of you, daughter. You've maintained your composure."

The Countess settled her hand on Eleanor's arm. The touch was as awkward as it was foreign. Her mother immediately drew away her cold, dry fingers and tucked the offending appendage against her waist.

"It is I who is ashamed."

The shock of those words left Eleanor speechless. Her mother was without even a modicum of impropriety.

"I did not have a good marriage with your father, God rest his soul." The Countess regarded Eleanor with a cool look. "He came from a strong clan before his family was elevated to the English nobility. It was his belief that all emotion was weakness, indicative of one who was base-born, and his family had worked too hard to climb high to be considered common. Murrays are strong. They do not show fear."

Eleanor bit back a bitter smile. She knew those words well and had spent a lifetime listening to them being recited. After all, she knew the story well enough. Her father had not allowed any of the *ton* to look down on them for being Scottish, for not having been members of the nobility since the dawn of time.

"I gave up a piece of myself when I married your father," said her mother. "I didn't realize..." Her eyes became glossy. She pursed her lips and gave a long, slow blink before resuming. "I didn't realize I would be making my children give a piece of themselves away as well."

This show of such emotion left Eleanor wanting to squirm on the bed with discomfort. This was immediately followed by a shade of guilt. After all, her mother was voluntarily peeling back a layer of herself to offer a rare peek within, and Eleanor could think of nothing but her own uncertainty on how to handle this foreign and precarious moment.

Her mother rose abruptly, alleviating the uncomfortable tension between them. "I aided in the suppressing of your feelings until you were rendered emotionless…cold. I did not see that until this incident." She sighed and the rigid set to her shoulders sagged slightly. "I'm sorry, daughter. And I will right that wrong tonight." She strode to the box and pulled off the cover.

Eleanor slid off the bed and peered into the opened parcel. Nestled within was a length of folded black silk.

"It's a domino and mask." The Countess gracefully scooped a black silk mask from the box. "There's a wig as well. To protect your identity."

To cover her hair. Of course. Anyone seeing the garish splash of red would immediately know Eleanor's identity. The color had come from her father and it certainly had not offered Eleanor any favors. Not like her mother's green eyes, which Eleanor was grateful to have inherited.

Eleanor stared down at the pile of black silk and her heartbeat gave a little trip. "Where am I to go that I should need a disguise?"

"I've paid a courtesan to teach you what I cannot."

Eleanor jerked her gaze to her mother in absolute horror.

"Oh, she wasn't always a courtesan," the Countess replied. "She'd once been a sweet vicar's daughter, which is how she is known to me. Difficult times do harsh things to women who have no other options." She pressed her lips together in a reverent pause. "The woman is discreet, and she will teach you to be more genuine, more receptive. Less like me. I don't want you to have a cold marriage or an austere life, in which every detail is perpetually calculated." The mask trembled in her mother's loose hold. "It's been so long since I've allowed myself to soften I fear I would be a poor tutor."

She pushed the mask into Eleanor's hands.

Her fingers closed around the silk without thought. "A courtesan?" she gasped. "I'll be ruined. *You'll* be ruined."

Her mother leveled her with a look. "Your father is dead, your brother is missing, I am getting old, and you are already two and twenty. The Season is halfway over and your one prospect has found another woman. You do know that if Evander is gone three more years he'll be declared dead and your cousin will inherit everything?"

Eleanor's thoughts flinched from the mention of her brother. It ached too much to think of his absence. He had left four years ago, to seek the adventure his father, the previous Earl of Westix, had once relished. In a world of turmoil and war, his prolonged absence gave them all cause for concern. Not that they had relinquished hope. Not yet, at least. But that did not mean they did not worry.

Her mother was correct in her harsh assessment. Eleanor's prospects were bleak.

The Countess was also correct regarding Eleanor's cousin, Leopold. He was a rapacious young popinjay, with an eye on Evander's title and any wealth he could squander on eccentric clothing and weighted gambling tables. Eleanor would get little from him before he managed to consume it all.

"Perhaps next Season will be better," Eleanor said. "I know I'm already nearly on the shelf, but—"

"There isn't money for another Season." Her mother pressed a hand to the flat of her stomach, just below her breasts, and drew in a staying breath. "Your father spent it traipsing around the world. Evander didn't leave to follow in his path—he left to repair it. To save us from financial ruin."

Eleanor maintained her composure—a near impossible feat when the world seemed to have tipped out from underneath her. "I didn't know…"

"I wouldn't have expected you to. It's not information I would have willingly shared. At least your father had the forethought to establish a trust in my name after we were wed. Which is why you've had the Seasons you've had so far."

The confident tilt of her mother's head lowered a fraction of an inch. Weariness etched lines on her face, and for the first time in Eleanor's life her mother appeared truly old.

Their situation was indeed dire.

Eleanor unfurled her fingers and regarded the mask crumpled against her damp palm.

"This may be your only chance, Eleanor," the Countess said. "Learn how to be less cold, how to appear more welcoming. Dispel the rumors and rise above the label they've placed upon you. Be in charge of your own destiny."

Her mother touched her face with icy fingertips. Eleanor did not pull away, but instead met the anxiety in her mother's stare.

The Countess's brow creased. "I want a better life for you."

Eleanor's heart pounded very fast. Surely her cheeks were red with the effort of it? "Do you trust her, Mother?"

The Countess of Westix nodded resolutely. "I do."

"Then so shall I." A tremor of fear threatened to clamber up Eleanor's spine, but she willed it away. "When do I start?"

The Countess turned to the window, where the sky beyond had grown dark. "Tonight."

Charles Pemberton was the new Duke of Somersville. The news was unwelcome, for it meant that in the six months it had taken him to return to London his father had died.

He stood by the desk in the library within the massive

structure of Somersville House, his father's letter clutched limply between his fingertips.

It did not feel right to sit at the desk, when for so many decades it had been the previous Duke of Somersville who had resided behind the great expanse of polished mahogany. The entire room had been off-limits to Charles for the majority of his life, and it left everything within him feeling too hard, too desolately foreign, to offer any comfort.

Charles regarded the letter once more. Not the one which had taken months to reach him where he had been exploring in a remote location on the outskirts of Egypt. That one had informed him that he must return home immediately. No, he held the letter which reminded him of a promise made—a promise woefully unfulfilled.

Rain pattered on the windowpanes outside, filling the room with an empty, bleak drumming. It was fitting, really, as it mirrored the torrent raging through him. His father had been the biggest part of his life—the reason Charles had sought to travel from the first. To witness the wonders of the world which had made his father so much larger than life in his eyes. To make his father proud of him for the first time in Charles's life.

And now the Duke was dead.

Ridiculous that the notion still had not thoroughly soaked into Charles's mind. Or perhaps it was his own guilt which prevented it. After all, he'd vowed when he'd left for his Grand Tour that he'd seek out the Coeur de Feu—the renowned ruby stolen from a French collector in the mid-sixteen-hundreds. It was said to be the size of a man's fist and to burn with a fire at its core—hence its name: the heart of fire.

It was the one artifact that had eluded his father, and therefore the one with which the previous Duke had become obsessed. It had been Charles's intention to seek out the stone, but he'd been so busy in the last years, experiencing new cultures, learning from the people there and their way of life. Time had seemed limitless and his father had seemed immortal.

Charles's legs were too heavy to keep him standing, and yet still he could not bring himself to rest in his father's cold chair. The grand home and all its fine furnishings might belong to Charles now, but he very much felt a stranger among his father's effects rather than their new owner. His new title fitted as uncomfortably as did the rest of his inheritance.

He looked down at the letter, which his father had left for Charles to read upon his return to London. It had been hastily written before the Duke's death and was crumpled from where it had been found, clutched in his fist. Even to look at it wrenched at Charles. He hadn't been there for the funeral. He hadn't been there to say goodbye.

The note was not filled with lamentations of time lost or proclamations of affection for Charles, who was his only living child. No, the letter contained only one scrawled line.

Find the journal and use the key to locate the Coeur de Feu.

Of course. The Coeur de Feu. Charles's greatest failure.

"The key" was a flat bit of metal the size of a book, with twenty-five small squares cut into it. The Adventure Club insignia had been stamped into the bottom right corner, indicating the key's proper direction for use. Its size matched perfectly with the various journals his father had had in his possession, all embossed with a gilt compass—the insignia of the Adventure Club.

The club had been started by his father and the Earl of Westix, and other members of the *ton*, several decades prior.

Charles had, of course, tried fitting the key into the journals. While the size of the metal piece matched perfectly with the books, it did not reveal anything more than garbled letters. Charles had tried to scramble the random offerings, rearrange them and put them together again. Yet none of his attempts created successful words—at least none that made any sense.

"Your Grace…" A voice sounded on the edges of Charles's thoughts.

Charles braced his fingertips over the desk atop one of the books, lest he leave prints on the polished surface. His father had always hated fingerprints on things.

"Your Grace?" the voice said again.

Perhaps the journals the late Duke referred to in his note were not within this collection. Westix had a stash, after all. Charles had been present and had seen his father's objections on how the artifacts had been split after the final venture of the Adventure Club fifteen years before—specifically the ownership of important artifacts and documents.

"My Lord," the voice snapped.

Charles turned in response to the familiar form of address. His valet, Thomas, was at his side with a parchment extended.

"With all due respect, Your Grace, you *are* Your Grace now."

Thomas was ever the loyal companion. The man had traveled around the world with Charles, never once complaining, no matter how dismal the conditions. And they had indeed been dismal at times.

Regardless, Thomas always managed a smile and a pot of warm water for a proper shave. And so it was that Charles knew his valet was not being disrespectful in issuing the gentle reminder.

Charles nodded appreciatively. "Yes. Correct."

A roll of thunder rattled the windows. Thomas cast a

disparaging look outside. "It would appear that Miss Charlotte is in town and she asks that you join her at her home immediately. Her servant also bade me give you this."

"Miss Charlotte? Lottie?" Charles asked with a note of surprise.

Thomas lifted a brow and handed the parchment to Charles. "Yes, Your Grace. She is apparently most eager to speak with you."

Charles unfolded the parchment and glanced at the letter.

Don't say no, Charles.

He couldn't help but smile at that. How very like Lottie. She always had been bold with her requests, even when they were children. It seemed like a lifetime since he'd last seen little Charlotte Rossington, the vicar's daughter from his local church near Somersville Manor. They'd grown up together, and had held a platonic fondness for one another ever since.

She'd grown into a beautiful woman, with dark hair and flashing blue eyes, and was so similar in coloring to him that people sometimes confused them as brother and sister. They'd been close enough to be siblings.

He hadn't seen her since just before he'd left for his Grand Tour. There would be much to catch up on. By his estimation, and with his knowledge of her sweet, charming nature, she was most likely married with the brood of children she'd always wanted.

The night was abysmal, but even the storm was preferable to a dreary house filled with ghosts and failed promises.

Charles folded the note. "Have the carriage readied, Thomas."

He smirked to himself as his valet departed. It truly had been far too long since Charles had seen Lottie.

Chapter Two

It had indeed been a considerable amount of time since Charles had seen Lottie. He nearly did not recognize the sultry woman standing before him in the sumptuously decorated drawing room. It was too finely appointed for a vicar's daughter—as was her tightly fitted gown of deep red silk far too tawdry. Especially when compared to the modest high-necked gown he'd last seen her in.

Gone was the wide-eyed innocence of her smoky blue eyes, and in its place was a smoldering vixen with a length of midnight curls tumbling over one nearly naked shoulder. A courtesan.

Charles stared a moment longer than was polite while the five years stretched out in the silence between them. Her fingers twisted against one another at her waist—a childhood show of nerves even her new guise could not mask.

"I'm sorry about your father."

"I'm sorry about *you*," he replied.

Lottie winced and looked away. "I didn't have a choice, Charles. There is no choice when your father dies and leaves you destitute."

Charles shifted his weight. The crisp new Hessians he wore pinched at his feet, and the slight discomfort was nearly unbearable when coupled with such agitation. "You could have wed."

Lottie's chest swelled and those damn fingers of hers started twisting again. "I could not."

"What *is* this prattle?" Charles paced over the thick carpet. "Lottie, you're lovely. You've always had the attention of men. How could you not find a husband?"

"I didn't say I couldn't find one."

"If you could find a husband why would you not—" Comprehension washed over him like cold rain.

Lottie scoffed at his apparent consternation. "*Now* you understand."

Oh, he understood.

Lottie had been compromised.

The little girl who had tagged along behind him until he had finally allowed her to join him at play. The girl he had regarded with the same undying affection one would a younger, more vulnerable sister. And some rake had ruined her.

"Who is the scoundrel?" he growled.

"No one I'll ever confess to you." She strode across the room, away from him. But not before he saw the hopeless misery in her eyes.

She still loved the man.

Charles followed her. "Why didn't you ask me for help?"

She drew a bottle of amber liquid from a shelf and pulled free the stopper. "Even if I could have found a way to contact you I have never been one for charity." She splashed a finger of liquor into a cut-crystal glass and pushed it into his hand.

He accepted the drink and took a long sip. Scotch. Very fine Scotch. "It wouldn't have been charity," he protested.

She regarded him with quiet bemusement. "Oh? And what, pray tell, would it have been?"

"Securing a future for you."

A sad smile plucked at the corners of her mouth. "I'm not your responsibility, Charles."

He settled his palm on her shoulder, the same way he'd done when she was a girl and had needed comfort: when her kitten had scaled a tree too high for her to climb, the time she'd skinned her knee and torn a new gown, the day her mother had died. He'd always been there for her.

Except, apparently, when she'd needed him most.

"You know I've always regarded you as a sister. I've always cared for you as if you were."

"But I'm not your sister." She waved him off. "You're going to make me cry with all that."

Indeed, her nose had gone rather red. She poured a second glass of Scotch and carried it over to a chaise, where she settled comfortably.

"I tried the opera first. I did well there, and…and offers began."

Charles took the seat opposite her and swallowed the rest of his Scotch at the word "offers."

Lottie pulled at a corner of the window coverings and peered into the darkness. "I resisted at first, of course," she continued. "But the expense of such a life was more than the income it generated. After a while, I couldn't refuse."

Charles stared into the bottom of his empty glass and savored the burn trailing down his insides, pushing past his heart and splashing into his gut.

"This is far grander than I've ever lived before." She indicated the room.

It was indeed fine. The dark wood furniture was polished to a shine, the walls were covered with a luxurious red silk, the floors layered with soft carpets.

"You intend to continue in this…this occupation for a while?" he asked.

She leaned toward the window and glanced out once

more. "No. At least I have the hope not to. Which is part of the reason I've called you here."

"What the devil are you looking for out there?" He got to his feet and glanced out the window to the quiet street below.

"A new opportunity." She beamed up at him and traded his empty glass with her full one.

A warning prickled along the back of Charles's neck. "I don't know what scheme you're up to, but please presume I'll want no part of it."

Lottie crinkled her nose and laughed, reminding him all too well of the girl she'd been.

"Nothing like that. Oh, Charles, you do know how to make me laugh."

She shook her head and the length of midnight curls swished against the disconcerting swell of her nearly exposed bosom.

"I'm waiting for a countess's daughter to arrive. A young lady who has fallen on rather unfortunate times. I'm to instruct her in the art of flirtation."

Charles eyed Lottie skeptically.

She put her fingertips to the bottom of his glass and lifted it higher, toward his mouth. "I could use the help of a gentleman," she said. "It would do well for her to have someone to practice on."

The glass was to his lips now, but he resisted and pulled his face away. "There's something you're not telling me."

"Plying you with drink isn't going to work, I take it?"

She gave a little mock pout he'd never seen before. The type of expression made by a petulant mistress rather than a well-mannered vicar's daughter.

He didn't like it.

"I think you know me better than that."

"Very well." Lottie lowered her hands and freed his glass. "She's the daughter of the Earl of Westix."

Charles lifted the Scotch to his lips once more. Of his own volition. And drank.

The Earl of Westix.

The Adventure Club would never have disbanded had it not been for the Earl. Charles's father would still have all the journals and would have been able to find the Coeur de Feu on his own had it not been for the Earl. Charles would never have been such a disappointment in failing to fulfill that one final wish.

And Lottie knew all of this. She knew, and yet she still asked for Charles to aid one of Westix's whelps.

"Oh, dear," Lottie said with a frown. "You're turning quite red about the face."

"Why would you presume I would be willing to help any offspring of that devil?"

"The lady has had quite the time of it." Lottie lifted her forefinger. "First her father died, some years ago, then her brother vanished, and now the man who had been courting her has proposed to another."

She held out her three extended fingers, as if the physical demonstration might alter his wits. Her pinky came up, bringing the total count to four.

"And because every woman deserves a second chance."

The latter was expressed so solemnly Charles knew Lottie was not only referring to Westix's daughter but to herself. No doubt she was aware that the best way to win his acquiescence was through staggering guilt.

She knew him too damn well.

"Just imagine it, Charles." She sat upright. "If there is one countess willing to pay for her daughter's education—the kind that cannot be obtained at any reputable institution—there will be more. Every mother wants her daughter to be desirable and to wed. Who better to teach such subtle seductions than a courtesan? I could even educate married women on the pleasures to be had in the bedroom—"

"Enough," Charles ground out. "For the love of every sacred saint, please cease this talk of intimacy."

He set his glass down and paced about the room, all too aware of Lottie's anxious stare. Helping her would be a betrayal of his father's trust, and hadn't he already failed him enough?

Charles's head snapped up as an idea struck him. But if he aided this Westix chit, perhaps she might be so grateful for his assistance she would assist him in locating the lost journals.

From her watchful perch, Lottie straightened in anticipation.

"I'll assist you," Charles said at last. "However, I'll do so on one condition."

She tilted her head in silent inquiry.

"You put on a shawl."

She rolled her eyes playfully. "Very well." She peered out the window and beamed victoriously up at him. "And your timing is perfect. She's just arrived."

Eleanor awaited her fate alone. She had been divested of her domino, wig and mask—all taken by the footman. Without the shield of those items she was left feeling exposed in her precarious surroundings, and far too vulnerable.

The double doors of the drawing room were closed and oil lamps cast a flickering golden light. A harp sat in the corner, its shadow stretching over the thick Brussels weave carpet like a great beast stretching for her. Childish fear nipped at her and left her with the urgent desire to lift her feet from the floor, lest it make a grab at her.

A glass of sherry sat in open invitation on an elegantly carved table beside the chair. If it hadn't been for the bust of a woman with her breasts thrust out that was set behind it, Eleanor might have accepted the proffered indulgence.

But, while she appreciated the consideration, she was quite certain she could manage her nerves well enough on her own without the aid of alcohol. In fact, she knew she could. Murrays, after all, were strong.

The double doors parted and a woman with tumbling curls of dark hair appeared. A crimson gown hugged her trim figure and a black lace shawl lay over the swell of her generous bust, lending her a far more decent appearance than Eleanor had expected.

"I am Lottie."

Her voice was as smooth and sensual as her face—the kind which left other women with a disquieted sense of inadequacy. Was it any wonder men paid for her time?

Eleanor hid the discomfiting thought behind a tight nod and had opened her mouth to speak when a tall man entered the room.

The low lamplight gleamed off his dark hair and shadowed his sharp jaw. His skin appeared golden beside the porcelain fairness of Lottie's, as if he'd spent much time in the sun. The brilliant blue of his eyes practically glowed against his gilded skin.

He was, by anyone's estimation, an extraordinarily handsome man.

Eleanor stiffened. "I was not told that a man would take part in my lessons."

Lottie smiled easily. "Darling, how would you learn to properly converse with a man if you hadn't anyone to practice on? Your mother knew it was a possibility and she trusts me." She regarded the man. "And I trust him."

He returned Eleanor's curious stare with a nonchalance so casual she felt foolish for voicing her fears.

"What is his name?" She spoke with equal indifference, as though she was entirely unfeeling. Except that she wasn't. Her insides trembled like set jelly and her bones ached from the rigidity of her muscles. "We haven't been introduced."

"I will allow my introduction when you permit yours."

The man's voice was deep and smooth. Eleanor lifted her chin a notch, uncertain if his response was meant in flirtation or insolence. Regardless, she wouldn't deign to reply. She had not come here to be mocked.

"This is a prime example of why I've employed his assistance."

Lottie threaded her hand through the crook of the man's elbow and drew him closer. He appeared to hesitate before Lottie gave him a firm tug.

"One can never anticipate what another will say." She gazed up at him pointedly. "He'll add a level of spontaneity to our lessons. And, I assure you, flirting with *me* for practice will be nowhere near as exciting as with him."

"Ladies don't flirt."

Eleanor's gaze flicked to the man as he was led closer. He was tall, his chest broad and his waist and hips narrow where his breeches encased his strong thighs. Heat touched Eleanor's cheeks, and something deep inside bade her to stand and raise herself to her full height, to meet whatever challenge his presence had thrown at her feet.

"Oh, but they do," Lottie said in a softly chiding tone. "It's slight, mind you. A subtle play of words slipping between two people as if it were a language only they knew."

Lottie was right, of course. Both about flirtation and about the subtlety of it, like a carefully memorized dance. Eleanor had done it with Hugh. Twice. Both times had been immediately followed by a rush of heady excitement.

And wasn't she the fool for having permitted herself to be so audacious?

Her heart flinched, the way it always did when she considered those rare quiet moments with Hugh. Lord Ledsey.

"This will proceed more smoothly if you are honest

with yourself and with me." Lottie kept her voice kind, taking the edge from the words. "There are things ladies are not supposed to do and yet still actually do—with finesse, mind you. I think we can both agree that flirtation falls within that category."

Eleanor's palms were sweating within the confines of her gloves. She wanted to run from the room, rip them from her hands and let the cold air wash over her hot skin. But she had been raised to be stronger than that.

"I'm amenable to that consideration."

"Excellent." Lottie's easy smile returned.

But it wasn't excellent. Not at all. The room was too dark, the walls too close, the expectation placed on Eleanor far too great. However, for all she did not wish to be at Lottie's town house, receiving this instruction, she was, at her core, a Murray—and Murrays did not show fear. Even when they tasted the metal of it in their mouths and were subjected to the tingling of it up their spines.

She would do this, attract a suitable husband, and then she would pretend as though it had never happened. She peeked at the man once more—a curious thing her eyes kept doing. Did he *have* to be so very handsome? And did he have to stare at her so unabashedly?

"The sherry is for you," Lottie pointed out. "If you'd like it for your nerves."

While tempted, Eleanor feared reaching for the glass might result in her brushing one of those marbled breasts gleaming in the lamplight. No, she would hold firm to her original resolve.

"Thank you, I'm fine."

Lottie clasped her naked hands together. "In that case, let us begin."

Chapter Three

Charles found the Westix chit prettier than he'd expected. Her hair was the same brilliant red as her father's, her eyes pale. Though whether they were green or blue or some color in between was imperceptible in the muted light. She was fair, her skin a lovely porcelain-white, and her back was so straight that looking at such rigidity made his shoulders ache.

It was evident she was attempting to appear brave, but he knew that all Murrays at their core were cowards. No matter how this woman tried to play it, she was exactly the same as her father.

"Let us start with introductions."

Lottie released Charles's arm and beckoned him. He stepped closer, the obedient dog in this ridiculous dance.

The delicate muscles of Lady Eleanor's neck stood out and a heavy awkwardness settled over the room.

"If he frightens you, I can send him away." Lottie spoke in the same careful tone she'd used with the parishioners a lifetime ago.

Dear God, he wished Lady Eleanor would confess her fear and he could leave. He ground his teeth. Except there were the journals, of course—the reason he'd agreed to this damned fool of a scheme. He needed her to like him.

Lady Eleanor stood abruptly, reaching the impressive height of Charles's chin. She tilted her face upward and peered boldly up at him. Green. Her eyes were green. And wide and attentive with a feline intensity.

"I am not so easily discouraged."

Conviction laced her words, but the gentle flaring of her nostrils told a different tale. She was indeed scared. In truth, how could she not be put off by such a bizarre scenario as the one they all found themselves thrown into? At least the girl had sense.

She stood close enough that the tip of one satin slipper touched the shiny toe of his boot, and her soft breath whispered over his chin with every exhalation. The sweet scent of jasmine floated around him. It was delicate and feminine, and seemed almost too gentle for the woman in front of him.

In truth, they were improperly close—as if the scene was not already indecent enough, with a lady of her breeding meeting a woman of Lottie's—

He couldn't finish the thought.

Yes, Lottie was a courtesan, but he could not consider her as such. Not when to him she'd always been just sweet and gentle Lottie. A woman now forced to bow and scrape to this spoiled brat.

"You needn't be alarmed." Lottie carefully drew Lady Eleanor back to a more respectful distance. "We do not intend you harm or ruination. We want to help—which is why I agreed to work with you. And…" Lottie indicated Charles. "It is why Lord Charles is here as well."

If Lady Eleanor hadn't been watching him so intently he would have given Lottie a curious look. She doubtless had her reasons for lying about his real title, and if her intention had been to set Lady Eleanor at ease, her effort proved successful. Lady Eleanor's shoulders lowered a notch and she nodded to Lottie.

"I should like to present Lady Eleanor," Lottie said grandly.

"I'm pleased to meet you."

Lady Eleanor's cool tone diffused the warmth of the greeting. Indeed, she appeared anything but pleased.

"I'd like to believe you mean that," Charles said, before he could stop himself.

Lottie shot him a hard look. Lady Eleanor met his gaze, brazen and without charm. "Perhaps that's why my mother has risked our reputations for my tutelage."

"He doesn't know the details of why you're here," Lottie said. "I should have explained it, but I—"

Lady Eleanor put up a hand to stop her.

"You must not have been long in London if you haven't yet read of the infamous Ice Queen." Lady Eleanor's brow quirked on an otherwise expressionless face. "A woman on the edge of spinsterhood, who lost her one chance at a proposal of marriage by the very coolness of her demeanor." Her eyes glinted like hard emeralds. "My mother has sent me here as she believes having Lottie teach me to flirt and project myself as being more genuine will dispel the rumors of my unaffected disposition."

"And what do *you* think?" Charles asked, his curiosity slightly piqued.

"I'm skeptical." Her reply came without hesitation.

Behind her, Lottie pursed her lips.

"Skeptical that you can be taught?" he prompted.

Lady Eleanor gave a tight smirk. "That it will have much impact. I must overcome preconceived notions sufficiently to entice a man to seek my hand in marriage. All in…" Her head tilted in apparent mental calculation. "All in the better part of two months."

Time was most certainly not in her favor. The woman was practical in her assessment.

"Does it matter who is on the other side of that proposal?" Charles studied her as he spoke, to see if she even bothered to flush at his statement. She did not.

"Women do not have the luxury of time and choice, as men do."

It was a simple reply, but it was the truth. Charles knew he had his own ducal obligations to tend to, but he did have time. Even if it took several years he could find the ruby, return to London and still acquire a wife within weeks of his arrival. Days, if necessary.

"Then we ought to get to work, oughtn't we?" Lottie stepped closer between them. "First, I'd like to observe how you comport yourself when introduced. Properly."

She regarded the Westix brat.

"Lady Eleanor, think of making eye contact and trying to look sincerely happy to meet Lord Charles."

Lady Eleanor shifted her weight from one foot to the other in reply. Clearly she was anything but happy to meet him. The feeling was mutual.

Lottie ignored the subtle display of sullen defiance. "Lady Eleanor, may I introduce Lord Charles?"

Lady Eleanor's gaze met his and raked into his soul. There was something in the way she gazed into his eyes, unapologetic and resolute. Not at all like the demure ladies of the *ton* he'd grown used to when he'd last lived in London. No wonder she put people off.

Lady Eleanor extended her hand, which Charles accepted and bowed over, kissing the air just above the knuckles of her white kidskin gloves.

When he straightened, she offered a stiff nod and said, "I'm pleased to meet you."

Her speech and manners were immaculate. Everything was as expected in polite society, except perhaps her bold stare.

Lottie nodded to herself. "Good. Proper." She put her finger to her lower lip. "But without feeling."

"I assumed feelings were not necessary with strangers," Lady Eleanor countered.

"They are when you want to encourage strangers to-ward matrimony." Lottie indicated Charles. "Let your eyes linger on his, but try not to be too direct, and give a smile when you say it's a pleasure to meet him. Convince him. He should believe everything you say." Lottie swirled her finger in the air and said, in perfectly accented French, *"Allez, on recommence."*

Charles bit back a groan. They might very well be there until morning.

"We'll be doing this all night, I presume?" Lady Eleanor's tone was not enthusiastic. "Being introduced *ad nauseam* until one of us finally pleads for mercy?"

"It will be me," Charles volunteered with a wink. If he was going to win her over and get those journals, a sense of camaraderie might go a long way.

She shot him a bland look in response, before turning her gaze to Lottie. "This is entirely ridiculous. I won't meet the same man over and over. It will not improve the poor image that most of the *ton* has of me, and nor will it change their minds. Call for my carriage." She closed her eyes, as if the act pained her. When she opened her eyes once more, her composure was fully restored. "Please."

"May I ask if there is something keeping you from this?" Lottie inquired. "Something you are afraid of?"

"I am afraid of nothing," Lady Eleanor stated firmly.

Lottie's brow pinched and she opened her mouth. But rather than offer a protest, she nodded and slipped from the room in a whisper of costly silk. A blanket of uncomfortable silence fell over the room and smothered any sense of companionship.

"You said you were skeptical." Charles lifted the glass of untouched sherry and drained it, needing the drink far more than she. Its sweetness followed the burn of alcohol and clung cloyingly on his tongue. "Perhaps you meant pessimistic?"

She eyed him warily and backed away, clearly aware of the inappropriateness of their being alone together. "Because I'm not playing along with this preposterous charade?" she asked.

"Because you're too afraid to even give it a chance." He didn't know if he was attempting to aid Lottie with this goading, or if he was doing it out of malice. Perhaps a bit of both.

Her gloved hands fingered the fabric of her skirt. "This is…abnormal."

While he agreed, he was not about to confess as much. He was, after all, there to aid Lottie. And if the chit left now he wouldn't have the opportunity to get the journals.

"I've learned that being unconventional often delivers stronger results than what is common," he said. "You came here because you want to prove everyone wrong. Why are you letting them be proved correct?"

The muscles along her slender throat tensed. "I came here because I have no choice."

Lottie entered the room with a man trailing behind her. "Your carriage is here. Ferdinand will see you out."

Lady Eleanor turned her attention from Charles and allowed the footman to help her don an absurd blonde wig, as well as a mask and black domino.

Lottie did not move from her path. "I do hope you'll reconsider."

Lady Eleanor gave Lottie a slow nod. Without another word, the Earl of Westix's daughter followed Ferdinand from the room.

Lottie's composure drained away and she sank onto the settee. "Well, that was an utter failure."

Charles watched the empty hallway where Lady Eleanor had disappeared. "I confess I fail to feel sympathy toward her—especially when she doesn't appear to find any fault with her current demeanor."

Lottie peeked at him through a curtain of dark hair. "You weren't exactly welcoming. What happened to the charming Charles I once knew?"

Her words made Charles wince. He hadn't meant his prejudice against Lady Eleanor to be so obvious. "Apparently we've all changed."

Lottie pressed her lips together rather than give him the cutting reply he deserved. "Will you try to speak with her?" She gazed up at him, her expression imploring. "I cannot, but surely you can. I know she walks in Hyde Park with her mother often."

It was on the tip of Charles's tongue to decline—to end this foolish charade. But once more the thought of the journals swam into his mind. Damn it. Not just the journals, but finding a way to assist Lottie.

He hated seeing her like this, catering to the rich with every part of herself. She didn't deserve this life.

"I'll consider it," he offered grudgingly.

Though in truth he'd already made up his mind. While he might hold contempt for Westix, and his whole blasted family, Lady Eleanor was the key to righting his great failure.

Nothing could ruin a lovely day in Hyde Park for Eleanor like unpleasant conversation. And truly there was no worse conversation than the general nagging of one's mother.

The Countess's face was hidden by an extraordinarily large white bonnet. Not that Eleanor needed to see her mother's face to know she was disappointed. The clipped tone of her voice provided all the evidence necessary.

"Will you not go again tonight?"

Eleanor wanted to cover her ears rather than endure her mother's tedious inquiry once more. She slid a glance behind them to her maid, Amelia, who knew well of the arrangement. After all, it was she who had aided Eleanor in her disguise the two days prior.

"The one lesson was enough, I assure you."

Eleanor kept to the left of the path to ensure her mother stayed in the shade. While the stroll did wonders for her mother's digestion, the late-afternoon sun wreaked havoc on her headaches.

The Countess made a sound of disagreement. Then she turned the expanse of her bonnet toward Eleanor and regarded her daughter with careful scrutiny. "Tell me again why it was so awful?"

Eleanor waited for a woman in a butter-yellow dress to pass before answering. "It was…uncomfortable…and odd. She wanted me to pretend to be introduced to a man there several times."

Her mother's face did not offer any conveyance of sympathy, or even shock that a man had been involved. Eleanor suppressed a sigh. She would have no support from her mother.

"Then you are happy to resign yourself to the fate of being a spinster?" Her mother's face had flushed a brilliant red. She snapped open her fan and waved it in front of her face to diffuse the onset of heat she'd been suffering from of late. "And you're happy with being relegated to the position of poor relation once Leopold has what little remains of our fortune?"

Eleanor had practiced the art of emotionless disinterest for so long it came naturally. Even still, at the mention of Leopold's name she found herself having to concentrate to keep from letting her expression crumple in censure.

"And what of love?" her mother asked.

"Love." Eleanor said the word as flatly as she felt the emotion was. She had never, after all, truly believed in it. "You've always said love is for fools and fiction."

Her mother stopped fanning herself. "You should toss aside all I've ever taught you. It will bring you naught but misery." Her gaze slid to the path behind Eleanor. "Speaking of misery…"

Eleanor turned to find a couple walking toward them. The two were leaning close to one another, deep in conversation. She'd recognize the man's wavy brown hair and bold nose anywhere. Hugh and his blonde-haired, perfectly beautiful betrothed, Lady Alice.

Eleanor's heart gave a turbulent knock against her ribs. If love really was for fools and fiction, then surely Hugh and Lady Alice were the biggest fools of all. And as Eleanor felt a pang of envy at such closeness, what did that make her?

The sun shone at their backs and lit them in a halo of gold. It obviously wasn't bad enough that their faces were glowing—their bodies had to as well.

They neared, and the knock at her ribs turned into a steady banging. She prayed heartily that they might continue to walk by without notice. She did not want added humiliation on a day already gone awry.

The couple slowed as they neared Eleanor and her mother.

Please pass by.

But, unfortunately, they did not pass by.

No, they stopped, and Lady Alice turned the lovely force of her open smile on Eleanor and her mother. If nothing else, Eleanor hoped that perhaps there might be some snideness to Lady Alice's tone—some nasty upturn to her mouth or a disagreeable conversation which would sanction a justifiable dislike of her.

"Oh, Your Ladyship, Lady Eleanor—it's so good to see you," Lady Alice said with delicate and authentic pleasure. "Lady Eleanor, your bonnet suits you so very well. Isn't it the loveliest day you've ever seen?"

The expression on Lady Alice's face was sweet enough to bring to mind visions of angels. She even paused to offer a smile for Amelia.

Eleanor inwardly sighed. Of course she would not be lucky enough to find fault with Lady Alice, who was, as she'd always been, agreeable, kind and absolutely perfect.

And she was right. It *was* a fine day. Even with Eleanor's stolen future standing so happily in front of her she could not deny the beauty of the day.

"It truly is lovely," she conceded.

"Good day, Lord Ledsey." The Countess of Westix's tone was cool in her address to Hugh.

Don't look at him.

If he replied to her mother Eleanor did not hear him. She intentionally gazed in the direction of the Serpentine River, where Lady Alice was looking with a wistful expression. The water glittered under the sun and reflected the wide stretch of the cloudless sky. A weak breeze swept from the river and brushed away some of the heat from Eleanor's blazing cheeks.

She would stare at the Serpentine for ages. Anything to avoid looking at Hugh. But, dash it, her traitorous eyes immediately disobeyed the direct order and slid over to the face which she'd one day anticipated being that of her husband. An ache began in the center of her chest, where her heart was still raw and wounded. She kept her smile small, for it felt brittle enough to crack if given too much effort.

Her mother had been so proud of Eleanor when Hugh had directed his affections toward her, and the pressure of the *ton* had eased from her shoulders. Lady Eleanor, with her garish red hair, had finally found a man who might be willing to wed her.

Except he had not been willing. And his newfound affection for Lady Alice had left her scalded with mortification. Eleanor should have expected such fickleness after his intentions toward her had come upon her so abruptly. At the time she had been too grateful to think on it.

She was not grateful any longer.

Hugh looked at Eleanor—a momentary flick of a glance, as if she were not worth his time. And when he had a woman such as Lady Alice on his arm surely she was not.

It was at times like this that Eleanor was thankful for her father's insistence that she never show emotion. Because at times like this Eleanor agreed that one must appear strong. She wore her indifference like a shield, staunchly guarding her wounds from prying eyes.

Hugh's hand came up suddenly and waved at a man several paces away. "Ah, here he is now."

Lady Alice gave an excited clap. "Oh, wonderful—he's made it after all."

The man stopped between Eleanor and Lady Alice. He was tall enough to block the sun from where it shone into Eleanor's eyes, but not so tall that she had to peer up at him foolishly. His hazel-green eyes crinkled nicely at the corners.

Hugh clapped the man on the back. "This chap went to school with me several years back. May I introduce the Marquess of Bastionbury?"

A part of Eleanor—a sad, pathetic part—perked up at the mention of his name. According to the *Lady Observer*, the Marquess was the most eligible man on the marriage mart. A man Eleanor had not yet had the opportunity to be introduced to.

The ladies all nodded their amenability. "By all means," said the Countess.

Hugh indicated Eleanor's mother first. "My Lord, may I present the Countess of Westix?"

Her mother offered a stiff curtsey and nodded.

Hugh's eyes met Eleanor's and her pulse gave a pitiful leap. "And the Countess's daughter, Lady Eleanor Murray."

Lottie's voice sounded in Eleanor's head, reminding her to meet the man's eyes. Eleanor nodded and held his handsome stare, but the smile trembled on her lips.

The Marquess nodded and then his attention slid away. To Lady Alice.

Hugh squeezed Lady Alice's slender arm with an embarrassing show of affection, which Lady Alice did not chide him for. "And now may I present Lady Alice Honeycutt, my betrothed?"

Lady Alice nodded and let her regard linger on the Marquess, much in the way a butterfly might over a choice bloom. A pretty blush colored her cheeks. "It is so very good to meet you, My Lord. I've heard such great tales."

Her smile was dainty and her eyes practically danced with the sincerity of her joy. She held out a hand to the Marquess, who readily took it and let a kiss whisper over her gloved knuckles.

The Marquess was genuinely engaged in Lady Alice's attention. Even her mother had a whisper of a grin teasing the corners of her stiff mouth. Lady Alice was warm and endearing, while still maintaining her cultured poise. An impeccable balance of breeding and manners and kindness.

And a glaring reminder of what Eleanor had been doing so very wrong.

In truth, Eleanor found Lady Alice's behavior bordering on inappropriate. Her father would have been appalled at such behavior, and no doubt would have been violent in his distaste for it. But he was not here now. He was dead, having left them with no fortune, Evander missing, and a wall of ice to melt.

Alice's open warmth was the line Lottie had mentioned in the lesson—the acceptable level of flirtation. Skirting propriety, subtle and delicately danced, therefore being socially acceptable.

Was this the kind of woman men wanted?

Eleanor didn't have to ask the question. She already knew. It was in the tinkling laugh Lady Alice did not suppress, in the measured, meaningful way her gaze met those she conversed with, and how men swarmed to her side, eager for any scrap of attention she was willing to offer.

Regret nipped at Eleanor with sharp teeth. Perhaps she ought to have let herself be introduced to Lord Charles several times more. She should have been more patient with the process.

"If you'll excuse us?" said the Countess. "We must be on our way."

Eleanor let her mother lead them in the direction of a group of the Countess's friends, where they clustered together in an array of colorful pastels, chatting under a tree by the river. Conversations blended around her, but her mind was unable to focus on any single one.

"Ah, there is Lady Stetton." Her mother nodded toward the shore of the Serpentine River.

Energy hummed through Eleanor's veins. She did not want to stop the steady rise and fall of her feet as she walked. To do so might give her mind cause to churn. And to think of all her failings—those she did not wish to ponder over.

"Do you mind if I go on a bit further with Amelia?"

Her mother eyed the path and gave an approving nod. "Join us once you've collected yourself."

Her mother swept off the trail and headed in the direction of Lady Stetton, leaving Eleanor and Amelia to continue onward. The absence of her mother's barrage of questions was a balm to Eleanor's racing brain, and she filled all her tumultuous thoughts with the rustling of trees and the twittering of birds.

"Forgive me," Amelia said in her gentle maternal voice. "But there is a man watching you."

Eleanor followed Amelia's stare to where a tall dark-haired man was indeed watching her, his eyes brighter than the clear sky overhead.

He smiled in invitation, his teeth impossibly white against his tanned skin. Her stomach sank. There would be no avoiding him, no matter how much she wished to.

She would have to speak to Lord Charles.

Chapter Four

Charles had anticipated that he might see Lady Eleanor. It had been his sole reason for a promenade through Hyde Park.

She was a beautiful sight, in a white gown with a pale green ribbon tied under her bosom and matching green ribbons on her bonnet. The color made her eyes stand out like emeralds beneath the brim of her bonnet. She had been pretty by candlelight, but by the light of day she was even comelier.

Her expression, however, mirrored that of a person being sent to the gallows. After the exchange of introductions Charles had overheard, it was quite evident that Lady Eleanor Murray was not having a good day.

It might have been kind to allow her to continue by and let her lick her wounds. If he were a sensitive man he might have allowed it. But he was not, and she had the journals he needed.

He stepped in front of Lady Eleanor and bowed. "Do you mind if I join you?"

Lady Eleanor hesitated long enough to suggest she did. Yet when her maid whispered inaudibly to her Eleanor subtly shook her head, and the brown-haired lady's maid stepped behind Lady Eleanor to make room for him.

"That would be lovely, Lord Charles."

Lady Eleanor's tone was flat and suggested it was anything but. Ever the charmer.

He ought to correct her, he knew—let her know he wasn't merely Lord Charles, but the new Duke of Somersville. Perhaps had she not been looking so crossly at him he would have been more inclined. But he owed this woman nothing.

Later. Perhaps…

He straightened and held out his arm to her, as was polite. She threaded her slender arm through his and rested her gloved hand atop the cuff of his jacket. Her light jasmine scent whispered at his senses. Although this time, in the afternoon's gilded light, with her dressed in delicate colors and gentle ribbons, the soft sweetness of her perfume seemed more fitting.

Lady Eleanor gave a little sigh. "I suppose you're here to convince me to return to Lottie's?"

"I thought I might give the idea a go," Charles replied.

Tree canopies spread over the path like an awning and blotted out the heat from the sun, leaving the air cool and fresh. Charles took a deep breath and let the quiet crunch of dirt under their feet fill the silence. Lady Eleanor's maid walked a few feet behind them, to grant privacy while still maintaining prudent proximity.

"Do you think you'll have any success in convincing me to return?" Lady Eleanor asked after a moment.

So much for any hope that she might make this easy. He glanced back over his shoulder, to where the Earl of Ledsey and Lady Alice still conversed with the dark-haired Marquess.

"If I were a betting man, I'd wager on it."

Eleanor's arm stiffened against his. "You saw?"

"I overheard," he said. "On my honor, it was quite by accident."

"What a wild coincidence…" she said blandly.

Charles did not bother to apologize.

"May I be frank with you?" Lady Eleanor asked abruptly. "Or rather, ask you to be frank with me?"

He inclined his head. "I believe our history dictates a level of candor."

Lady Eleanor glanced around them. The path had gone empty and they were all but alone. At least for a few moments. Or as alone as one might be with a chaperon in tow.

She stopped and stared up at him with her catlike green eyes. Perfectly sculpted red curls framed her porcelain forehead. In fact, everything about her was so carefully refined it made him long to see something skewed out of place.

"What is so unappealing about me?" she asked.

She asked it bluntly, almost casually, the way one might ask what would be served at supper that evening.

He hadn't expected such a question and found himself quite without words. After all, she was Westix's daughter, and certainly that brought her a plethora of ill traits.

"I truly wish to know so that I might see how to improve," she said. "I am from excellent lineage, and my manners are impeccable. I move in all the right circles. I know I don't have the kind of beauty Lady Alice possesses, and that my hair is…awful. But what else is it about me, about my person, which is so heartily distasteful?"

She turned her head away before he could see any kind of expression cross her smooth face or come to her eyes. She quickly began to walk once more, as if she regretted what she'd said. Her speech had been one of hurt, but her tone had been without feeling.

Perhaps there was more to his enemy's daughter than Charles had wagered.

He resumed his stroll beside her at the slow pace she'd

set. But, for all her steady pace and dispassionate voice, her hand trembled when it returned to his arm.

"You want my honesty?" he surmised.

"Yes."

Charles hesitated. These words would be important, ultimately forming her decision to return to Lottie's and setting the foundation for a friendship which might allow him access to those damned journals.

"May I begin first by saying that while Lady Alice is indeed lovely, so too are you."

Lady Eleanor looked up at him sharply, her eyes wide and the fullness of her pink lips slightly parted. After all her careful hiding behind an emotionless mask, the shock on her face was a surprise.

"I do not find your hair 'awful,' as you say."

In truth, its color was vibrant and beautiful. Any distaste stemmed from the reminder of her relationship to a man whom Charles so bitterly detested.

Lady Eleanor turned her head away and regarded the path once more. Several more people had filled the area around them, and he kept his voice intentionally lowered to ensure their privacy.

"It is your demeanor which is unwelcome."

Lady Eleanor did not react.

"Are you sure you wish me to continue?" he asked.

She exhaled and nodded. "Yes. I believe I need you to."

And in truth she was right. She *did* need to hear what he had to say. For her own good, and to increase her desire to return to Lottie's for lessons.

He went on as bade. "You are cold, as they say. Polite? Yes. But you have no *joie de vivre*…your delivery is without feeling. You have no…*passion*."

"Passion is vulgar."

"Passion is necessary," he countered. "It's what colors our world, what provides change and excitement. A woman like you, so without passion, is like a painting without depth. You will go through life in an endless routine of changing gowns and attending luncheons and soirees until they all blur together. You will meet every encounter with bored uninterest, to the point of teetering on disdain, as if nothing will ever be enough to please you. And one day, when death comes knocking at your door, you will look back on the nothing of your existence and realize that you never once lived a day in your life."

It wasn't until the entire, ugly and honest truth was out that he realized the depth of the cut in his words.

Lady Eleanor had stopped. The shade of trees had thinned out and her bonnet was dappled with splashes of gold. She turned toward him, pulled her arm from his, and slowly lifted her face. Her eyes gleamed in the light, glowing like gemstones with the gloss of what appeared to be carefully restrained tears.

The realization struck Charles in the chest.

He had gone too far.

He opened his mouth to apologize, but Lady Eleanor spoke first.

"My mother and her friends are waiting for me."

She nodded to the women on the riverbank. The entire group looked their way—and immediately snapped their heads in the opposite direction once they realized they'd been caught.

Lady Eleanor gently cleared her throat. "Thank you for your candor. Good day, Lord Charles."

She ducked her head down, hiding her face with the rim of her bonnet, and slipped away. Her gait was stiff, her back ramrod-straight and her shoulders squared. The maid hurried along after her.

Charles watched Lady Eleanor walk away, feeling very much the cad. He'd assumed such a speech would render him victorious, and yet his joy had been marred by something rather unexpected—the stab of guilt.

Later that evening Charles sat among a collection of his father's greatest acquisitions. If Charles hadn't thought it possible to feel any lower than he had after his honest assessment of Lady Eleanor, he'd underestimated what coming home to Somersville House would do. Especially as he surveyed the unboxed treasures.

There was a sarcophagus containing an intact mummy, found in a sealed-off tomb in the Valley of the Kings. The paint stood vivid blue against un-flecked gold, as if it had been created only weeks ago rather than centuries before. Its discovery had earned his father a private audience with the King. Then there was a gold scarab encrusted with priceless jewels, of which the *ton* had talked for three months.

Charles hefted an ancient tome into his grasp. The pages within the leather binding were unevenly cut and yellow with age. They crackled when handled. But the drawings and words within were still dark with ink. The discovery of this particular book had left scholars in a state of frenzy.

Every item found by his father in a foreign world and brought to London had been met with praise and acclaim. And Charles had been witness to it all his life—first as a young boy, peering from the stairs, later from the corner where his governess had grudgingly allowed him to sit, and later by his father's side, as an honored son. That was, until the Duke had begun to suffer from gout and declared himself too old for travel.

Charles set the tome down gently on the desk and regarded the key, studying its flat, cool metal surface.

It had indeed been a sad day when the Duke of Somersville had had to put away the old floppy hat he'd worn during his Adventure Club days.

At the time of its dissolution, the club had still been obsessed with locating the Coeur de Feu. Each man had gone about his own adventure, following leads on its location and documenting his journey. It had been when they returned home that everything had dissolved around them, their trust ripped apart by perfidy and speculation.

The Duke and the Earl of Westix had been the wealthiest of the men in the club, but they had not been the brightest. Only one man, whose name was never mentioned, had been cleverer than the rest, and had put his findings in code. And, while the previous Duke of Somersville had somehow obtained the key, and had known of its purpose, he had not known which of the journals was needed.

Charles had already been through all the journals at Somersville House, of course. He'd found nothing but descriptions of places the members of the club had gone, and accounts of treasures acquired. Until his father's effects were returned from their country estate there was nothing more to look through.

Regardless, Charles was certain the one he needed lay in the Earl of Westix's home.

He let the key slip from his grip and the metal sheet fell silently against the thick Turkish carpet. There was a story behind that carpet as well, only he couldn't recall it at the moment.

Every item in the house had a story—had come from a different homeland, after a new adventure. He put his face in his hands and let the coolness of his fingers press into the heat of his skin. They all had far better stories than his own—the son who had watched with adoration the father whose magnificence he would never measure up to…the sole heir who had cast aside his promises in search of his own adventures.

His father had been larger than life, experiencing every day to the fullest. Charles couldn't believe he was gone, leaving him with no more chances to fulfill his promise and finally gain what he had always wanted—his father's respect and pride in his accomplishments rather than always standing in his father's shadow.

A knot formed stubbornly in Charles's throat.

"Your Grace?"

A man's voice nudged gently into Charles's awareness. He looked up and met the dark gaze of his valet.

"Your Grace, you asked to be reminded when it was near time for you to depart for Miss Lottie's."

Charles nodded. "Thank you, Thomas. I'll be down in a moment."

Thomas glanced at the treasures surrounding Charles. "Several doors down there is another room filled with the items you discovered on your own travels."

The trouble with good valets was the way they oftentimes were far too perceptive.

"They aren't the same." Charles looked at a jade pendant of an elephant with gilt tusks.

"You are a good man, Your Grace. He would be proud of what you've accomplished in such a short period of time."

Charles nodded absently. His father wouldn't be proud. Not after his failing to locate the Coeur de Feu. No, his father would be disappointed.

The thought sliced into him as he recalled his father's last words, hastily scrawled with the desperation of a man with only moments left to live. And once again he felt the crushing weight of disappointment, because they'd been about the damned ruby.

Thomas bent in front of Charles and lifted the key from the floor. "When you're ready, Your Grace?" He carefully set it on the desk beside the massive tome and departed.

Charles sighed, but the weight in his heart did not lighten. He had committed many wrongs in his life, and all the treasures of the world wouldn't make it right. Getting those journals from Eleanor would be a start.

In truth, she had wormed her way into his thoughts several times since their discussion. Her forthright demand for what she might do to improve herself had taken him aback. And yet it had been refreshing. It was a rare thing indeed for a member of the *ton* to request an opportunity to better oneself. Not in dance or watercolor or singing, but in the general composition of their personality.

Charles got to his feet and strode out the door. He stopped at the top of the stairs and gazed down to the entrance hall below, where polished marble gleamed in the candlelight. He'd stood there so very many times before, watching his father prepare to leave for another trip.

When he was a boy he'd held onto the ornate railing, his small fingers curled around the cool wood, as if clutching it would keep his father from leaving again. When he was an adolescent he'd propped his elbow on its bannister and let his imagination carry him to the places his father would go, where Charles knew with the whole of his heart he would also venture someday.

And this was where Charles had seen his father for the last time…

The bustle of servants began to calm and Charles found himself alone in the foyer. His blood danced in his veins at the thought of the impending adventure awaiting him—the foreign lands, the excitement of experiencing everything he'd ever heard about from his father and had spent a lifetime dreaming of.

The back of his neck prickled with the awareness of being observed. He turned and looked up the curving stairs to where his father leaned heavily on a carved ivory cane just at the top.

They'd said their farewells already. Promises had been

made to pursue the Coeur de Feu, *and wisdom and advice had been passed from father to son.*

The Duke did not make his way down to offer another goodbye. Instead he stood at the top of the stairs, leaning on the cane gone yellow with age, and nodded down at his son.

This time it was the Duke of Somersville who was seeing Charles off. And this time it was not just information which had been passed from father to son, but a role...

The memory wrenched at Charles's heart. Not because he hadn't been there to offer his father a final farewell when the Duke had passed on, but because he had failed.

There would be no moving on with Charles's life until the gem was found. The dukedom could wait. It had been unattended for the previous six months, after all. Charles was young. He had time for life to wait as he finally fulfilled his promise.

The steel of determination set in his spine as he climbed into the waiting carriage. He would get those journals by any means necessary.

Chapter Five

Late evening was often the hour of illicit deeds. Eleanor's deed posed no exception. She slipped into the town house on Russell Square in Bloomsbury, utilizing the servants' entrance for discretion.

It wasn't until the footman had led her into the drawing room that she allowed him to take the domino from her shoulders, the wig from her head and the mask from her face.

While last time divesting herself of her disguise had left her trembling with vulnerability, now it rendered her lighter, freer. Perhaps now she saw the lessons for what she hadn't fully understood previously that they were: a second chance. Possibly her only chance.

Not just in acquiring a husband, but in living her life. Having passion, as Charles had said. Being a painting with depth.

The very idea of it prickled over her skin. She had restrained her emotions for so long, the very idea of letting them free was exhilarating.

Her mother had been equally eager to have her attend another lesson, especially after she had been seen in Hyde Park, speaking with a mysterious man. Eleanor had remained closed-lipped about Lord Charles, and her mother had been too pleased with the development to press for more information.

Eleanor watched the door with anticipation—waiting for it to open, for Lottie to saunter through it with her sensual confidence. And for Charles to follow behind her.

Perhaps Eleanor ought to have been offended by the bluntness of his words—certainly they had stung. But they had also thrown open the doors of her comprehension. What might have been the harshest criticism had also been the introduction to opportunity.

A glass of sherry, she noticed, was sitting once more on the small table beside the buxom bust. She leaned over the marble woman, considering... Her eagerness to change, however, did not extend far enough to allow her to reach between the pert nipples and claim the glass.

The doors swept open and Eleanor lurched around like a child caught doing something naughty. Lottie passed into the room like a queen. The length of her black curls cascaded down her right shoulder and the blue silk gown she wore made her skin gleam like the flawless surface of a pearl. Charles entered the room behind her and bowed low.

"Good evening, Lady Eleanor."

He rose and bestowed upon her a charming smile, which she ought to have ignored but which set her heart tapping at an odd rhythm.

"It's good to see you again."

There was a genuine note to his tone, indicating he was indeed happy to see her. Her cheeks went warm.

"So wonderful to have you back." Lottie clasped her hands together and pressed them over her chest.

"Forgive my previously disparaging attitude," Eleanor said. "I didn't understand how valuable a chance this was. If your generosity is still extended, I am eager to avail myself of and continue with the lessons."

Lottie waved at the air. "Oh, pish—there's nothing at

all to forgive. And of course I'll continue with your lessons. I'd never have taken you on unless I truly wanted to instruct you." She touched the underside of Eleanor's chin, the way a mother might do a cherished child. "You are going to be magnificent, dear one. You need only to believe in yourself."

The touch and her proximity were startling, but the affection behind both was innocent. It served to endear Lottie to her all the more.

"Shall we start with introductions?" Eleanor asked gently.

Lottie gave an appreciative laugh. "By all means, let's." She cleared her throat and straightened, her demeanor taking on a regal bearing. "Do you remember what I told you?"

Eleanor nodded. "Make eye contact, smile, be sincere." The way Lord Charles had just been.

Suddenly the understanding of it all washed over her with even more clarity.

"Perfect." Lottie waved Lord Charles closer.

He obligingly stepped forward. The strength of his muscular thighs was visible beneath the light-colored fabric of his pantaloons.

Oh, dear.

A sudden thought occurred to Eleanor. Was Lord Charles a client of Lottie's? They would cut a fine pair, with their dark hair and beautiful blue eyes.

Except he was smiling at Eleanor as if she were the only woman in all the world. How very devastating of him. And how very different from their last meeting.

What had changed? Her stomach twisted. Was it that he felt sorry for her? Did he find her so piteous that he had taken it upon himself to make up for it with flattery?

"Lady Eleanor, may I introduce Lord Charles?" Lottie indicated him.

Eleanor extended her hand and Lord Charles bowed over

it. His fingers curled around hers and his mouth kissed the air above her gloves. Though his lips never touched the kid-skin, she swore she could sense the heat of his mouth over her knuckles, like a caress against her skin. The sensation was not unpleasant.

When he rose from his elegant bow she let her eyes meet his and linger. "It's a pleasure to meet you, Lord Charles." She infused the words with everything she could dredge up—gratitude at his temerity in being honest with her the prior day, the kind of charm he offered her, even her hope of becoming a better person than she might otherwise be.

His smile broadened. Was it truly possible for one's teeth to be so brilliantly white?

Lottie laughed somewhere a world away. A joyous sound that dragged Eleanor back to the sumptuous red silk detail of the drawing room, where that nude bust stared boldly at her behind the temptation of a sherry glass and a wide gilt-framed mirror reflected Eleanor's own flushed cheeks and sparkling eyes.

Was that truly her in the mirror?

She quickly looked away, to ensure she was not seen staring at her own reflection.

For a moment she had allowed herself to be drawn into the alluring pull of Charles's presence, sharing his confidence. For a moment, she had been someone else, open and sincere. The realization, however, brought back the sensation of being completely vulnerable. She had worn her expressionless mask for so long that without it she was naked.

"Oh, Lady Eleanor, that was so very marvelous."

Lottie nodded appreciatively at Charles, and the look between them was intimate, conveying so much more than a friend aiding another.

Immediately a wave of humiliation curdled the success Eleanor had mustered. What a fool she'd been, blushing at a courtesan's lover as if he might find her truly enchanting. Hadn't she already learned her lesson once before when it came to men who offered interest in her?

"Shall we try again?" Lottie asked.

Eleanor nodded, even though the shine of her new-found opportunity had greatly diminished. Not that she'd expected Lord Charles to find her truly interesting. But he'd said she was lovely.

Was she so desperate to be found attractive? Especially with a woman like Lottie in the vicinity?

"Lady Eleanor, may I introduce Lord Charles?" Lottie said in her silky voice.

Eleanor lifted her eyes, but found Charles's gaze harder to meet this time. "It's lovely to meet you." She heard the rigidity in her own voice and lifted her hand awkwardly.

Charles did his part with the same smoothness as before. Again and again and again he demonstrated his mastery over his part of the introduction. Again and again and again Eleanor found she could not with hers.

The flare of hope began to dim. She was lacking once more. Inadequate.

Lottie's question from the prior lesson surfaced in her mind once more—the way it had many times since the query had been issued: What was Eleanor afraid of?

Eleanor had the answer. Or rather the answers. For there were many. After living behind the shield of her apathy for so long, to lower it was frightening. To be sincere was to be vulnerable, and to open herself to what rejection might do to that fragile, exposed part of her.

She could not stomach such embarrassment again. She could not be a failure.

Charles was home late that evening from Lottie's. They'd worked with Lady Eleanor for longer than before. All to no avail. He was weary of introductions. Indeed, Eleanor's disappointment in herself had been evident in the flush of her cheeks, despite her otherwise cool demeanor. And, though she was Westix's daughter, he had not been able to help the swell of sympathy.

She had persisted, patiently facing each new introduction with a determined set to her brow. He'd wished he could give her the passion she so lacked, could encourage the flame of life in those green eyes.

Charles's butler, Grimms, took his coat, hat and gloves as he entered Somersville House. "Good evening, Your Grace." Grimms offered a formal bow. "I believe you'll be pleased to learn that your father's effects have arrived this evening. All have been placed within the library."

Charles's exhaustion fell away, to be immediately replaced by excitement. He hadn't anticipated the arrival of his father's items from the country estate for at least a few more days.

"Thank you, Grimms."

The butler inclined his head, showing the glossy skin atop his head where his snow-white hair no longer grew, and strode off.

Charles immediately made his way to the library, and found a mountain of wooden crates beside one of the curio cabinets laden with his father's treasures. At least twenty boxes, by his estimation. Going through the lot of them would take a considerable amount of time.

"Welcome home, Your Grace." Thomas entered the room and held up a metal hook with a grin. "I heard you were back and thought you might require some assistance."

"Your timing is impeccable as always, Thomas."

Charles stepped back from the pile to give his valet better access. Thomas pulled down the top box with a grunt and shoved the point of the hook into the narrow gap under the lid. He pushed, and the top lifted off with a splintering crack.

Inside were stacks of papers and journals. Enough to take the night to get through—if Charles was lucky.

Thomas regarded the contents within the box and lifted his brows. "Fancy a brandy?"

Charles ran a hand through his hair. "I think that might help."

His valet quit the room, leaving Charles alone with piles of correspondence and notations written in the Duke's neat, narrow writing.

The first few layers were accounts for the country estate—a detailed overview of funds spent and rents collected. Those were followed by letters from museums and from scholars, thanking the Duke for his contributions to their institutions.

Charles stopped and took the time to read those, awash in his father's greatness. Interesting how even when he had been alive Charles had always felt on the outside, looking in with awe.

Eventually he carefully set the correspondence in a stack to one side. Next he lifted a large journal from the box. The gilded compass on the front indicated that it had been part of the Adventure Club. Unfortunately, the pages were too large to fit the key.

Charles opened the cover, regardless. The spine creaked and crackled in protest at its disuse. Clearly the journal was older than the others he'd gone through previously. Indeed, the first page placed the previous Duke thirty years ago, somewhere off the Nile in Egypt. A careful perusal revealed only his father's handwriting.

Charles strode to the desk, hesitated, and then reverently sat upon the chair his father had occupied for so many decades. The leather was cold beneath him, and stiff to the point of providing little comfort. He would have Thomas find him a more accommodating one the following day.

For the time being Charles settled back rigidly and perused the aged book. He'd read all the Adventure Club's journals in his possession, and traveled their adventures vicariously. This was the oldest he'd seen, and the first written only by his father.

Thomas came in and placed the brandy before Charles. "Shall I open another box?"

Charles shook his head. "This will do for now. Thank you, Thomas."

The valet nodded and left Charles alone with the journal.

The brandy remained untouched while he delved into the words written by his father.

The pyramids rose before me, dotting the horizon with triangles, their tips pointing toward the sun. These wondrous fossils of an age long dead are rife with treasures beyond my wildest dreams, ready for presenting to England.

Thus far my findings have been well received, at least by the English. It would appear there are some within Egypt who begrudge my presence. People who declare the excavations pillaging and deem these sites sacred.

For those unable to apply reason, certain documents can be replicated to allow us the access we require.

It was a perfectly constructed plan from one of our members—a man who has proved himself a genius in his approach to dealing with these obstacles as well as finding treasure.

He shall surely be a worthy asset among us, especially in gaining access to the most guarded treasures.

Charles paused in momentary confusion. Surely his father didn't mean he'd bribed people and forged documentation? There had been many instances when Charles had heard descriptions of finding tombs and temples long-ago abandoned and left to fall in on themselves in the middle of nowhere.

Charles's father had been a good man, with a name honorably built on the findings of great pieces which he'd shared with England. He'd been a hero—one who would never have stooped to such low levels as deceit and theft.

Not his father.

Charles read through the rest of the journal, which described the findings within the tomb in considerable detail. No further suggestion or implication was made of any untoward acts.

The absence of such eased the twist in Charles's stomach. Surely his father's earlier words had been written merely as a precaution, in the event that he'd need to go beyond the rules a little in order to bring an item home. The Duke had been an honorable man whose efforts had always been morally sound.

Charles closed the book and lifted the glass of brandy. He drank half in one great swallow before settling back in the seat. His mind nudged from his father to the distraction of Lady Eleanor.

There was something strange about the way the lesson that evening had gone—how she'd seemed so fully connected one minute and then separated the next. Regardless, she had appeared to be positively affected by his more pleasant demeanor.

He would need to meet with her again and ensure she did not fall prey to discouragement. She had to continue her lessons with Lottie and her association with him.

He was surprised to find he rather looked forward to it.

Chapter Six

Eleanor didn't much care for a walk in the park two afternoons later—any more than she'd cared for the soiree she'd been forced to attend the prior evening. Not when all she could ruminate on was her utter failure.

And Lord Charles.

Blast it. Why had he regarded her with such appeal? And why had she reacted to it so?

She would be meeting with Lottie again that evening. Perhaps Lord Charles, too.

The very idea of it made her insides flutter and her palms grow damp. A sensation that was as pleasant as it was disconcerting.

She thought again of how he'd looked at her...when everything had faded to a dull focus and her world had seemed to right itself. A grin played over her lips.

Eleanor strode along the worn paths of Hyde Park with Amelia walking at her side. While her maid had been all too eager to join Eleanor that fine spring day, she seemed to sense her mistress's need for solitude and remained in pleasant silence.

"Lady Eleanor."

A familiar, warm voice interrupted Eleanor's musings. Her stomach churned with myriad emotions: trepidation, fear, and most of all excitement. They all swooped and tangled together into a nervous whirl.

"Lord Charles."

She turned in his direction and nodded politely as he bowed. There was just enough time for her to salvage her composure before he straightened.

"I hoped I might find you here," he said.

He wore a pair of fine buckskin breeches and they gave him a casual, comfortable appearance. It was altogether very attractive, that look...

"You were looking for me?" She lifted a brow in the manner her mother often affected, hoping her face mirrored skepticism and not hope. Hope would be foolish.

Amelia quietly shifted to walk behind Eleanor, allowing her a modicum of privacy with Charles.

"I feared you might be disappointed after the last lesson," Charles said.

"I wasn't pleased," she conceded. "I'm not doing as well as I'd hoped."

He held out his arm to her. "May I walk with you a moment?"

There was no hesitation on her part, as there had been previously. She slipped her arm through his. "Of course. Thank you."

As they began to walk together she could not help but notice the solidness of him beneath his sleeve. And he smelled of foreign spices—something pleasant and exotic she could not quite place.

"I'd like to be frank with you once more," Lord Charles began. "That is, if you are inclined to hear my opinion on the matter?"

"I am," she replied, despite the jangle of her nerves. "I wish to learn."

But, while she was being truthful in expressing her wish

to learn, the idea of hearing more criticism of her person dragged her lower into herself.

"Why do you wish to learn?" he asked.

"To obtain a husband befitting my station," she replied readily. After all, it was what was expected of her—what was necessary.

"I think there's more to it than that."

His response took her aback, and the subsequent silence left her contemplation hanging between them. It would be easy to push the answer down inside her and bury it beside the rest of her emotions. But wasn't she trying to unearth them all? Wasn't she trying to be warmer? More approachable? Didn't she want to have depth?

"I don't want to live a life without passion," she said, in a quiet voice only he would be able to hear. "I enjoy reading so I can experience the emotions of the characters, to revel in their liberation to express them. But they are fictional and do not suffer the consequences we do. I have always been envious of the ability to express oneself so completely. I want to be free to *feel*."

Her heart raced at her confession. She had given merit to the truth and said it aloud for the first time in all her adult life.

Charles smiled warmly. "I think you are on the right path, Lady Eleanor."

"Why, then, is it so difficult?" she asked.

"You did well initially the last time," he answered. "But then you changed. I feel there was a reason for that, and I hope I might be able to help you identify what it might be."

Eleanor was glad to be walking beside him, with the brim of her bonnet covering her face, lest he see the heat blazing through her cheeks. After all, such things were impossible to mask, no matter how one schooled one's face.

She knew exactly what had been responsible for the

change in her at their prior lesson. It had been her own foolishness. The way she'd so easily reacted to Lord Charles's kindness, the recollection of her mistakes, and the reminder of how painful it was to love.

"Have I overreached in my frankness?" he inquired.

Eleanor realized she'd been contemplative for too long. "No."

"How did you feel when you made the first introduction?" Charles asked.

Beautiful.

Desired.

"More genuine," she answered. "As though you were meeting me as a person and I you, rather than just performing the stiff formality of introduction."

"I thought as much." There was a note of delight to his tone. "I felt the connection as well."

Eleanor hated the little flip her stomach gave, and hated how difficult it was to force herself not to turn toward the allure of his handsome smile.

Lord Charles deftly guided her around an aging couple in front of them who walked at a much slower pace.

"And how did you feel after?" he prodded.

Foolish.

Embarrassed.

"Exposed…" she breathed, almost choking on the suffocating memory.

"Ah, yes."

This time she did glance up at him and found him nodding to himself.

"You do realize the appeal of such openness?" he asked.

"No," she said slowly.

"The stiffness of your formality is what you've conformed to. It's not who you are. The feeling of exposure is what comes when you let your shield slip and grant others the opportunity to see who you are."

His explanation served to heighten her sense of vulnerability.

"I don't think I like that." No, she *knew* she did not like that.

"Because it feels foreign?" He paused. "Lottie once asked what you were afraid of. Perhaps this is your answer."

"Perhaps." It was all she would allow. The full truth would stay locked within her.

A gentleman tilted his hat to Eleanor from a passing carriage, catching her eye. Only then did she realize it was Hugh, with Lady Alice. Clearly they had been in her line of sight for some time on the road ahead and she was seeing them only now.

Interesting...

So, too, was the lack of heady anxiety seeing the two of them typically produced in her.

"When the shield slips away," Charles was saying, "it lets a man glimpse the true woman beneath."

"And you saw me?" she queried.

"I did." He said it softly, as if he were considering something.

"What did you see in me?"

Her pulse ticked wildly. After their last conversation, did she truly want to hear this?

"You're bold...you meet challenges head-on rather than cowering back from them. And there *is* passion in you. It's simmering below the surface, but it's there and it's beautiful."

"Do you find *me* beautiful?" Eleanor immediately regretted the brashness of her question.

Lord Charles stopped walking. Improper though it might be for him to stop her rather than her stopping him, the offense fell away when she met the blue of his eyes and felt the way they seemed to swallow her whole.

"I do," he said earnestly.

But Lord Charles was not a man she ought to want. Not a man who should make her stomach flutter with such confusing emotion. Certainly not a man who stayed in the company of a beautiful courtesan.

"Do you think other men will find me so?" she asked.

A muscle worked in his smooth jaw and he stared down at her for so long she felt all the hope in her begin to wilt.

"Yes," he said at last. "Yes, I do."

She breathed a sigh of relief and gently nudged them both forward into a walk, to avoid attention after being gone too long. Already she knew her mother would have more questions about the mysterious man at Hyde Park.

"So I ought to allow myself to show flashes of vulnerability?" she surmised.

"Yes."

She was indeed fortunate to have a man like Lord Charles at her side in this process of social edification, someone insightful and honest. The entire process had begun to pry apart her instilled ideals. Where once politeness and emotional stoicism had dominated her world, now she began to find an appreciation for the candor of her conversations with Lord Charles, and even the instructional detail Lottie provided.

The idea of the two together nipped once more at Eleanor. A reminder, yes, but still a curiosity.

"I confess lowering my shield, as you put it, is difficult," she confided. "I was raised to keep my emotions reined in, that only the common show emotion."

"Most of us are raised to eschew passion and exuberance," Charles replied. "But not to the degree you were."

Eleanor considered his words before replying. "My father was Scottish, and worried he might be judged by the *ton* for it. But he was also a man used to controlling everything. Including his emotions."

"Including you?"

Eleanor flinched at the idea, and at the truth behind it. Everything had always had to be just so with her father. The servants, her mother, the preparations prior to his adventures, even the silly little club he'd been in with his friends and his need to dictate how everything went. She had never really considered the element of his control, and how far it had truly extended.

"Might I ask you something?" she inquired.

"Of course."

Charles's arm was warm under hers...strong. A deep, dormant part of her was tempted to stroke her fingers over his forearm. She shoved the thought aside and held her hand stiffly in place.

"It's not my place to know," she said. "I am merely curious."

"Ask your question, Lady Eleanor."

Very well. She drew in a deep breath and asked the question she couldn't get out of her head. "Are you one of Lottie's lovers?"

Charles's mouth twitched with the beginnings of a laugh. He and Lottie! Lovers!

Truly, the idea was preposterous to imagine. Lottie with her sharp tongue and how well she knew him. He would have all the trouble in the world with a woman like her. And not the kind he might enjoy.

He pressed his lips together to suppress his mirth but a choking chuckle emerged from his throat.

"Lord Charles?" Lady Eleanor peered up at him from beneath the rim of her bonnet. Her brows had pinched downward in an expression of apparent concern.

"Forgive me." He shook his head. "No, I am not one of Lottie's lovers, nor will I ever be."

Lady Eleanor pulled her head forward once more, shadowing her face with that damned bonnet. Her arm on his had gone stiff again.

"I see my mother ahead." Eleanor nodded to a group of women visible through the trees. "I should join them."

Charles found himself disinclined to leave Lady Eleanor's company—a surprising realization. After all, she *was* Westix's daughter.

"I didn't mean to laugh," he offered by way of quick apology. "Lottie and I grew up together as children. I've always viewed her as a sister. So you see I could never possess any romantic inclination toward her. In fact, the very idea… It was unexpected and I found it amusing. Please know I was not laughing at you."

Why was he working so damned hard to reassure her?

"I truly must go." She glanced toward the group of ladies once more. "But I want to tell you how I appreciate the honesty of our discussions. I've never had anyone I could speak so candidly with before. I find it…refreshing."

Her expression was soft—hopeful, even. Had she truly not had anyone she could be sincere with? If that were the case, she had gone her entire life hiding behind the severity of society. Was it any wonder she worried now at pulling down her mask? Especially being the daughter of the Earl of Westix.

Charles was glad he had accepted Lottie's offer to aid Eleanor. It appeared she was as much a victim of her father as they had all been.

"I enjoy our conversations as well." Once the words were out of Charles's mouth he realized he'd spoken with truth. He did appreciate them. Which was an idea that would have rendered his father truly disheartened. The daughter of the Earl of Westix was still a part of the terrible Earl.

She gave Charles a smile that hovered between pleasure and reticence. Her teeth sank into her full lower lip in a most becoming way. Most ladies did it purposely. Lady

Eleanor, however, was not the type to attempt so silly a girlish gesture with intent, which made the action all the more alluring.

And, God, but didn't she have a sensual mouth? Full and shaped for kissing, with a slight cleft in her bottom lip. How had he not noticed before?

He watched as she headed in the direction of her mother. Had it been his imagination, or had her cheeks been stained with a blush before she left him…?

Several hours later he found himself in Lottie's drawing room as they awaited Eleanor's arrival.

She was fascinating, this daughter of his enemy. Through their conversations he was beginning to obtain a comprehension of what had established her unbending fortitude. Her brazen questions had helped him glean a hint of the woman beneath. There was strength there, of course—an inner strength he did not often see in most people—but there was also a hidden hunger for life, something she was afraid to unleash.

"You're smiling," Lottie accused. She pointed at his face. "Did you find what you need for the Coeur de Feu?" She stood up a little taller with excitement. "Do you know where it is?"

Reality crashed into his ruminating. He was consorting with the enemy—*enjoying* it, no less—and was not a single step closer to obtaining the stone.

Charles ground his teeth in frustration and shook his head. "It still eludes me. Damn them for making this so difficult."

"If it isn't the stone…" She pursed her lips and captured him in the line of her scrutiny. Her mouth fell open. "Is it a lady?"

Charles smirked and turned away to fill a glass with liquid resilience, seeing the possibility of a Lottie-mandated inquisition. "I assure you, it is not."

"Oh, pish. You can't fool me." Lottie's voice drew closer as she did. "Everyone is susceptible to love. Even *you*." With the last word, she tapped the tip of his nose.

Love. The idea was laughable. Of all the people to love, the offspring of the Earl of Westix was the last on Charles's list.

He splashed a bit of Scotch into his glass and slid a sideways glance in her direction. "I find your jaunty assessment reprehensible."

"It's all part of my charm." She propped a hand on her hip and grinned impishly up at him. "Aren't you supposed to wed now that you're a duke?"

"After I've found the stone," Charles muttered into his glass, and took a sip of his Scotch.

The butler appeared through the double doors. "Lady Eleanor has arrived."

Charles kept his face impassive, lest Lottie manage to notice any change in his features. While he did not hold affection for Lady Eleanor, he *was* anticipating seeing her with pleasure. After all, she was softening toward him through their discussions. It would take a few meetings more, but if things continued he would no doubt convince her to give him the journals.

It was only a matter of time.

Chapter Seven

Being open was extremely difficult for Eleanor at her next set of lessons, despite the allure of it. Her first bout of tedious introductions proved her absent genuine appeal, and the second didn't let the feigned enjoyment reach her eyes.

In truth, pleasantness was a trying feat to perform when one's stomach was knotted into a storm of anxiety.

Charles nodded encouragingly at her. "Perhaps think of a humorous thought or event."

"You know ladies are not to give in to the effects of mirth. It's common." She hated her father's words on her own tongue, and yet she could not fully cast them aside. "And it's impossible to think of anything comical with the two of you staring so expectantly at me. As if I'm…on display. It's most unsettling."

Lottie tapped a finger on her bottom lip in contemplation before jolting upright suddenly. "I have an idea. Do excuse me."

Charles met Eleanor's gaze in the empty room—too beautifully blue, too familiar. The unease in her stomach tightened.

"Smile at me," he said. "I promise not to ravish you in the time Lottie is gone."

He winked at her, the rogue.

Eleanor stretched a smile over her lips once more. Her mouth trembled with the effort.

Lord Charles cocked an eyebrow in a debonair display of consideration. "You look like you're trying too hard to smile."

The man was insufferable.

"I *am* trying too hard to smile," she exclaimed.

"Well, it's coming across as a blend of grimace and snarl, as though you intend to tear out my throat."

A smile did come to her lips then, natural and easy. "And what if that was my intention?"

"I prefer nibbles to bites," he answered. "Just below my ear, if you should like to know."

Eleanor's tongue went thick in her mouth and stuck fast, paralyzing the prospect of saying anything witty or even vaguely intelligible. Her stare drifted to his neck, where strong muscle showed at his tanned throat. Was he serious? About nibbling his neck?

After all, how *did* one nibble against another's skin? Was it in dainty pinches between the front teeth, as when she ate at the edges of a delicious marzipan flower, too pretty to eat and too delicate to keep? Or perhaps an act akin to the nip of one's lip in a moment of consideration?

And how would it feel? To the one being nibbled and the one doing the nibbling?

Lottie reappeared suddenly with a basket carefully propped against her hip. "I believe these ought to elicit some warmth."

She set the basket carefully on the ground. Eleanor leaned close and lifted the blanket on the top to reveal a lazy gray tabby nestled along the bottom. Half a dozen puffs of gray-and-white fur wriggled over her soft belly.

"I thought Silky had been getting fat on her complacent life here in London." Lottie stroked the mother cat's head, affectionately rubbing her ears. A contented purr vibrated in the air. "Turns out she was merely in a delicate way. Aren't they terribly precious?"

She scooped up one of the furry bundles with her cupped hand and cradled it to her chest. The mother watched vigilantly as her baby was taken. A squeaking cry came from the ball of fur, repetitive and desperate.

Lottie pressed a kiss to the tiny gray head and grinned at Eleanor. "Would you like to hold one?" She cradled her hands around the small bundle and its cries fell silent as it snuggled against her.

An eager excitement dashed through Eleanor. "The mother won't mind?"

"Silky is grateful for the reprieve, and I know you'll be gentle."

At Lottie's words, the gray tabby licked her paw and scrubbed at her face, confirming her mistress's claims. Eleanor did not wait for a second invitation. With the same care she'd seen Lottie utilize, Eleanor lifted up the wriggling warmth of a new kitten.

The pitching mewls of protest began immediately and a fat belly writhed against her palm. The kitten's claws dug into Eleanor's skin like miniature needles, but she was not so easily deterred. She cooed quietly to the baby and tucked it against her chest. The mewling ceased.

"Focus on how you're feeling right now," Lottie said in a low, soothing voice. "The kitten offers no judgment, no scrutinizing assessment. You are protection and you are comfort to her. Let yourself cast aside your fears and embrace the quiet delight of such a treasure. There is no need to ever be afraid of being who you are."

Eleanor set her attention to Lottie's words. The kitten's belly rose and fell with even breaths beneath a delicate set of ribs and its blue eyes blinked slowly closed. How very precious. And how true were the words of instruction.

There was nothing to be afraid of here, in the presence

of people she trusted, while cradling a small cat who had fallen asleep cupped between her palm and her chest.

"Lady Eleanor…"

Lottie's smooth voice nudged into Eleanor's enjoyment of a kitten lying fast asleep just above her heart.

"I'd like to introduce you to Lord Charles."

Eleanor looked up and found Charles watching her with a smile quirking his full mouth. She beamed up at him. "It's lovely to meet you, Lord Charles." The kitten shifted at the sound of her voice and climbed higher on her gown with its needlelike claws. Eleanor couldn't help but giggle at its clumsy movements. "I'd curtsey, but I am otherwise detained. I do hope you'll forgive me?"

"If you swear to look at me like that again someday, I will forgive you any transgression."

There was a low softness to his tone and it pulled at something deep within her chest. He was watching her with a pensive expression that made the skin around his eyes tighten in a very alluring manner.

"Lady Eleanor, you are a beautiful young woman, but when you smile you are wholly and completely captivating."

Captivating?

Her?

She'd always been prim, proper and well-behaved. Perhaps beautiful, if she were inclined to believe his prior compliments. But captivating—never.

"Thank you." She said it in a clear voice, which was a wonder in and of itself when the rest of her had turned suddenly weak and trembling.

She turned her attention where it was the safest in application—to the slumbering ball of warmth nestled against her chest. Emotions held exceptional power. She'd spent her entire life fighting against them, squeezing, strapping and binding them into a solitary, biddable place. How could she simply let loose the stays? Would they not all explode in a riot of chaos?

There was perhaps only one way to find out: to cast her fate to the stars and allow Lottie to help pull free the ties.

Charles had grudgingly admitted that Eleanor was a pretty woman. Even her red hair, which some of the *ton* had described as gaudy, he found uniquely fascinating in the way it set off the creaminess of her skin. But when she smiled, truly smiled, it transformed her face into a beauty no one could deny.

Good God. If she greeted every man with such open affection, and if they all were granted the glint of those bewitching green eyes, Lady Eleanor would be in no danger of consigning herself to a spinster's life.

The kitten had settled itself contentedly against the elegant curve of her collarbone. Funny that Charles hadn't noticed before the lovely smoothness of her fair skin, the graceful arch of her long neck.

Lottie caught Charles's eye. She lifted her brows in a confident manner which radiated the unctuous touting of her victory.

For her part, Lady Eleanor had dropped her attention back to the furry body cuddled against her.

"Now that you've been properly introduced, perhaps we ought to progress to conversation," said Lottie, and carefully lifted the kitten from her lap and replaced it alongside its mother.

Lady Eleanor removed the kitten from her chest and laughed softly as the beast tried to crawl back up her arm. After a few moments she freed the creature and returned it to its mother. The smile hovered in her eyes and left a particularly lovely flush to her cheeks.

Lottie gently set aside the basket in a quiet corner of the room and pulled the blanket over it. Lady Eleanor elegantly rose to her feet and he saw the familiar stiffness take up residence in her shoulders. But then after a lifetime of wearing such rigidity it could not be cast aside with the ease of a cloak. It would take time…practice.

Except all the time it took to perfect was time Charles was without the journals.

He had been sitting on the floor beside the ladies, but now pushed himself to his feet without ceremony. After all, there was no proper protocol for the etiquette involving ladies on the ground playing with animals.

Now standing, he offered a courteous bow. "How are you this evening, Lady Eleanor?"

The transformation was immediate. The light in her eyes was shuttered, leaving stark politeness in its place.

"I'm well, thank you." Her words were devoid of the friendliness they'd been brimming with only moments before. "And how are you?"

"Well, thank you. I wonder if I might be fortunate enough to claim you for a dance?" He grinned down at her in the hope that she might relax more. "Forgive me for being so bold, but I must say you look lovely this evening."

She gave a perfunctory smile. "Thank you. I'd be honored to dance with you."

A thick and uncomfortable silence thudded between them.

Lady Eleanor's brow puckered. "This is terribly awkward…"

"Perhaps I may offer some suggestions." Lottie appeared beside them. "You are a reader, from what I understand?"

Lady Eleanor's face lit up. "I am."

"And do you immerse yourself in the stories when you read them?"

"Oh, indeed," breathed Lady Eleanor.

Charles stared in wonder. Was Lady Eleanor truly being *wistful*?

"Close your eyes and imagine being a character in one of your favorite books during a romantic scene."

The expression on Lady Eleanor's face relaxed, and when she opened her eyes once more there was intimacy in her expression. Lottie nudged Charles and nodded at him.

He offered Lady Eleanor the lazy half smile women had always seemed to hold in high regard. "Good evening, Lady Eleanor. You look enchanting. I trust you are well?"

Lady Eleanor peered up at him through a veil of black lashes. "Quite, thank you. And yourself?"

Good God. "All the better now."

A tinge of color swept over her cheeks. A glint of something mischievous shone in her eyes. When she looked at him like that, as if she were teasing him with a secret, he could stare at her all day. It was suddenly too easy to imagine her laid out on a chaise longue, the top of her gown falling from a naked shoulder, that glorious red hair spilling over the swell of her breasts.

"Dance with me this evening." He hadn't said it as an invitation or an offer. It was a command, and one he wished he had the right to make.

She met his eyes and held his gaze. "With pleasure, My Lord."

He held out his hand and she took it, her kid leather gloves soft in his palm.

"Superb..." Lottie's voice stole into the private moment.

Charles eased back at once, granting room for her to approach. The interruption was exactly what he had needed.

Westix.

The reminder blared through his mind. She was the daughter of his enemy. He was here for the journals. What the devil was he doing, letting himself be swept away by a mere smile?

"Lady Eleanor, how simply marvelous." Lottie clapped aloud, as if it were an opera that played out before her instead of a conversation. "You let a piece of yourself free. I saw it on your face. One such look to a man will make him feel important. He will not be able to stop his thoughts from fixing on you, focused and wonderfully enraptured."

It appeared Lottie had a strong grasp of what made up the male mind. Charles did his best not to be affronted by her perfectly accurate assessment.

Eleanor inclined her head graciously, accepting the praise with humble pride. "Your instruction has been integral, Lottie." Those green eyes turned on Charles and her mouth opened in preparation to speak.

A knock sounded at the great double doors. The footman entered and announced that Eleanor's carriage had arrived.

"Has it been an hour already?" she exclaimed.

"It has, unfortunately," Lottie replied. "Shall we expect you tomorrow?"

Lady Eleanor settled the blonde wig on her head, albeit slightly askew. "Please do. Especially if I might see the kittens once more."

Lottie laughed, and Charles felt his own lips teased into a smile by her gleeful hope.

"You may certainly see the kittens once more." Lottie delicately straightened the wig, so all the bounty of that red hair lay hidden by the coiffure of pale tresses.

Once Eleanor had departed, Charles turned his attention to Lottie and found her watching him with a small smirk, her hand propped against her hip.

"You were in rare form tonight, Your Grace." She lowered her head and teased him with a coy expression. "I think you've changed your mind about Lady Eleanor."

Indeed, he had not. A lovely smile or no, the woman was still the offspring of the Earl of Westix. Even if he'd made her life as difficult as he'd made Charles's. And, while Lottie was aware of Charles's need to acquire the journals from

Eleanor, she didn't know it was his primary reason for accepting the opportunity to aid her in this bizarre venture.

He brushed at a bit of kitten fur on his sleeve and didn't deign to reply.

"Hmmm…"

Lottie nodded slowly, her head tilted in purposeful observation, her gaze sharpening too perceptively for his taste. As though she knew something he did not. And he didn't like it one bit.

Chapter Eight

The following evening Charles took his time, deliberately not arriving early at Lottie's. He refused to feed her implication that he might harbor affection for Lady Eleanor. Indeed, he rejected the very idea. Why, his father would turn about in his grave at such a consideration.

"Any more discoveries in your search for the stone?" Lottie asked, once they were settled in the drawing room.

A servant entered and placed a glass of sherry on the small side table, the same as was done every night when Lady Eleanor came.

"She never drinks it." He nodded to the full glass.

"It's there if she wants it." Lottie shrugged and turned her attention back to him. "And that's a no on the stone, I assume?"

He had uncovered nothing of use in the pile of boxes from the country estate. Not that he'd expected his efforts to yield what he needed. After all, his father would have easily uncovered the ruby's location if the necessary information had been in his possession. No, Westix had to have it. Why else would the late Earl have refused to relinquish any of his items?

Charles tapped his finger impatiently on the mahogany

tabletop holding various bottles of liquor. "If only I had *all* the journals."

If only he were close enough to Lady Eleanor to ask her for them. But he'd made far too much headway with her to risk losing all by asking too precipitously. Especially with Lottie's future at risk.

"Have you ever considered approaching the Countess of Westix for them?" Lottie asked.

He gave a grunt of dissatisfaction. "And have Lady Eleanor discover who I am?"

"She'll find out eventually. Do you truly think you can keep up this charade and fool her forever?"

"It was your decision to introduce me as Lord Charles."

Lottie threw her hair over her shoulder and gave him a saucy look. "I hadn't planned on you getting so close with her."

The doors opened, saving him from having to respond. The subject of their conversation entered in a whisper of silk, her cheeks pink from the chill of the night air.

"I have been invited to Lady Covington's masquerade ball this Tuesday. Do you think I might be ready in time?"

"I have no doubt you will," Lottie answered with great enthusiasm. "Being masked will make it all the more convenient. It will keep you from being overly formal, help you to be more yourself. You will be *wonderful*."

"Wonderful" was not a word in Charles's vocabulary at present. After all, a suitor would distract Lady Eleanor from Charles and impede his opportunity to become well enough acquainted to beseech her for the journals.

"My mother is delighted with the change she claims she sees in me already," Lady Eleanor continued, oblivious to his lack of enthusiasm. "She is convinced I'll be an enormous success and has already secured a time for me to meet with a modiste tomorrow afternoon, to have a new costume fashioned." Lady Eleanor hesitated and bit her lip in a rare show of nervousness. "Are you quite sure I'll be ready? I've had more failures than successes, and I don't think I can carry a kitten with me in my reticule."

Lottie settled a comforting hand on Lady Eleanor's shoulder. "We have several more lessons before the night of the masquerade, and your mask will help embolden you. Mark my words, you'll be magnificent."

"Have you chosen your costume?" Charles asked, more boorishly than he'd intended.

Something rather unpleasant knotted in his stomach, and he didn't like it any more than he relished the opportunity slipping through his fingers.

Lady Eleanor had distinctly caught his note of disapproval, because her attention fell on him and her brows flinched. "An Ice Queen."

Lottie clapped in pleasure. Charles drowned a groan with some brandy. He could envision her all too well, sparkling in a wash of white, pale blue and glittering crystal, and giving the brilliant smile that transformed her prettiness into real beauty. Suitors would be crawling about her like ants on a dropped pastry.

Even in his fog of personal misery he couldn't ignore how clever the costume truly was. After all, what better way to make her entrance into the good graces of the *ton* than by throwing their own very moniker for her in their face?

"Pray tell, what do you envision for your gown?" Lottie asked, with excitement gleaming on her face.

Charles did not bother to listen to the reply—not when his mind was spinning around the discomfort of his own internalizations. He had several days before the ball. If he pressed his luck the odds might be in his favor. But if he pressed too hard he might ruin his chances.

There was always the option of the truth, of course. Lady Eleanor did not yet know who he was, nor what his identity might mean to her family. He was unsure how Westix's family regarded his father.

So, either he could tell Lady Eleanor the truth and ask her outright for the journals, while hoping for her compliance. Or...

Or he could have Thomas find out when Lady Eleanor would be at the modiste and he could go to Westix Place to meet with the Countess. Lady Eleanor need not ever be aware of their meeting.

Once he had what he required, and if the information necessary was indeed in the journals, he would be gone once more and the deception of Lord Charles would be inconsequential.

"Lord Charles, are you well?" Lady Eleanor's voice pulled him from his thoughts.

"Of course."

He set his unfinished brandy down. If he was going to call on the Countess of Westix the next day he had to begin preparations. After all, Thomas was good, but even he needed time.

"If you'll excuse me? I must take my leave."

Lottie's mouth fell open. "Now?"

"Yes. There are matters which require my attention. I am unsure if I can make it tomorrow evening. Or the night following that." Charles straightened the lapels of his jacket rather than allow himself to meet the shocked stares of the two ladies. "Forgive me."

"Please do stay, Lord Charles." Lady Eleanor approached him.

The sweet jasmine scent drew his attention. He met her imploring expression.

"I can't do this without you." Her smooth forehead furrowed. "I feel as though I'm finally beginning to comprehend what's expected of me. But I need *you*."

She needed him. Such a caress to his ego. But needing

him in the flippant way she did would not grant him what he wanted.

"You have been ideal to practice with," she added. "And I've truly appreciated it."

Part of him wished they had more time, that there might be more of an opportunity to procure her trust and friendship. And yet her father Westix remained lodged in Charles's mind. Westix and the wrong done to Charles's own father.

This woman was not for him. Marriage was not for him. Not when the need to explore ran in his blood and the Coeur de Feu still needed to be found. He required those journals with urgency.

Utilizing that thought, Charles steeled himself for what he must do. "Forgive me, Lady Eleanor." He bowed low, more to break the hold of her gaze than for civility's sake. "You are in superb care with Lottie, and you will excel at flirtation at the ball. I am certain you will be the Diana of the matrimonial hunt."

Without another word, he straightened and strode from the room, set on seeing his promise fulfilled.

Eleanor had developed doubts about attending the modiste appointment that afternoon. Life had been so very different when she hadn't been aware of their dire financial circumstances. And so, when her mother had fallen prey to the crippling effects of another one of her headaches, Eleanor had been all too eager to cancel the appointment and remain at home with the ailing Countess.

That choice led to a fascinating series of events—beginning with Eleanor taking tea with her mother in the drawing room. Oftentimes taking tea soothed the rougher edges of the Countess's debilitation.

Their butler, Edmonds, entered the room, with a silver tray perched atop his fingertips. He stopped before the

Countess, presenting the tray with his usual grace. Her mother lifted the card from it between the pinch of her fingers and her lips tucked down at the corners.

Eleanor sat higher in her seat, attempting with what she hoped was discretion to read over her mother's shoulder. Without success. The print on the card was too small from where she sat.

The Countess nodded at Edmonds. "Send him in and tell Bessie to bring in another setting for tea."

"As you wish, my lady."

"Someone will be joining us?" Eleanor inquired politely.

The Countess cast a dubious look her way and lifted a brow. "Don't think I didn't catch you craning your neck. I appreciate you taking to your new lessons with such sincerity, but please ensure your manners do not suffer."

Chastened, Eleanor regarded the bits of tea leaf floating about the bottom of her dainty porcelain cup.

"If you must know," her mother began, "our visitor is His Grace the Duke of Somersville."

Somersville… The name was familiar.

"He and your father were at university together. They had their…" her mother swept her hand through the air with a disdainful gesture "…their *club* together. Until they fought like children over some of the items they'd found and ruined the club along with their friendship."

She sighed and rattled off the details with the ennui of a person reciting a list of tedious daily tasks.

"The Duke died in his sleep several months past. I'd heard his son was out adventuring and has now returned to claim his title, his estate, and most likely the dusty relics from our study."

The slight roll of the Countess's eyes was all the explanation Eleanor needed to know what her mother thought of the Duke. She understood now why she recalled the name. Her father's face had turned purple every time the name

Somersville had been mentioned. There had even been an incident when the Duke had paid a visit and shouting had been heard from the study.

Whoever the new Duke of Somersville was, he was not a friend of the family.

"Why did they quarrel?" Eleanor spoke in a quiet voice to keep their conversation from carrying down the hall, where the Duke might overhear.

Her mother took a careful sip of her tea. "Mummies' bones, fragments of old pottery and the like. The lot of it is a bunch of dreary rubbish, if you ask me. I gave the previous Duke nearly everything he asked for after your father died, having no purpose for it myself. It would appear his son is under the illusion that I have been inclined to retain some." She set her cup in the saucer. "The Somersvilles are nothing if not persistent. I know if I decline seeing him now there will be another card tomorrow and another the next day until I finally concede."

Unwelcome Duke or not, this would be the first person Eleanor had met since she'd begun her specialized edification with Lottie and Lord Charles in earnest. Her nerves disturbed the mirrored surface of her tea with a perceptible tremble. She set her cup down, lest it rattle in its saucer.

Should she use this Duke for practice? A test prior to her grand attempt at Lady Covington's masquerade ball?

Her father would be appalled if he were alive. And *that* was the final reason she needed to convince herself it was a good idea.

She ran through the instructions in her head. *Be kind, be genuine, make eye contact, smile. Pretend you have a kitten in your lap.*

She looked down at her empty lap. For the life of her she could not recall the feelings the kitten had evoked. But she could make out the perfect seedcake on her plate, and had the sudden urge to nibble a piece before the Duke arrived.

Was that the kind of nibbling Lord Charles had alluded to?

The thought popped in her head, unbidden and unexpected. A newly familiar heat rose in her cheeks. It was rather shameful, really, how often the memory of that conversation played itself in her mind, and the curiosity it aroused.

"Eleanor, have you heard a word I've said? What ails you, child?"

Her mother's admonishment sliced through the endless winding of Eleanor's wayward musing.

"And why in heaven's name do you keep staring at your lap?"

"I'm looking at the kitten."

The words slipped from Eleanor's mouth before she could stop them, and earned her a baffled, reproachful look from her mother. Fortunately it was at that exact moment that the dastardly Duke of Somersville entered their drawing room.

Lottie's most important words whispered in Eleanor's mind: *Believe in yourself.*

She looked up—but the warm smile gliding over her lips froze and swiftly faded.

For it wasn't the Duke of Somersville at all, standing before her.

The man who strode proudly into the room, with his fathomless blue eyes and immaculately tailored jacket, was none other than Lord Charles.

Chapter Nine

*D*amn. Charles had not expected to see Lady Eleanor beside her mother, the Countess of Westix. He was, in fact, so surprised he almost asked why she hadn't gone to the modiste as planned.

He bowed low to cover his shock. "Good afternoon, Your Ladyship."

Lady Eleanor's mother was a handsome woman, with a fine bone structure beneath a face almost untouched by age. Her green eyes were sharp with the scrutiny of assessment.

"Allow me to introduce my daughter—Lady Eleanor Murray."

Her words were hesitant, as if she hadn't wanted to say them. He might be a duke, but the Countess found him wanting.

Lady Eleanor offered a smile so hard and brittle it made the baring of her teeth in those earlier sessions appear friendly by comparison. "It's a pleasure to meet you, Your Grace." And by "pleasure" she unmistakably meant not at all anything remotely pleasant.

Rather remarkably like when Charles had first met her.

"Do sit down." The Countess indicated the empty place setting for him.

Truth be told, he'd rather take tea in the company of vipers at this point than the ladies of Westix Place. The vipers would doubtless prove less dangerous. But he had arrived with a purpose, and he could not back down simply because events had not transpired as expected.

He gave his thanks and settled himself opposite the ladies on a dainty rose-colored chair. "You've added new wall coverings." He nodded to the spread of saffron-yellow silk along the walls, with painted birds flitting about its glossy expanse.

"Several years ago," the Countess stated dryly. "It's been some time since we've been graced with your company. Would you have some tea?"

Graced indeed. Charles nodded. "Yes, strong, if you please."

While the Countess's attentions were otherwise occupied, Charles chanced a glance in the direction of her daughter. Red stained Lady Eleanor's cheeks and her eyes glittered with a hidden emotion she would not permit her face to convey. Regardless of her hiding what she was feeling, he knew it was not good.

Forgive me, he mouthed.

She cut her gaze from him.

"Your Grace…" The Countess offered him a cup of black tea.

The Countess of Westix *did* pour a good cup of tea. So long as it wasn't laced with poison.

"Thank you. Your tea is always top-notch."

"You flatter me." She did not appear flattered. She appeared as though she wished to be anywhere but there. "I presume there is a reason for your visit?"

He ought to ask for the journals and be done with it. It was, after all, why he'd come. A quick glance at Lady Eleanor's tightly pressed mouth and her blatant attempt to keep from meeting his gaze were evidence enough of her anger at his ruse. Asking for the journals would surely leave her further incensed.

The Countess plucked a lump of sugar with the sugar tongs and lifted her brows with impatient expectation.

Damn it. There was only one thing he might do and possibly retain his budding relationship with Lady Eleanor and get the hell out of this mess.

Charles held his cup and blew at a curl of steam while he gathered his composure. "I intend to court your daughter and came to seek your approval."

The Countess's mouth fell open and the lump of sugar splashed into her tea with an indelicate plop. "Surely you jest?"

The skin along the back of his neck prickled with Charles's awareness of Lady Eleanor's observation. He glanced in her direction and found her staring at him not like a woman eager to be courted by a duke, but a woman wholly and completely bewildered.

Frustration tightened through him. Why the devil hadn't she gone to the modiste?

"I do not jest," he said levelly.

"I was not aware you had even been introduced." The Countess of Westix stirred her tea, seemingly quite recovered. "You are the son of the Duke of Somersville and a member of the Adventure Club. I have seen the accounts of what transpired within that club." Her lip curled with censure. "I am well aware that you have begun traveling, as your father once did, and I can assure you that you will never acquire leave to court my daughter."

Charles's heart thudded harder in his chest. The Countess of Westix had seen accounts of the club's adventures. The journals. She *did* have them.

Her face had gone an unpleasant shade of red and she had folded her lips on themselves in an obvious attempt to stop herself from saying more. "Is that all, Your Grace?"

She drew out the last words, making the title seem less of an honor and more of an offense.

"Yes, I believe it is." Charles set his tea on the table, regrettably untouched, and got to his feet. "Thank you for your time, Your Ladyship." He let his gaze finally fall on Eleanor and found her staring up at him, her expression unreadable, her cheeks a bright red. He nodded in her direction. "Lady Eleanor."

He bowed to them both.

"Good afternoon, Your Grace." The Countess of Westix lifted her tea to her mouth, took a sip, and looked out through the window into the gardens with an air of clear dismissal.

Charles took his leave, stopping only to gather his hat and coat from the footman, and even those he was sorely tempted to abandon in an attempt to flee all the faster.

Having faced such utter failure in his alternative attempt to collect the journals from the Countess, he was now forced back to his initial idea—to win over Lady Eleanor and convince her to give it to him.

He only hoped he had not pushed her away with the unexpected shock of his offer to court her and with the greatness of his lie. But, more than that, he hated it that this new change in plan might somehow see her hurt.

After an hour of her mother's fuming, and far too many seedcakes, Eleanor made her way to her room. No longer was she in shock—she was angry.

How dared Lord Charles—*His Grace the Duke*—put her in such a position?

She'd had to lie, of course, building on his perfidy in order to protect Lottie, who had doubtless had no part in this. Eleanor could not abide the idea of that sweet woman receiving punishment from the Countess of Westix for Somersville's deceit. But why had he asked to court Eleanor?

Why not wait until the ball, allow himself to be properly introduced to her, and *then* ask to court her?

The idea of him doing exactly that swam in her mind. Him impossibly handsome in some roguish costume, her in a glittering gown made for an Ice Queen, taking a turn about the room, dancing, laughing, speaking at length.

It was a whimsical dream. Most likely a foolish one.

A nudge of something uncomfortable crawled into her mind. She'd mentioned she would be at the modiste. How terribly odd that he should arrive unexpectedly to offer courtship when he had known she would be out.

She recalled the look of choked surprise when he first saw her. He had not expected her to be there.

For all his bravado in speaking out to her mother, Eleanor knew one thing for certain: he had not visited in order to ask to court her. He'd been there for something else, and she would find out exactly what he was after.

Chapter Ten

Charles hadn't thought Lady Eleanor's back could possibly get any straighter. But then she hadn't known him to be so blatant a liar and a fraud before. His stomach swam with unease as he peered through the door crack to where Lady Eleanor was perched tightly on a chair in Lottie's drawing room.

This was not going to go smoothly.

Lottie nodded at him, and he knew it was time to make their wrongs right. She strode in first, with Charles following behind her, as they'd always done.

Lady Eleanor rose from the stiff-backed seat she hadn't truly needed and turned a blank face in his direction. Despite her implacability, her cheeks were flushed with a brilliant red, as they'd been during tea. She was not as unaffected as she would have liked herself to be perceived.

Charles stepped around Lottie. "Lady Eleanor, I can explain. If you'd give me—"

"I understand well enough." Her eyes flashed behind her emotionless mask. "You thought I'd be at the modiste, and you presumed to impose upon my mother in my absence so your identity might remain a secret. My presence startled you into offering to court me rather than admit your true purpose."

Well. There wasn't much more to add to it than that. She'd surmised it quite succinctly. Surprisingly and rather unfortunately.

"You lied to me when I confided in you."

Her voice gave a delicate tremble. The slight break in her tightly reined composure cut into him more deeply than any slice she could make with her tongue.

"Why were you there?"

Charles remained mute, unable to tell her, unable even to open his mouth under the weight of the truth.

Lady Eleanor scoffed. "You can't even *tell* me? After you lied about why you were there? After you lied about your title? After you lied about finding me desirable enough to court?"

"It was me," Lottie said softly. "I didn't tell you he was a duke. I only meant to keep you from casting him out due to your fathers' association. I knew he would be ideal to assist you and I trust him implicitly."

Lady Eleanor regarded Lottie for a long moment. When she finally spoke, Charles knew the words were meant for him.

"Your trust is more steadfast than my own. But then he did not seek to avoid you as a means of taking advantage of your mother. He did not make a fool of you."

Lady Eleanor drew in a long, slow breath and carefully let it out, the inhalation and exhalation both very apparent in the silence of the room. "I need your help, Lottie, or I would leave posthaste. The Duke of Somersville, however, is no longer necessary, and I find his assistance bothersome. Will you be so kind as to ask him to leave?"

The request smacked Charles in the chest like a punch. This woman who had confided in him with their candid discussions, who had smiled at him with all the warmth of a summer sun, was now casting him out. But then, he truly deserved it. His deception had been deplorable and his cover attempt unforgivable.

Lottie pulled her head back, as if she too had been viscerally struck by so powerful a request. She turned to Charles, all pretense of poise and her newly adopted sensuality giving way to wide-eyed shock. Her mouth opened and closed without issuing either an order or a protest.

Charles would not be able to call himself a gentleman if he left Lottie in the awkward predicament of having to choose between her sole pupil and source of income and her lifelong friend.

He bowed first to Lady Eleanor, and his heart dragged into his stomach as though it had been affixed with a weight. "Forgive me my transgressions. I understand that they were egregious and hope you do not seek to exact your frustrations upon Lottie, as she truly wants nothing more than to help you succeed." Next he bowed to Lottie. "I shall take my leave."

Lottie nodded, her eyes luminous with regret and quiet gratitude.

He strode from the room with all the confidence a cad such as he could muster. His error had been egregious indeed, and the cost had been heavy. Aside from jeopardizing the opportunity to reclaim the journals, he had also compromised his ability to help Lottie in her new endeavor. There was also the loss of Lady Eleanor's hard-won trust.

The entire ordeal left his stomach knotted and a dull, aching sensation in his chest.

Rather than show him out, Lottie's butler escorted him to the library. "Miss Lottie will wish to speak with you once Lady Eleanor has gone."

Charles gave him an appreciative nod and sank into an oversized chair beside the hearth. He stared into the flames, watching them writhe and twist against one another as a similar inferno blazed within him.

At long last, the door to the library groaned open.

"She's gone," Lottie said in a somber tone. "And she's quite upset. I do not believe she trusts often…but I think—I think she did trust you."

Charles closed his eyes against the pain of Lottie's words. There was more truth to what she said than he wanted to admit. He knew Lady Eleanor had indeed spoken to him in confidence. Their conversation on the path flashed back to him, when she'd thanked him for his honesty and expressed her genuine appreciation for having an opportunity to speak frankly. She'd given him her confidence and he'd responded with betrayal.

He'd hurt her.

The thought made something in his heart wrench painfully.

Regaining his composure, he rose from the chair and faced Lottie. "I should have told her the truth about my title."

Her brow creased. "I never should have put you in that situation. I worried it would frighten her off."

"I never should have gone to her mother." Charles put into words his deepest regrets. "Nor should I have attempted to hide my true purpose by asking to court her. Rather than flatter her, I have deeply offended her." He shook his head. "I do not know how to fix this, Lottie."

She sighed—a weary, defeated sound. "And you have not acquired what you need to find your lost stone."

Charles blinked. The journals. Yes. He had not even considered them in light of his misdeeds. *Damn.* But how the devil did Lottie know…?

"How did you know I needed information from her?" Charles asked.

Lottie gave him a sad smile. "Because I know you far too well, Charles. Your hatred for Westix is strong enough that there would need to be a motivation greater than myself to lure you into aiding me in this endeavor."

Charles truly was a cad. He ground his back teeth, but it did not quell the disgust tightening through him.

"But you still assisted me." Lottie patted his forearm. "I know if I'd come to you for help when I needed it all those years ago you would have been there."

"I would have been," Charles said resolutely. "I still would now."

Lottie's mouth tucked at the corner. "You needn't worry about me, but I *would* like you to make things right with Lady Eleanor."

Charles scoffed. "I doubt she will speak to me ever again."

"I disagree." Lottie tapped her lips in thought. "Go to the masquerade ball."

Charles wished he had a glass of liquor in his hand—something strong enough to burn away the ache in his chest. "She has no desire to see me."

"Nor talk to you, nor hear your explanation. But if you're at the ball with her…" Lottie smiled and gave a musing nod at her own plan. "She can't refuse a dance with you—unless she isn't planning to dance at all, which we know she won't do. It will be the perfect opportunity to explain yourself."

Truly, the idea was preposterous. His actions had only proved correct everything she'd grown up learning: it was best for him to stay behind an unaffected shield and to dim all emotion.

"I would suggest honesty this time." Lottie leveled her gaze at him. "What other choice do you have?"

A heavy sigh pressed from his lungs. "You're right." He owed it to his father to try again to get those journals. And he owed it to Lady Eleanor, whom he had never thought he would be beholden to, to explain the breach of her hard-won trust.

"Of course I am." Lottie gave a nonchalant shoulder-lift at her victory. "So you'll go?"

"As long as I can get an invitation on such short notice."

Lottie laughed at that. "You're the new Duke of Somersville, just arrived into London after a five-year absence during which you traveled the world in search of ancient treasure. You could show up in rags and they'd still welcome you."

No doubt his appearance would set all the tongues wagging. He cringed at the idea. "I'll go as a pirate," he said grudgingly.

Lottie's expression became serious. "I know you loathe balls, and other such social functions, but Lady Eleanor is going to be nervous. She could use a friendly face to settle her nerves." She tilted her head in consideration. "Or at least a familiar one. Someone to help ward off the legions of suitors who will seek her attention."

Charles narrowed his eyes. *Legions of suitors.* He nearly scoffed again. But then recalled his idea of her gown, of how she would appear as an Ice Queen with her fire-red hair. Lottie was correct.

"I've said I'll go," he said gruffly. Grumpily, really, if he was being honest. "So I can have another shot at getting my father's journals," he added for good measure.

"Of course. For the journals."

Lottie gave him a coy look he did not think he liked. But, while he didn't appreciate her implication, or the annoying way she tapped his nose after she said it, he was looking forward to another opportunity to claim the journals.

And, blast it, he was anticipating with pleasure seeing Lady Eleanor as well.

To make things right, of course.

Or so he told himself.

* * *

Eleanor's decision to be an Ice Queen for the masquerade ball had been the product of the mind of the woman she *wanted* to be, not necessarily the woman she truly was. In her mind, wearing the dazzling pale-blue-and-white gown would make her heedless of people's opinions. She'd thought she might sweep into the ball like a queen, make the wittiest of remarks and confidently meet the eye of every eligible peer in the room.

She could not have been more wrong.

Everything she'd recently learned cautioned her against giving in to the desire to frost over, while every innate defense within her demanded she curl up inside herself. What was left was a very miserable and socially confused Eleanor. Her mother's expectant stare did not help, and nor did the pressing watchfulness of the masked attendees.

Why, why, *why* had she insisted on trying to throw the *ton*'s words back at them? And why had her mother insisted on her having the costume made?

Now Eleanor was merely a fool draped in a costly gown and the burden of intense disappointment.

No one had approached her…no one had asked her to dance. No one had even bothered to acknowledge her or beg an introduction. The weight of failure crushed in on her. She tried to stave off such thoughts, and instead repeated the rules Lottie had given her.

Smile. Be sincere. Make eye contact. Believe in yourself.

Those last words made her want to give a choke of laughter. For how could she believe in herself when she didn't even feel comfortable behind a physical mask?

Even as she tried to relax, every muscle in her body locked up, followed by the stiffening of her limbs and the straightening of her back to an impossible level of rigidity. The shield was up, locked so tightly in place that it could not be brought down by all the kittens in London.

"Lady Eleanor."

The smooth, masculine voice was entirely too familiar. Her stomach twisted in anger and her heart gave a walloping thump against her ribs. She turned and met the brilliant ocean-blue eyes of the Duke of Somersville.

A fascinating thing happened then—for, despite the hostility of her ire, and in spite of the lies of omission and blatant betrayal offered by the Duke, Eleanor immediately felt herself soften.

"Your Grace." She offered a slight curtsey.

"You did dress as an Ice Queen after all."

His mouth quirked up. The arrogance in his expression scraped over her ragged nerves.

"Evidently," she replied.

"Ah…an unforgiving Ice Queen," he amended.

Eleanor glanced over the black fitted breeches, ruffled shirt and old-fashioned black jacket. The growth of hair on his jaw was unshaven, giving him a dangerous air. In fact, all of him appeared rather dangerous and far too alluring.

"And what are you? A rogue? *Lord Charles?*"

The Duke of Somersville swept into an elaborate bow and straightened. "I am a humble pirate."

"Shouldn't you possess at least a modicum of humility in order to refer to yourself as humble?"

He smirked. "Touché! You make me regret leaving my sword at home. I hadn't realized I'd be up against so sharp a wit."

Eleanor found her lips curling into a smile. She was flirting, she realized, and comfortably. What was more, she was enjoying herself immensely, even though she was furious with him. How could he make her do that when she was so irate still?

His expression turned serious—a rather becoming look with his whisker-darkened jaw. "Dance with me, my unforgiving Ice Queen."

She studied him for a long moment, the answer hovering on her tongue. "If I refuse...?"

"I daresay your mother might be glad of it. But you won't refuse me. To do so would be considered rude, and the Ice Queen, while unforgiving, is anything but rude." He held out his arm to her.

"Am I so predictable?" She slid her arm through his.

"No, actually." He grinned at her, his teeth all the more startling white against his whiskered jaw. "Not at all."

The quiet amusement in his tone created a slow, pleasant warmth in her stomach as he led her through the room toward the dance floor.

"It was inexcusable for me to lie to you." His voice was little more than a low hum beneath the chatter of surrounding conversations.

The quiet joy in her ebbed. "You made me a fool."

Heat scorched her cheeks and suddenly she regretted her decision to dance with him. She would take ill manners over yet another humiliation at the hands of this man.

"No." His eyes locked on hers. "I was the fool. I have enjoyed our friendship and now I've ruined it." His brow lifted and he turned his head slightly to the side. "Almost ruined it?" he asked hopefully.

She wanted to sigh in exasperation. How was she supposed to keep her wits about her when he looked at her so beseechingly?

She clenched her jaw. If he wanted to continue their friendship she would get what she wanted from this son of her father's enemy: *answers*.

"Why did you do it?" Before he could answer, she added, "And I warn you not to lie to me this time."

Several people stared at them as they passed, their eyes alight with interest...watching. But then they were always watching, were they not? How could she be genuine when she was so very much on display?

Eleanor's body began to stiffen once more.

The Duke of Somersville's arm tightened, drawing her closer to the strength of his body. "I vow to be completely truthful going forward. You have my word as a gentleman."

He came around to face her, preparing for the opening of the dance. Her heart fluttered. The waltz.

She had only practiced it before with her dance master. In fact, she had been sorely tempted to decline each time she practiced because of the dance's vulgarity.

Though the patronesses of Almack's had sanctioned it, and given their permission to the *ton* in doing so, Eleanor had never actually performed the steps at a ball. No doubt her father would have locked her in her room for all eternity for even considering doing so now. And with the Duke of Somersville, no less.

The Duke gave her an encouraging nod and she stepped toward him, placing her left hand on his jacket as his arm came around to lightly touch her shoulder blade. The brush of his gloves whispered over her back, where her skin was bare.

A shiver tickled through her. It was easy to understand why the waltz was considered so scandalous.

He gave her a half smile, boyish and lazy and altogether too charming. It set her heart pounding before the dance could even begin. How would she endure an entire set thus?

She found herself so near to him she could make out every single eyelash around his eyes…could see the beautiful blue was flecked with a subtle pale green she'd never noticed before. The exhalation of his breath teased against the length of her neck like a gentle breeze, tantalizing and intimate. Her stomach quivered and her nipples drew tight where they pressed into the security of her stays.

"Why did you lie to me?" she asked, determined not to let herself be swept away by his attractiveness, determined not to let his transgressions pass without accountability.

The opening notes of the waltz cut in, and the Duke lifted his arm to meet the fingertips of her raised right hand.

His expression became earnest. "I was afraid if you knew whose son I was you would hate me."

She paused a moment in the dance. "Why would I hate you?"

"Because of our fathers' past."

"Did you hate *me*?" Eleanor lowered her arm. "When we first met?"

He held her waist at a respectable distance—for the waltz, that was—and began to spin around with her. "I didn't know you."

The world whirled around and around and around in a heady rush. "You know me now," she said breathlessly.

"Yes, I believe I do."

The spinning stopped for a moment and they resumed their careful hold on one another, her hand atop his hard shoulder and his at the nakedness of her back.

His exotic scent was no longer foreign to her, and was uniquely appealing. Conversation was difficult to focus on when it was all too easy to let her gaze wander to his full mouth. And when he held her thus, lightly, almost in a caress.

She liked this, she realized. The closeness to his strong body, the wonderful smell of him, the enticement of intimacy. Was this what marriage would be? A blend of comfort and excitement?

It was far more than she'd ever anticipated a marriage could be.

"What I've learned about you makes me want to know even more." The Duke stared down at her, drawing her attention from his sensual mouth. "Lady Eleanor, you fascinate me."

Her face warmed in a blush. Was he intentionally trying to distract her?

Stay focused.

"How?" She spoke quietly, only half hoping he would hear.

"You dress as an Ice Queen to force the *ton* into acknowledging their own gossip and yet you wonder why you fascinate me?" He chuckled. "But that isn't all you want to ask me, is it?"

The enormity of her previous anger and hurt crushed the delicate mood of flirtation. She wanted to ask him why he'd offered to court her. If he'd been sincere, or if he'd merely been covering his appearance with a viable excuse. But she realized she was not willing to hear the answer.

"What was your true purpose in calling on my mother?" she asked instead.

They began to twirl once more, and the room whirled by in a spinning array of resplendent gowns and murmured conversation. Eleanor held tight to ensure she did not fall. Their eyes locked, held, and she fell into the moment, tumbling head over heels into the palpable intimacy charging between them.

It was more dizzying than the dance, and the rush of emotion nearly overwhelming.

"I'm looking for a precious stone," the Duke of Somersville replied. "A ruby as large as a man's fist. It shines as though a fire were lit at its center."

The spinning stopped, but Eleanor's rapid pulse did not slow. Not when she was so close to Charles...not when her body had grown accustomed to his touch on her back. On her skin.

"The Coeur de Feu," she whispered.

The Duke of Somersville stiffened. "You know it?"

"Of course. A magnificent ruby named the Heart of Fire for the way light flickers at its center. It's lost, from what I understand, though there was one person my father was certain knew of its location."

The Duke's gaze fixed more intently on her. "You know a great deal of it."

"Young ladies may be made to remain silent before their fathers, but it does not mean they do not listen. My father spoke of little else in the last year of his life. His inability to locate it consumed him. It was the one thing he could not control." Bitterness seeped into her tone.

"You know about the journals, then?"

The step the Duke of Somersville had been performing fell behind by half a beat, a move subtle and practically imperceptible. Had they not been so close she might not have noticed. There was something bright in his eyes. Excitement? Desperation?

He blinked, and recovered with a smooth smile. But it was too late. She'd seen exactly how important those journals were to him.

And she knew where they were located.

Chapter Eleven

Charles ought to be vexed by Lady Eleanor's lengthy silence. She glanced up at him with a coy look borrowed from Lottie and his heart missed a beat. While on Lottie he found the expression irritating, on Lady Eleanor it held a considerable amount of appeal. It also meant she knew something and was holding her cards close to her chest.

The snag of crystals against his fingers told him that her gown lay against his hand. The warmth of her seeped through into the tips of his gloves, reminding him of the nakedness of her back where the gown did not cover it, and how badly he wished he could stroke her silky skin.

She gazed up flirtatiously from beneath her mask and her full breasts rose and fell with her exertion. Despite all that had transpired between them she appeared to be at ease with him once more. Perhaps he had not fully ruined his opportunity. If that was indeed the case, he was an absolutely lucky devil.

"You know where the journals are, don't you?" he asked in a disaffected tone.

Deep down, he was anything but. He wanted those damned journals with such ferocity he could practically feel the smooth worn covers against his palm. He was too close to fail.

"I plan to read them," Lady Eleanor answered, with the simplicity of one discussing the weather. "To see what is so intriguing it would make a man lie."

The twirling began again, and he held her by her slender waist to keep them together. Their gazes locked, the way they might if they intended to kiss, and his blood raced with frenzied force through his veins.

He smirked at her confident reply. "You won't find what you need by simply reading them."

"Won't I?" She tilted her head.

"There's a key to decipher a careful series of coded letters," he said. "At least to obtain what is needed to locate the Coeur de Feu."

"I presume you have the key you're referring to?"

Her lips were pursed in a shrewd expression. He wanted to push his mouth against them and drag the tip of his tongue over her lower lip until she opened for him with a soft, eager breath.

Damn it. She was the daughter of his enemy, the keeper of what he needed. She was a means to an end, not a plaything.

"I do." His reply came out lacking the smugness he'd intended.

"Of course you do." She tossed her head, a haughty move so carefully blended into her steps anyone might assume she'd done it as part of the dance. "How very convenient."

There was something in their verbal *tête-à-tête* he was rather enjoying. Her blend of astute observation and bold flirtation was enticing, and the glint of those green eyes certainly caught his attention.

"You look as though you are planning to make a bargain with the devil," he said.

"I very well might be."

His hand went to her waist again, while the other held

hers at shoulder-height as they paraded around the dance floor, forced to regard one another from the side.

"Go on," he pressed.

"You have the key," she said. "And I have the journals."

"What do you want for them?" He spun her around.

"My request is twofold. Firstly, I want us to work together." Her voice was gentle, breathy…the way a lover's might be after a particularly passionate tryst.

"I'm a pirate, mind you—not a devil." He winked at her and reveled in her pretty flush.

The orchestra began to slow until the last notes faded away almost regretfully.

"And I'm not truly an Ice Queen." She curtseyed to him as he bowed.

She was indeed not an Ice Queen. The title of Ice Queen belonged to her mother, who now glared at him with all the hatred in the world. The Countess of Westix truly was a woman befitting a man like her late husband.

"What is the second part of your request?" he asked as he offered her his arm to lead her back to the watchful viper.

"If I am unable to find a husband you must agree to marry me."

His step faltered. Was she serious?

But the Countess of Westix was not the only person who awaited Lady Eleanor's return. Several men milled about the Countess, chatting in idle conversation while keeping their focus firmly planted on the glittering form of Lady Eleanor.

They snapped to attention like well-trained pups at her approach.

"I do not think the latter concern will be an issue," Charles offered.

"Only because the elusive new Duke of Somersville danced with me." She tutted. "Besides, it should not be a true concern. And to think just this afternoon you were willing to court me."

The wry twist of Lady Eleanor's lips told him she had seen through his ruse. It also told him well enough how she felt about it.

"Think on it," Lady Eleanor said as he bowed a final time and released her to those so wholly unworthy of her company. "I'd like an answer soon."

"Tonight," he said.

It was an audacious suggestion, for it meant they would either have to be alone together at some point, in order to speak candidly, or he would be dancing another set with her. One or the other would certainly set a flame to the possible kindling of a scandal.

Charles turned from depositing Lady Eleanor among the pack of puppy-eyed suitors and all but bumped into an angel on his departure. But not truly an angel, for surely no celestial being had so robust a bosom as the one being tilted with obvious calculation in his direction.

The angel curtseyed. "Your Grace."

He nodded, unable to scrape up her name from his memory. Her face certainly was familiar, with its pink apple cheeks and bright blue eyes framed by a white feathered mask.

"You remember me, don't you?" She blinked up at him with feigned sweetness. "I came to Somersville Manor often."

Ah, yes, now he remembered. The Carston chit. The very one who used to dump dirt in Lottie's hair and rudely point out the quality of her worn dresses when they were all children. Charles worked hard to keep cultured impassivity on his face, when he wanted so badly to give in to a scowl of dislike.

"Lady Sarah." He nodded at the woman and hoped her

costume was indicative of a bettered nature—for her own sake. "I trust you are well?"

She giggled behind her fan. "You *do* remember. And I'm quite well, I thank you." She leaned closer. "The other ladies are envious of our acquaintance. Many are clamoring for an introduction."

True enough, several faces were turned in their direction, all framed in a sea of curls and coiffures.

Dear God.

Attending Lady Covington's masquerade ball had been a dire mistake. In doing so he had publicly declared himself an eligible bachelor, with a new dukedom, and plopped himself squarely in the middle of the marriage mart. Invitations would be overwhelming Somersville House the following day, and no doubt all the mothers would be seeking to thrust their daughters into his path.

"This will be a very exhilarating set." Lady Sarah looked wistfully toward the dance floor and blinked up at him once more.

Charles gritted his teeth and made a silent apology to Lottie for what manners dictated he must do next. "Would you care to dance, Lady Sarah?"

She put her hand to her chest, as if the request had taken her by surprise. "I'd be honored, Your Grace."

She fluttered her lashes at him once more, with such vivacity he wondered if one of the feathers had come loose and was stuck in her eye.

Lady Sarah slipped her arm through his, tugging herself a bit closer than was necessary. While she paraded him through the ballroom like a prize won, Charles caught sight of Lady Eleanor, making her way to the dance floor on the arm of the notoriously eligible Marquess of Kentworth.

Charles had to focus once more on not scowling as he settled himself in front of Lady Sarah. He'd been wrong when he had declared himself merely a pirate. For now, being forced to dance with an angel while watching an Ice Queen with another man made him feel very much like the devil himself.

Eleanor's newfound appeal to the *ton* had more to do with the new Duke of Somersville offering to dance with her than the results of her social edification. However, her suitors made one realization glaringly obvious: not all men were like the Duke of Somersville.

Where he was warm and encouraging, sometimes even teasing, and with the most pleasant hint of flirtation, other men were—well, they were dull.

The Marquess of Kentworth was an exceptional dancer, and yet he'd prattled on so about his physical prowess that her eyes had nearly rolled from her head. The tall and awkward Viscount Rawley had come next, with a nervous bow, and during the course of their dance had dropped a scrap of paper with the dance steps written on it in blotted ink.

Following supper, which she'd been unfortunate enough to be forced to attend with Viscount Rawley and his many dietary allergies, had come the very anticlimactic affair of unmasking.

It wasn't until she was subjected to Earl of Devonington, though, that she had finally had quite enough. She might have fallen asleep dancing the Scottish reel, with his boring chatter over his hunting dogs, had it not been for the many numerous times he trod upon her toes with his surprisingly dainty feet.

The final notes of the dance finally whispered through the air—far sweeter than any Eleanor had heard before. The Earl of Devonington gave a final deft leap and came down hard on her foot. The very one he'd crushed so often earlier in the dance.

He led her back to her mother with a comment on hunting that teetered precariously on the inappropriate and a promise to call upon her the following day. It was then Eleanor decided she needed a moment to herself, lest she go mad.

It had been wonderful, initially, to have the attention of so many gentlemen when she had previously been so woefully ignored. But easy conversation had not come with the others as it had with the Duke of Somersville. The carefree comfort she possessed when she spoke with him had not come as readily either.

The set she'd danced with him had set the night twinkling with promise and excitement. Everything thereafter had fallen rather flat.

Only when she was alone could she finally acknowledge the bold request she'd made of him: to marry her in the event that another man could not be found. She'd done it out of necessity, of course, to ensure her own financial security. At any rate, it did not seem likely he would need to follow through.

And yet she knew the offer had been unwise. Not only would her mother never allow such a union, Eleanor did not know what to make of the emotions swimming in her stomach when he was near, the sensation as exhilarating as it was frightening.

It was far too easy to recall the brush of his hand over her naked back, the way their eyes had locked while the world spun around them, as though their souls were joined. It was fanciful and ridiculous and altogether reckless.

She strode from the withdrawing room into the empty hall while thinking of the waltz. While thinking of him. They'd been so close—near enough for her to note the way his eyes crinkled at the corners when he smiled down at her, the way their bodies touched and how incredibly strong his broad shoulder had been under her hand. Even now the exotic spice of him clung to her skin and gown, the way the residual warmth of a good dream might linger into wakefulness—as if she could still savor him.

"What is it that puts such happiness on your face, Lady Eleanor?" a smooth, masculine voice asked.

Eleanor turned to her right and found the Duke of Somersville approaching her. "Your Grace..." Her heart fluttered like a freed moth in her chest.

The Duke tilted his head regretfully. "I'd ask you for a second set if you weren't so popular."

"You mean if it wouldn't be so scandalous?" she chided.

"I think I'd very much like to be scandalous with you."

He grinned at her, his lips parting over his perfect teeth and making him appear very much the pirate. Heat burned its way up from Eleanor's neck and scalded her cheeks.

The Duke of Somersville did not move closer to her, and yet the intimate glint in his eye made her feel as though he'd just closed the proper proximity.

"Why, Lady Eleanor," he said with feigned concern. "You appear to have overexerted yourself on the dance floor. Perhaps you ought to forgo this set and venture to the veranda for a bit of air?"

Her breath caught. Had the Duke of Somersville just suggested she meet him for a tryst?

And was she truly considering it?

Chapter Twelve

Charles did not wait for Lady Eleanor's reply before he bowed and took his leave. The suggestion of her joining him on the veranda hung in the air between them, ripe with temptation.

He let the stretch of time work in his favor and strode with a purposeful gait through the ballroom, nodding at the few attendees he recognized favorably and ignoring those he did not. Masquerade balls could be very convenient for avoiding unwanted social interactions.

And for creating enticing ones.

Everything in him wanted to turn and look behind him, to see if the sparkling Ice Queen of the ball followed, his invitation answered. He had to force his head to remain straight ahead, fixed on the doors to the terrace.

Several people milled about outside, in search of either fresh air, a moment unseen by an escort, or a liberating break for solitude. It was not improper for one to go outside alone at a ball, even less so at a masquerade ball, where minor transgressions were glanced over. It was his suggestion which had been improper, bordering on indecent.

Though it was not his place to crave it, he wanted a moment with her alone, somewhere she would be only his.

Where suitors would not be present, seeking a dance or some of the attention she'd doled out with charming smiles and genuine attentiveness. The idea of her being solely with him eased some of the curious knots tightening in his stomach.

He stepped through the doors onto the veranda. The music was muted by the closing door, and the quiet of night overtook him.

The door opened behind him, but Charles did not look to see who had arrived. A tingling at the back of his neck told him that his senses had picked up everything he needed to know.

Lady Eleanor had arrived.

He didn't have to turn, but he did, for he would not miss the sight of her striding toward him.

"Ah, Lady Eleanor."

He'd meant to say more, but the words died on his tongue. Moonlight caught and twinkled in the crystals on her dress and hair, making her shimmer. The white cloth blended with the fairness of her skin, so only the pale blue fabric of the gown and slit sleeves showed, as delicate as a moonbeam across her skin.

"What a happy coincidence, meeting you here," he said, finally finding his voice.

She inclined her head respectfully and set the copper of her hair shining. "Your Grace…"

She stood beside him at the railing on the terrace and rested her fingers on the thick band of marble, a mere fraction of an inch from his own. How he longed for such separation to be closed between them, so he might delicately run a finger over the back of her gloved thumb. A slow stroke, easy and sensual—but one he would not make.

"I assume you've had a pleasant evening?" Her casual tone indicated no nervousness at being with him outside, alone.

"I have," he answered in earnest. For it had been so when she was dancing in his arms. "It would appear you have become quite popular."

Lady Eleanor's eyes danced in the night. "Is it not enough for you to be a humble pirate, but you must also be one prone to jealousy?"

Jealous? Him? It was so ridiculous a notion Charles could only scoff.

Eleanor lifted her brows and fixed her attention to the garden—a convenient distraction. He edged his hand closer, drawn by an unseen force, and grazed the back of her thumb with his forefinger before he realized what he was doing. The fine quality of their gloves glided against one another.

Eleanor gave a quiet gasp and met his stare, her eyes luminous. Blood rushed through his body and he found himself wishing to pull the gloves from them both, to caress the silky heat of her naked skin on his.

Gloves. Confound it.

He could have shaken his head at his own thoughts. He'd been too long abstinent from the fairer sex if he was thinking merely of removing gloves and touching hands.

No, not just gloves. He wanted to peel the dazzling dress from her body and watch the true beauty of her being unveiled in a way no crystal or diamond could ever rival. She would be lovely. He needed only to see how the dress hugged her curves to know as much.

"Why are you looking at me like that?" she whispered.

Her breath was sweet and her lips were parted with innocence, with temptation…

The touch of their fingers was not enough, damn it. He wanted more—needed more.

Though he knew he shouldn't, he drew his arm around her waist, as he'd done when they'd danced the waltz. They stood together in the semi-darkness, far too close, with nothing between them but the sparking of mutual attraction.

Lady Eleanor did not pull back from him as she might once have done. She stared deep into his eyes, as if she saw every level of his soul…as if she could stay thus for hours.

He touched her cheek and cursed his gloves once more. Her lashes swept downward in pleasure at the caress. He shouldn't be doing this—holding her, wanting to kiss her. The right thing to do would be to release her and make his way back into the ballroom.

Even as he thought of the right thing his body acted on the wrong thing. He tilted the delicate edge of her jaw upward, turning her face to the moon, the better to see her beauty in the cast of silver light before he lowered his mouth to the warmth of hers in a delicate kiss.

Her body eased closer against him and her lips opened ever so slightly, granting him the opportunity to gently suck her lower lip. And the Ice Queen melted in his arms.

Eleanor was lost in the Duke of Somersville's kiss. His mouth was hot, and surprisingly soft, and the kiss was followed by the gentle drawing of her lower lip between his.

Despite the coolness of the night, her skin blazed with the most delicious heat and settled into a low, eager throb between her thighs. His fingers trailed behind her head, cradling the weight of her hair. Then—dear God—then his tongue swept into her mouth and brushed across her own.

Sweet heavens.

Her nipples hardened with a pleasant needling against the silk shift she wore beneath her gown and every bit of her skin seemed to dance with awareness.

The Duke pulled away and gazed down at her in a way no man had ever done. "My God, you are beautiful," he said in a low voice.

"Will you kiss me again?" she asked breathlessly.

His gaze settled on her mouth and his lips lifted in a languid half smile. "Not here. Not now." He swept his thumb over her cheek. "I do not want your absence noticed."

She fought the urge to protest. She wanted to be kissed again. Again and again and again. Until the entire night faded away in the hungry pulse of heat still throbbing insistently through her.

"You shouldn't look at me like that," he said.

"Like what?"

"Like you wish I would kiss you again."

Her knees went soft at the deepness of his voice, at his obvious attraction to her. "You *could* kiss me again," she offered.

He put his hands behind his back and eased away to a proper distance, such as should exist between a lady and a gentleman. "I would not ruin your reputation, Lady Eleanor. I've seen the effects of ruination and would not wish it on a lady I hold in such high esteem."

A lady he holds in such high esteem. Her heart should not swell so girlishly at mere words, and yet it did, expanding in the most delightfully happy way until her chest seemed near bursting.

His scent hovered on her skin and mixed with the warm pleasure still tingling over her lips. It was divine—a heady, exotic combination of spices and adventure. The scent of a man who had seen the world she had only ever imagined.

A glance toward the door confirmed that the dancers were walking away from the finished set. She would need to return before the next began.

"Have you come up with your answer for me yet? Will we work on the mystery of the journals together? Will you…?" She flushed, unable to ask the most pertinent question aloud again.

"Will I marry you if no one else will have you?" he finished for her.

When he said it she realized how sad it sounded—how desperately pathetic.

"It would be my honor to work with you." His face was entirely earnest.

The very idea of working alongside him to solve the mystery left her pulse racing in her veins. The adventure… the excitement…

"And the other thing…" He paused. "I will need more time to consider."

Disappointment crushed in on her, but she suppressed the emotion with the stiffness she'd clung to for the better part of her life. This was a reminder not to allow herself to get too close to him, to remain at a distance no matter how he encouraged her to open to him.

"I shall bring one of the journals with me when I come to Lottie's tomorrow evening," she said. "But only one until the remaining terms can be met."

"Understandable."

He brushed the length of his forefinger over the back of her gloved hand once more. Her skin warmed at the caress. *Distance.*

After all, she could not afford to be reckless.

"I do not wish to hurt you, Lady Eleanor."

He said the words so softly she almost did not hear.

"You must go." He bowed low. "Enjoy your evening, beautiful Ice Queen."

"And enjoy yours, jealous pirate."

She bobbed a quick curtsey to him and strode to the doors. It was a wonder she was able to walk at all with her legs trembling the way they did, with knees that seemed too weak to hold her upright.

But she did make it to the doors, and through the crush of people, until she practically ran into the chest of a man who did not move aside for her to pass. How very rude.

"Excuse me, please." Eleanor curbed the irritation from

her words and looked up. Anything else she might have said died on her tongue.

Hugh looked down at her with a quiet smile on his lips. "Will you dance with me, Eleanor?"

In days past she would have readily accepted, maybe even harbored the hope that he might cast aside Alice, as he had Eleanor. But not now—not tonight. Not after the Duke of Somersville's searing kiss had relegated the memory of Hugh's kisses to a place of easy forgetting.

"Do forgive me, Lord Ledsey, but I am on my way to speak with my mother now." Her regret did not come across as earnest—not even to her.

Hugh's pale blue eyes regarded her carefully. Compared to the rich depth of the Duke of Somersville's blue eyes, Hugh's appeared rather pallid.

"Perhaps later, then." He bowed to her, his tone cool. "You look beautiful this evening, Lady Eleanor."

While his words and actions were polite, there was an air about him that set little bumps of unease running down Eleanor's spine.

"I thank you." She was suddenly desperate to escape from Hugh, and found herself grateful for Lady Alice having interrupted their courtship.

At last Hugh moved aside and gave Eleanor leave to pass. Her mother was clearly waiting without patience, her face dour.

"You've certainly taken your time," said the Countess of Westix in a flat tone. "Was that Lord Ledsey I saw you talking to?"

Guilt prickled at Eleanor, but then memories of the pleasure of Charles's kiss wiped away any negative sensations. The kiss, the kiss, *the kiss*. She could swoon at the very thought of it, at the memory of the protective strength of the Duke's hands around her, the heat of his mouth on hers, his tongue grazing—

"Did you not hear what I said?" Her mother's brow rose. "I certainly hope you aren't imagining more kittens, or some other such nonsense."

Eleanor pursed her lips, thoroughly chastised despite the humor threatening to bubble up in her throat. The thing about the kittens *had* been rather amusing.

"Forgive me," she said. "The Earl of Devonington was not exactly light on his feet. I needed to recover."

She said it quietly enough, but her mother rebuked Eleanor with a sharp look.

"I have it on good authority that he was very taken with you." The Countess clapped her fan against the palm of her gloved hand. "You could do far worse than the Earl of Devonington."

She delivered a stare so pointed, it jabbed through Eleanor's daydreams.

"For instance, the Duke of Somersville."

Chapter Thirteen

If one measured success in such things as multiple callers, and flowers sent with heavy cream-colored note cards, it could be said the following day that Eleanor's appearance at Lady Covington's masquerade ball had been victorious.

And most intriguing of all the flowers she received were the brilliantly red tulips sent with a note stating only: *An admirer.*

The man who had sent the red tulips did not call, and nor did he send a servant so that she might guess who he might be.

The butterfly of hope in Eleanor's chest fluttered about. Surely it had been Charles.

While she ought to be simply pleased with her new-found suitors, she could not help but place him above others in her mind.

There were several others who did call—including the much sought-after Marquess of Bastionbury, whom she'd danced with later in the evening. Though following the magic of dancing with the Duke of Somersville, the Marquess of Bastionbury's appeal had regrettably been thin.

The Earl of Devonington called too, and took a short lifetime to finally depart, with the Countess of Westix practically tugging him back in.

The day trudged on, taking an eternity, until the sun finally began to sink behind the clouds. Most of it had been a blur—a background to the thoughts at the forefront of her mind: *an admirer.* The Duke of Somersville. And that kiss.

Surely he had sent those vividly red tulips which proudly spoke the love of their sender?

Finally night descended on London, and at long last Eleanor was finally able to slip into the domino and blonde wig with her black mask.

Amelia winked in the mirror at her mistress. "I don't think I've ever seen you beam so, my lady. Is it...?" She paused for a long moment before speaking. "Is it the Earl of Devonington?"

Eleanor's mouth fell open in horror. "Most certainly not!"

Amelia pressed her hand to her chest. "Pardon me for saying so, my lady, but I'm glad it isn't him who has you in a whirl."

"*Am* I in a whirl?"

"Your cheeks have been flushed all day and you've had a dreamy smile on your face, like you're floating through the world while the rest of us simply walk." The maid grinned down at her. "Are you going to confess to your trusted maid who it is?"

Eleanor's stomach clenched. As much as she loved Amelia, she couldn't bring herself to say the Duke's name aloud. Not when her mother's ears managed to extend through the entire house.

And a good thing too, for no sooner had Eleanor decided to keep quiet on the topic her mother strolled into the room in a glittering evening gown. Eleanor got to her feet and met the Countess's lifted brow as she regarded her daughter's masked appearance.

"What are you doing, Eleanor?"

Amelia bobbed a curtsey and left the room, silent as a

mouse, the way a good servant ought to be. Oh, how Eleanor wished her maid was still there to share secret confessions with, rather than the Countess of Westix. Eleanor knew too well the determined glint in her mother's eye.

"We're going to Almack's tonight." The Countess spoke in a voice brooking no refusal.

The brilliance of Eleanor's excitement wilted into an ache of crushing disappointment. "I thought I was to go to Lottie's?"

Her mother waved her fan dismissively. "You needn't go there anymore. What she's taught you has evidently paid off. Several gentlemen are quite taken with you. Most especially the Earl of Devonington. He's asked to take you to supper later this week at Vauxhall Gardens."

"I don't want to go anywhere with him." Eleanor spoke the obstinate words levelly.

The Countess narrowed her eyes. "You are lucky to have his attentions, Eleanor. He's one of the wealthiest peers in London and would keep you in the lifestyle to which you are accustomed. Beyond it, really. While the others have merely flirted, he has spoken to me directly about his intentions to court you."

Eleanor said nothing. How could she? Her mother was right, of course. The Earl of Devonington was impossibly rich, and high in the instep as a result. He was clearly very interested in Eleanor, and he had the means to let her live even better than she did now. Her life would be just as the Duke of Somersville had predicted: an endless blur of soirees and luncheons until they were all strung together in a life without purpose.

Her stomach twisted at the thought of being wife to a man like the Earl of Devonington, with his pompous sneer and devastatingly painful little feet. While several months prior she would have been pleased with Devonington's interest, she understood now that she wanted more.

Needed more. A suitor who matched wits with her—one who would turn her blood molten in her veins and make her melt with desire for intimacy.

"Nothing to say?" asked her mother.

Eleanor had much to say, but she had never given herself leave to allow her mother to see the depth of her feelings, to hear the truth of her opinions. Her blood rushed with such fervor through her veins it roared in her ears.

"Forgive me, Mother," Eleanor said. "I feel I would benefit from more of Lottie's instruction. I should like the opportunity to meet a suitor who appeals to me more than Devonington…one whom I might find happiness with."

Goodness, but her knees had begun to tremble, and she found herself wishing to be seated still.

The Countess's eyes sharpened with perceptible shrewdness as she regarded her daughter for a long, stifling moment. "You aren't dressed properly and your hair has not yet been done." She relaxed and sighed. "I daresay you wouldn't be ready in time. Almack's closes its doors to all patrons in the next hour. If you will agree to sup with Devonington at Vauxhall, I believe I might forgive your absence tonight."

Eleanor's heart leapt at the opportunity. "I agree."

Her mother gave a smug smile. Apparently they had both just won a victory.

The Countess of Westix brushed at her immaculate gown. "I shall inform Devonington tonight of your decision to dine with him, and convey your disappointment at not being able to attend Almack's. I shall say that you have truly been overly exerted by the events of today and last night. I will also see if Aunt Lydia and your cousin Lady Violet might be free to act as chaperons for you." She turned to leave and stopped. "You are smiling, daughter."

Eleanor pursed her lips to quell her blatant display of delight.

The Countess softened slightly and nodded. "I like it."

"Thank you, Mother."

The Countess of Westix swept from the room without further comment, letting the door shut quietly behind her. Eleanor rushed to her dressing table and pulled out the journal she had obtained from her father's study earlier that day.

But the eagerness of her joy was dampened by the presence of guilt. Her mother trusted her, and Eleanor intended to spend the evening with the very man her mother most despised. Eleanor bit her lip and slid the battered book into a bag. Her mother wanted Eleanor to be happy, though, and this made Eleanor far happier than anything else ever could.

Amelia appeared in the room once more and bobbed a curtsey. "The Countess has departed and the hackney has arrived for you." She glanced at the bag.

Eleanor resisted the urge to pull it behind her back.

Amelia winked. "You needn't worry, my lady. You could hide a body in here and I'd not tell a soul."

"You knew?" Eleanor asked.

"Nothing in your room goes unnoticed by me. It's my job, my lady. It's all part of protecting you."

Eleanor had never thought of Amelia as a protector. A maid, yes, but never a protector. The idea was a nice one—to know Amelia was on her side should she need her.

"Thank you," Eleanor said with genuine gratitude, before slipping away.

Only when she was inside the hackney did she notice a similar hired coach just pulling away from the home opposite her own, with a lone man sitting inside. Eleanor peered through the darkness at the face in the other coach's window. There, lit by only a sliver of moonlight, was a face she would recognize anywhere—Hugh, the Earl of Ledsey.

* * *

Charles arrived early to Lottie's by special request, and filled her in on the events of the ball—including Lady Sarah's preposterous costume of an angel. Lottie's smile wavered, however, at the mention of Charles dancing the waltz with Lady Eleanor.

The clop of hooves came to a stop outside and he glanced behind the window covering to see a woman in black slip out of a hackney. His pulse kicked up a notch in wicked delight. Lady Eleanor had arrived. And no doubt the journals with her.

Or one of them, at least.

Lottie twirled one dark curl thoughtfully on her finger and pursed her lips.

He dropped the curtain. "What is it?"

Lottie's brows lifted in feigned confusion.

Charles pointed to the hair curled around her digit. "You are twirling your hair and pursing your lips. Which you always do when you have something you want to say. So speak your piece and be done with it."

She sighed and spread her hands over the green silk gown she wore. "Have a care for why you're here, Charles. Why you're helping."

He frowned. "I am not following..."

The footman appeared at the door and announced the arrival of Lady Eleanor.

"Bring her in," Lottie said to the footman before turning back to Charles. "She is meant to wed, not to be distracted by you."

Something deep in Charles's chest gave a little snag. There was Eleanor's second condition, which he had not yet answered: his amenability toward marriage to her. He'd thought of it for a good length of time, and frankly did not see the possibility of her not being wanted.

"I'm well aware of that," he replied.

"Good." Lottie beamed widely at him. "Then I'll let you have your time with Lady Eleanor once we have had a chance to celebrate her success. Assuming she brought the journal."

Before anything further could be said Lady Eleanor entered the room, appearing unlike she ever had before. A gleam lit her emerald eyes, reflecting the grin on her face, and her cheeks were rosy with good health. She'd already removed her cloak and mask. Her bright red hair was tied back in a simple knot, and free of the ghastly blonde wig.

"Oh, Lottie," she breathed. "Thank you for your incredible instruction. Your tutelage has been invaluable."

Lottie gave a squeal of excitement and caught Lady Eleanor in a hug. "I'm so very delighted," Lottie gushed. "I heard how brilliant you were. Have you had any proposals yet?"

If Lady Eleanor had been surprised by the physical affection of Lottie's impulsive hug, she did not show it. Instead she returned the hug and laughed. It was a sweet, joyous sound that Charles found to be quite pleasant.

"It has only been one day," Eleanor said.

Lottie released her and put a hand on her hip. "Does that matter?"

"Well, I did have many callers, and Mother has stated that the Earl of Devonington would like to take me to Vauxhall. I also received several lovely flowers."

Lady Eleanor slid a glance at Charles and smiled, as if they had a shared secret. And perhaps they did—he knew how eager she had been to rid herself of the Earl's company. But even with the knowledge of her disdain for Devonington, he could not stop the gnaw of irritation grinding at him.

"Have your feet quite recovered?" Lottie asked with a chuckle.

Lady Eleanor rolled her eyes playfully. "Not enough to chance another set with Devonington any time soon. I was lucky to beg off from Almack's this evening, or I might have been in the same situation once more. But, I had something to bring tonight."

She hefted a bag from her side. Charles stepped forward and accepted the welcome heft of it into his grasp.

"One of the journals," Lady Eleanor said. "As promised."

He pulled the stiff leather handles of the bag, splitting it open at the middle to draw out a battered journal with an embossed gold compass on the front. A true journal of the Adventure Club.

Relief washed over him. *She had brought it.*

"You remember our agreement?" Lady Eleanor said.

Her sly glance indicated that she still anticipated an answer for her second condition. Charles's gut tensed. Surely agreeing to wed her if she had no other alternatives was no great deal. Her victorious night at the masquerade practically guaranteed that he'd never have to make good that promise.

He looked up from the journal. "I do," he replied smoothly.

He pulled the key from his jacket pocket. It had been worth the discomfort of its sharp edges jabbing against him to ensure it remained safe.

Lady Eleanor came to his side, teasing him with her delicate scent, which had clung to his clothes the night before.

"Shall we get started?" He handed her the key.

An impish smile touched her lips. "I confess I've read through a little of this one. Even without the key it made for interesting reading."

The flat metal sheet rested in her hands, held just at the empire waist of her evening gown. A mere inch below her bosom. Much as he wanted to delve into the contents of the journal, he could not stop his attention from glancing over the bounty of her creamy breasts, encased in a swath of pale green silk—the lucky cloth.

"Will you open it?" she asked.

"Yes." He pulled back the cover to the first page of neatly written script.

"It isn't my father's handwriting." Eleanor settled the key so it fit snugly within the page.

"Nor my father's." Charles studied the key. The letters revealed through the slits spelled out WDIFLSJSNLIDF-NEWSZDIJLBEK.

Eleanor shook her head. "It makes no sense—no matter how I try to combine the letters."

"It was the same with my father's journals," he replied. "But there must be at least one or two pages where it works. It has to be here somewhere."

"This is so very interesting…" Lottie peered down at the book.

Charles knew Eleanor would prefer to be alone with him, to get his answer to her request. Part of him wished to be with only her as well, yet part of him feared it. Thoughts of Eleanor had burned through him since the masquerade ball, of kissing her and how much he longed to touch her.

Then there was the answer she still awaited.

He cradled the weight of the journal in his hands, its leather soft and cool against his palms, its secrets scrawled on fine paper. He knew he had to have them all.

He would have no choice but to agree to Eleanor's terms—and hope to God he was correct that she would never press him to make good on his agreement. And that he could stay his growing attraction.

Chapter Fourteen

Eleanor found using the key to be far less fascinating than reading the journals themselves had been. And Lottie found not a jot of it interesting, despite her initial claim. After only several pages she cast a flippant excuse and made her way from the drawing room.

Eleanor's pulse sped up a notch. She and Charles were alone. She would have her answer.

"We ought to forgo all the pages with images…"

Charles spoke beside her, near enough for his warm breath to tickle the sensitive skin of her neck. Each time he did so delightful prickles of pleasure danced over her, like the little bubbles of champagne floating up the sides of a glass.

"Good idea."

There would be no words on those pages, of course. Though she also suspected he feared some of the drawings would be too vulgar for her. And they were. She'd seen them herself, but she would not confess as much.

She tried to turn the page showing a roughly sketched tower, but it caught on her glove and she turned several pages rather than only the one intended.

"You should take off your gloves."

He took the book from her and set it aside with the key.

Her heartbeat tripped over itself. Charles took her hand in his and slipped free the button at the heel of her palm. The blunt edge of his forefinger ran up her inner wrist. Eleanor sucked in a breath. When had the skin there become so sensitive as to make such a simple touch feel so terribly intimate?

"Your Grace…" she whispered.

"Charles." His voice was low, quiet—a silken caress in her mind. "Call me Charles, Eleanor."

Her mouth went dry and she found she could no longer speak. Instead her eyes remained captivated by his and she nodded. He pulled at the gloves and they slipped off, unveiling her palms to the cool air of the room one glorious inch at a time until her hand was bare and in his.

There were small calluses on his palms, but his long, tapered fingers were cool and smooth against the heat of hers. He held her hands between his, letting their skin press together.

Eleanor's breath came faster, and she wondered idly if he could feel the wild thrum of her pulse against his skin. His fingers moved over hers, restlessly exploring, including the carefully rounded edges of her nails and the highly sensitive dip of her palm.

Eleanor watched the graceful slide of his hands over hers and tried to keep from closing her eyes at the blissful sensation of their naked flesh against each other's. He put his hands to hers, palm to palm, so his fingertips extended an inch over her own, and slid his fingers between hers.

There was a sensuality in the act of joining them together which left her flushed and her insides trembling.

She gasped. "Your Grace, this is—"

"Improper." He released her and cleared his throat. "Indeed, it is. Forgive me."

He laid her gloves gently on the table and passed the

journal to her. She took it with trembling fingers. Her skin still hummed with the tantalizing warmth of his caress.

"And it's Charles."

He winked at her, appearing unaffected by an encounter which had left her hot and flustered, with that strange thrumming racing through her veins. He reached over her and used those magnificent hands of his to find the page they'd last left.

"Do you have an answer for me?" Her voice had gone breathy and it made her sound altogether foolish to her own ears. "For my second request?"

"Say my Christian name."

His voice was a low, sensual purr that stroked over her. Dear heavens, he was going to make her faint dead away before the hour ended if he kept up with such intimate flirtation. Even still, her mouth went dry at the suggestion behind the command.

"Your answer, if you please… Charles." His name lingered between them and tasted sweet on her tongue, like tea cakes or marzipan.

"Yes, Eleanor." He glanced down, as though almost shy, and regarded the journal. "My answer is yes."

He lifted the key from where she'd set it aside absently and held it up, so they might work together again. The thin piece of metal fluttered in his grasp and giddiness charged through her at the way he too was clearly affected.

The idea that she was causing him to feel the way she did, shaking with excitement and breathlessness, served only to make every part of her tingle with awareness.

He leaned closer to her side with the key, close enough that their shoulders brushed as he moved the metal from one page to another. The warmth of his body seeped through his jacket and whispered against the exposed skin of her arm. She wanted to edge closer to him, until she was firmly pressed against his tall frame.

Eleanor turned the pages almost without seeing them, absorbed in his nearness, in the wonderful exotic spice of his scent. She hoped he was concentrating on the key, as she found herself incapable.

His gaze alternated between the book, and her. More specifically, her mouth, as though he longed to kiss her as he had the night of the masquerade.

She turned one more page and her gaze fell on a vivid painting of a woman wearing little more than scarves. A swath of red fabric was tied over her breasts and a long purple skirt was slung around her naked waist, with slits high enough to reveal her thighs. Her arm was extended upward, with her middle finger and thumb pinched together, and she stared directly out of the page with dark, fathomless eyes and long, enviable lashes.

The woman was beautiful, but the exposure of her person obscene. Far more so than any other image Eleanor had seen thus far. She would have dropped the book had Charles not grabbed it from her.

Too many questions whirled through her stunned mind for her to fix on any one in particular, and she regarded Charles with a look of confusion. Well, perhaps panicked confusion, if she were being entirely honest.

"There are things in here a lady should not see."

She knew this, of course, but she hadn't expected such a state of nudity.

Eleanor swallowed. "Who was she? A…a courtesan?"

"Ghawazi." He closed the book and cast her a regretful frown. "Women who dance."

"She's so exposed…"

The horror began to fade and a raw curiosity pulled at Eleanor. She reached for the book. Charles did not stop her from taking it. She pulled it open to the page and stared down at the image once more—the image of a woman whose sole source of income relied on performing. Eleanor was not so foolish as to believe women such as her only danced. And yet there was no shame painted on the woman's lovely face. There was only pleasure and satisfaction.

Eleanor considered her own ungloved hands. How ridiculous to be so overwhelmed by bare fingers when this woman was nearly naked and seemingly glad to be so.

"This is not appropriate." Charles reached for the book.

"Nor is my being alone with you," Eleanor countered. "Or being in a courtesan's home, or reading through this journal, or having kissed you on the terrace, or our agreement. And yet I seem perpetually to do all the things I was taught long ago that a lady ought never to do. And I am enjoying it."

Her body trembled with the realization of what she'd said. It had burst from her with more emotional truth than she'd permitted herself to experience in a lifetime. It was powerful, this liberation. Powerful and euphoric. And she suddenly found herself craving more.

Charles had struggled for the whole duration of his time with Eleanor. It had all been so much easier when he had been able to regard her with distaste, as the daughter of the man who had destroyed his father's dreams.

But now, as he witnessed her determination to overcome her failings, and as she looked to him for his candor and advice, and after he'd sampled the sweetness of her lovely mouth, it was impossible to hate this woman.

What the devil had consumed him to have her call him Charles? And yet the way she said it, soft and hesitant and far lovelier than his name had ever been spoken before.

He'd been distracted by the closeness of her person to him—near enough for him to sense the heat of her, to breathe in the subtle jasmine notes of her scent—and that damnably low-cut bodice had distracted him every time he'd tried to read the letters in the key.

And after such a declaration from this woman, of her newly found enjoyment of life, he was drawn to her. He looked up and saw the passion lit up in the depths of her soul. He moved toward her as a moth to a flame, unable to stop his hands from caressing her lovely face.

He should stop. Leave. Call Lottie. Anything.

His mind raced with ways to free himself from the grip of his own temptation when Eleanor pushed onto her toes and pressed her lips boldly to his own.

He accepted the kiss, meaning it only to be a simple caress of her soft mouth on his own, something chaste and innocent. Just one and then he would back away, as he ought to. He needed to leave her for another man—one who would be a proper husband to her. And yet that first capture of her lower lip was swiftly followed by the greedy brush of his tongue.

A soft whimper sounded in the back of her throat and she sank against him, giving herself fully to the kiss, to him. His body roared with the want of her, the want to have her closer still, to remove so much more than her gloves. *But she was not his.* And then her lips parted and her tongue swept into his mouth.

His shaft strained against his fitted breeches and blinded all logic in his mind. He'd been a fool to allow so much time to elapse since he'd last had a woman. Too much of his focus had been spent on acquiring accolades and foreign treasures and not enough care had been paid to his person.

Everything in him begged he make up for the oversight now, with this pliant beauty in his arms and her wild vein of passion he'd helped unveil.

Charles trailed kisses down her chin to her slender, graceful neck and gently nipped the area just behind her jaw. Her moan hummed in his ear and sent pleasure rippling through him.

It wasn't enough. He wanted more. Needed more.

He needed *her*.

He should not, and yet he did.

His thoughts splintered apart his rationale and his lips wandered down the delicate line of her collarbone, lower still to the enticing swell of her bosom. Her fingers threaded through his hair and she gave a quiet gasp when his lips grazed the low neckline of her gown.

More.

He tugged gently at the silk until it slid low enough to reveal the tempting pink of one partially exposed nipple.

"Charles…" Eleanor whispered, her voice throaty with desire.

He didn't know if it was encouragement, but she kept a tight enough grasp on his head for him to be held in place and to assume it was not a protest. He pressed his thumb just above the pink nipple, popping it free from the confines of her stays, and closed his mouth over it.

Eleanor drew a sharp intake of breath and clung to him.

He held her more tightly, pressing her firmly against him, and drew the tip of his tongue around the pert nub. Her body writhed against him, implying that she wanted him every bit as much as he wanted her.

And, God, did he want her.

No. Need. He *needed* her. So much so he was swollen to the point of pain.

A single thought floated to the forefront of his mind: *her innocence*. Its loss would pull away the rest of life's opportunities for her, the way it had for Lottie.

No. Eleanor had need of a husband and it could not be him—not when adventure called to his blood, when he had unmet promises to fulfill.

Charles straightened and pulled her neckline back into place. "Forgive me," he said raggedly. "I forgot myself."

Eleanor glanced down, her lashes hiding not only the brilliance of those green eyes but also her emotions. When she looked back up her thoughts were closed off to him.

She lifted her head with the haughty elegance she'd exhibited weeks before. "Did I do something wrong?" she asked.

"No, thank God."

Her brow lifted. "I don't understand."

"Eleanor, that *couldn't* have gone further."

"I believe it could have."

He stared at her a moment, stunned beyond wit and words. "I'll not strip you of your virtue. Especially not when you are seeking a husband."

The small muscles of her neck tensed and she gave a stiff nod. "I understand."

She lifted the journal from where it had fallen on the ground, forgotten in the blaze of passion.

"I believe I will read through this on my own, as the key does not appear to have revealed any secrets to us."

He caught her hand and could not help but sweep the pad of his thumb over the incredible softness of her palm. "Are you sure you wish to do this? What is within those pages is not anything a lady ought to read."

She drew her hand from his. "I am not as fragile as you believe me to be."

She was sliding away from him emotionally, leaving him cold in her wake. "Will you be at Hyde Park tomorrow?" he asked.

"My mother did not know you in order to recognize you before," she replied. "I cannot believe she will be thrice fooled now that she's seen you enough to make the connection."

Devil take it, that was an excellent point.

"But you'll come tomorrow?" Was he bargaining with her?

She tilted her head, her expression sweetly pleasant. "Perhaps."

Footsteps sounded outside the door before Lottie entered, with Eleanor's cloak and wig draped over her arm.

Eleanor began to assemble herself for her immediate departure. "Thank you again for everything, Lottie."

Lottie pulled her into another gentle embrace. "The pleasure has been mine, Lady Eleanor. I hope our time together has been beneficial."

The footman appeared to announce that her hackney had arrived. Eleanor inclined her head at Charles and gave him a seductive smile that set his heart pounding.

"Thank you for the tulips, Your Grace."

And with that, she was gone.

The tulips?

"Did you teach her to smile like a coquette?" Lottie asked. "If so, I'm quite impressed with you."

"That was of her own creation," Charles replied.

"Well, then, I'm quite impressed with myself." Lottie winked at him. "Did you come to any exciting revelations?" she asked.

Too many to share.

"Nothing in the journal," he answered earnestly.

She nodded slowly and then smirked at him. "Tulips, Charles? Mind you do not lose your heart to the girl."

"Lose my heart?" Charles scoffed at the preposterous notion. "I merely have an interest in seeing her succeed. And I assure you the tulips were not from me."

Though, dammit, he could not help but sift through his memory to think on who might have sent them.

Lottie shrugged, as if she did not believe him. "I have a favor to ask you regarding Lady Eleanor."

He gave a tense nod, suddenly fearful that Lottie might suggest he never come back to assist Eleanor.

"Will you go to Vauxhall the night she is to meet Devonington?" Lottie wrinkled her nose with distaste. "I do not like the man."

"I'll be there."

Charles poured himself a finger of Scotch. He didn't much care for the man either. But then, he hadn't liked any of the suitors vying for Eleanor's affections. Not a one of them was worthy of such a woman as Eleanor Murray.

Least of all him.

Chapter Fifteen

The dinner at Vauxhall Gardens could not have been more terrible. Eleanor made her way to the carriage line through the thick crowd, desperate to be done with it all.

A day with the promise of heavy rain had left the London air thick with moisture. Her skirts hung with damp stickiness against her legs, her hair felt as though it were plastered against her brow and the evening chill seemed to have taken up residence in the marrow of her bones.

And, as if the atmosphere were not already uncomfortable, the company had been far worse.

The Earl of Devonington held tightly to her arm as he escorted her through the throng of people seeking to avoid the impending storm. It had been he who had been utterly deplorable. He'd eaten with relish at the carvings of ham, famously thin, apparently taking great quantities to satisfy his monstrous appetite.

Watching the glistening slivers of pink meat disappear between his wet lips had resulted in obliterating her own appetite.

And now he had allowed Eleanor's cousin Lady Violet and her Aunt Lydia to become lost in the crowd.

A clap of thunder sounded overhead and Devonington

flinched on her arm. He patted her hand. "It's merely thunder. No need to be afraid."

Drops of rain trickled from the skies and the civility of the crowd dissolved quite suddenly into chaos.

A man lunged between Eleanor and the Earl, ripping her arm from where the Earl had gripped it.

Devonington looked down at his waistcoat and cried out. "The wretch stole my watch!" He bolted after the man without a backward glance to Eleanor.

She stopped in stunned shock. He had left her. Alone. She steeled her spine and pressed forward in the crowd, eager to get to her carriage and end the awful night.

A man further behind them in the crowd caught Eleanor's attention. He rose taller than the other men, his dark hair glossy in the subtle moonlight, with a profile all too familiar. Her breath caught.

Charles.

Rain pattered down with a vengeance and the crowd reacted in kind, becoming rougher and more forceful.

She blinked through the heavy droplets.

Was it truly him?

Had he come for her?

The man turned and she nearly cried out with joy. It truly was Charles. He scanned the crowd, his expression intense, before his stare came to rest on her. Eleanor's heart leapt at the connection, and pounded even harder when he fought through the wall of people, heading in her direction.

She shouldn't be so eager, of course. After their last discussion he had made it quite obvious he wanted her to seek another husband. He had agreed to her condition, but clearly did not intend her to remain unmatched.

The churning sea of bodies tugged her hard to the right, and for one cold, lonely moment Eleanor was at the mercy of wherever the panicked crowd forced her. Shouts filled the air as people cried out for lost companions, while others shoved for advantage. She searched the sea of faces but did not catch sight of Charles again. The glow of hope dimmed.

Then a strong arm settled around her shoulders, blocking the worst of the jostling, and Charles's familiar scent fell around her like a warm embrace.

"I have you, Eleanor."

The voice was smooth and confident. Immediately any distress with Eleanor's situation evaporated.

Charles was there with her and all would be well.

Charles shielded Eleanor from the crowd with his arms, taking on the worst of the bumps to protect her. He did so gladly, grateful for the opportunity to come to her aid, to see her liberated from the company of Devonington.

The arrogant ass of a man had been so loud while speaking that almost every word he'd uttered had reverberated around the expanse of the private boxes. Eleanor, her cousin and the older woman with them had appeared quite perturbed.

Now she was free of the Earl, and standing before Charles with a quiet smile hovering on her lips.

"I have had my footman bring my carriage around toward the back, where it might be less crowded," Charles offered. "May I escort you there?"

"It would be my pleasure to have you do so, Your Grace."

"Charles, please."

He led her away from the edges of the crowd. Those large green eyes flicked up at him and held his stare.

"Charles." She glanced to his mouth and quickly turned her head away, looking toward the direction they headed.

The rain had ebbed to a few trickling drops and the roar of the crowd faded behind them. Ahead, one light glowed in the distance like a brilliant ball of fire. Another lit up several feet away, followed by another, and another.

Eleanor stopped and Charles followed suit. "They've continued to light the lamps," she said.

"It would appear the rain is beginning to abate." He kept his hold on her. There was no longer a need to do so, but there was certainly a desire.

Several more globes of light lit up in the distance.

"It's amazing, isn't it?" she asked. "Like magic."

He looked down at her and found her lovely face awash in the gilded glow of those many lamps. "Indeed."

She shifted her gaze from the lamps in the distance to his face. Dots of rain had left a sheen on her skin, giving it an otherworldly, luminous appearance.

"Why are you looking at me like that?" she whispered.

"Because you're beautiful."

She did not lower her head in demure acceptance of his compliment. Instead she tilted her head up. "No longer an Ice Queen?"

The blazing memory of that kiss, her passion, scorched through him. "God, no. Rather the opposite." He dragged his fingertips over a wet lock of her red hair. "You are fire, and your kiss is quite unforgettable."

"Then you've thought of it?" She slid him that coquettish look.

"I have." Time and time again…until the tease of the memory became as unbearable as the aching in his groin.

She turned to him and set a hand on his chest. The rain had resumed its steady fall, pelting them with frigid drops, and yet so intense was the heat in her eyes he scarcely registered the cold.

"I've thought of nothing else."

Her voice was quiet, intimate, the same as it had been that day when he'd kissed her. He recalled it all too well now…taking the pinkness of her nipple into his mouth and reveling in her cries of pleasure.

"Nor have I," he groaned truthfully. It had even distracted him often from his task of finding the ruby.

Rain soaked them both, leaving their clothes clinging to them and giving shape to her curves beneath the loose-fitting gown she wore. He could see a narrow waist and full hips to match the breasts he knew to be round and firm.

Her gaze took on that boldness he so enjoyed. "Will you kiss me, Charles?"

Lottie's words came back to him at that unfortunate moment. *She is meant to wed, not to be distracted by you.*

Yes, he'd promised to marry her if there was no other interest, but he wouldn't be any more a good husband to her than his father had been parent to him. He should take her from this place. And yet even as he thought as much he found himself already leaning into her, drawn to the promise of her lips.

Her mouth was warm against his, despite the chill of her skin. Their lips met in a single chaste kiss before their tongues brushed one another's.

Charles's blood raced insistently through his veins, hot with need. Aware of the possibility of being seen, he pulled his evening cloak around her and held her gently to him as he led them both down one of the infamous dark paths of Vauxhall Gardens.

Once they were veiled in shadows, Charles kept his cloak over them both and tilted her face toward his. She licked her rosy lips. With a hungry growl he drew her more tightly against him and kissed her. He sucked her lower lip into his mouth and ran his tongue over it.

The feminine curves of her body arched against him, so the ache of his hard shaft pressed into the softness of her stomach with the most exquisite torment.

She trailed kisses down his jaw to the line of his neck. Her breath sounded loud in his ear and he felt the warmth of his lips parted over his skin as she gently nibbled at the sensitive skin there. He had to clench his teeth to keep from giving in to a long, hungry groan.

"Is that what you like?" she asked.

Dear God.

"Eleanor…" he said her name on a rough exhalation.

Her hot tongue touched his neck, followed by a delicate little nip and a sucking kiss. His body blazed with the tingles of lust. Did she know what she was doing to him?

He found her body under the cloak by touch, roaming his hands over her sweet shape. He reveled in the slenderness of her waist, the curve of her bottom, which he caught in his hands. She arched her hips forward and his shaft pressed against her stomach once more, causing friction against the intensely building pressure.

He murmured her name, though he'd intended to speak in protest. They should not be doing this—especially in a place they could be so easily seen. Yet even as he thought such things his hands did not cease their eager exploration.

She pulled her head away from him as his palms found the weight of her breasts. Her lashes swept downward, her face registering all the pleasure she felt. Confound it, he could not help himself. His thumb brushed the swell of her breast until a moan told him he'd found her nipple beneath the thickness of her stays.

She was so passionate, so receptive. Had he ever wanted anything the way he wanted Lady Eleanor Murray?

Yes, he had. The stone.

Everything he'd sacrificed already and would sacrifice in the future. The stone, his promise—it had to be everything. Before the dukedom, before Eleanor. She needed a husband—not to be pawed by him.

It was for exactly that reason that he drew away and straightened. "We cannot keep on with this," he said.

Eleanor simply nodded. Her eyes sparkled with longing and her mouth remained reddened from the force of their kisses. She did not protest this time—perhaps because she understood that together they were far too dangerous.

Charles quickly adjusted his placket once his cloak had fallen back around him. He could only hope the raging swell of his manhood would soften quickly.

Eleanor took his offered arm, her hand trembling slightly when she set it atop his, and together they made their way to the waiting carriage.

The cool air cleared the fog of Charles's passion. He would not allow himself to ruin Eleanor—especially when he knew he could not in good conscience marry her.

Once he had the rest of the journals from her, he would unearth the whereabouts of the Coeur de Feu and then leave to reclaim the stone, fulfilling his father's promise. In the meantime he would have to keep his distance. For Eleanor's sake.

Chapter Sixteen

Charles couldn't take it anymore. Or rather he couldn't take the lack of progress anymore. He'd applied hours to searching through the journals from their country estate to no avail.

Placing the key on the page, reading something indistinguishable. Then placing the key on another page and reading something indistinguishable. And yet again placing the key on the page and reading something indistinguishable.

In truth, it was as he'd expected. He'd gone through every book and piece of paper in the stack of boxes. What he needed was doubtless in the other journals Eleanor had.

He would need to see her again in an effort to secure more of them. After all, he had said yes to her request to wed her if there was no one else willing to. The journals were his due.

And yet the very idea of being in the same room with her left his mind whirling with a stream of memories he could not shake.

Their secluded tryst under his cloak blended with that last time at Lottie's. When he'd kissed her. Actually much more than kissed. He had pulled down her bodice and drawn her nipple into his mouth. He almost groaned at the memory, for such a little bud it was—berry-pink compared to her alabaster skin, firm against his tongue. And the way she'd cried out and clung to him…

Regret twisted in his chest. He shouldn't distract her from the marriage mart. Especially when the only vow he truly intended to fulfill was the one he'd given his father.

He stared down at the great mahogany desk he sat at—his father's. Even the new chair Thomas had procured did not alleviate the sense of strangeness in the room, the sense that Charles did not belong there. Perhaps he never would adjust to this room being anything more than his father's study.

Charles lifted his gaze to take in the richly appointed room with its blend of luxurious furnishings and cherished artifacts, all amid the piles of opened boxes from Somersville Manor.

His father had seemed invincible, too vibrant ever to die. And yet he was truly gone. After a lifetime of seeking his father's approval, of wishing for the bond Charles had seen other fathers and sons share, it would never happen now.

Not that his childhood had been without privilege. Charles had been brought up with nothing but the best of everything, and his father had never asked anything of him.

Nothing until the stone. And in that one request Charles had failed.

He rose abruptly from the desk, unable to stand the crush of his father's success around him, the scalding reminder of how Charles was so very imperfect.

"Thomas," he said aloud. His valet appeared immediately. "Have my carriage readied. I'm curious to learn if I've been blackballed from White's yet."

As it turned out Charles had not been ousted in his absence, and was, in fact, welcomed eagerly into White's as if they'd known he was coming. No doubt Thomas's doing.

Upon entry he had a brandy in his hands and the hearty

welcome of several members. Conversation centered on Napoleon's impending exile and the hardheadedness of General Thouvenot, who seemed to have a dogged determination to keep the fortress of Bayonne in French control, despite Napoleon's surrender.

The conversation fed an inner part of Charles he'd long forgotten he needed—a chance to come to a place like White's and let his mind relax, away from all of life's complexities. There was no mention of Lottie and her fall from grace, nor of unmet promises to dead fathers, nor even any reminders of a woman who set his soul aflame.

No, White's was about men. Sports. Drink. Politics.

"Somersville!" The Marquess of Kentworth waved him over from where he stood near the broad fireplace with the Viscount Rawley ever at his side. The volume of Kentworth's voice indicated that the man was thoroughly in his cups.

Charles sipped at his own ball of fire and made his way to his old university chums. They'd certainly had some fun together in their heyday, and he was more than ready to reminisce over those fond memories rather than dwell on the dismalness of his current life.

"How are you, old chap?" Kentworth smiled at him, revealing the dimple in his right cheek which had always set the ladies aflutter.

"Relegated to London society." Charles lifted his glass in silent toast.

Kentworth bellowed a laugh. "Aren't we all?" He drank deep from his overfull glass, sloshing some over the rim.

"Rawley." Charles nodded at the tall, thin man, who gave the shy half smile that had followed him into adulthood.

"Have you found all the gold in Africa yet?" Kentworth asked with a bleary grin.

The question rankled, teasing at Charles's already tense nerves. He hadn't gone to seek fortune. Fortune he had in abundance, thanks to generations of cunning investments and the well-known financial accoutrement of the Somersville ancestors. But then Kentworth's demeanor had always edged near the obnoxious when he was foxed.

"I don't believe gold is precisely what Somersville was seeking," Rawley said.

Kentworth squinted and nodded. "Of course, of course… Antiques and other things of the like—correct?"

Charles chuckled in an attempt to be more good-natured than he felt. "Mmm…other things of the like."

"I bet you found yourself a good bit of sport around the world, eh?" Kentworth said with a wink.

Before Charles could answer, or Rawley could intervene, Kentworth gulped more of his drink and put up a finger to indicate that he was prepared to speak again.

"You recall that bit of ice we danced with at Covington's masquerade ball?"

That bit of ice.

Charles clenched his jaw. "I might…" he replied slowly.

"The one with the glittering dress and the bright red hair?" Kentworth tilted his head as if the details weren't important. "She rather surprised us by being quite unlike the prim and prudish miss that Ledsey had led us all to believe she was. After all, the chap was once considering marrying the ewe."

"Lady Eleanor was quite impressive." Rawley nodded in agreement and took a measured sip from his own glass.

Kentworth lifted his drink in the air. Somehow it was already half drained. "If I were the marrying sort I'd make a bid for her myself. Though she won't be long on the market."

"Why do you say that?" Charles's stomach flipped. A ridiculous reaction. He should be grateful to be saved from having to work his way out of his promise.

"Devonington is going to make an offer." Kentworth

snorted. "He may not be much of a boxer, but the old goat is full of spirit—I'll give him that. And I can't say she'll be inclined to refuse, considering she's got enough dust on her already to be lobbed on the shelf, and he's got enough wealth to make the heavens sing on command."

Charles's drink soured in his gut. Kentworth went on to prattle about some other such nonsense, but Charles had stopped listening.

Devonington was going to ask for Eleanor to marry him.

He was an earl with an unrivaled fortune. He had a strong name with titles that could be traced back to the Conqueror. The man was a bloated beast, and his conversation was a dead bore. But eligible ladies long on the market—ladies like Eleanor—might easily be pressed by their desperate families to accept such a proposal.

Kentworth was right. The odds of her refusal were low indeed—especially with the Countess of Westix shouting in Eleanor's ear.

Of course, she might refuse—but then she might do so in order to come to Charles, for him to make good on his promise. And he could not follow through.

Either way, he did not like the outcome.

Charles finished off the rest of his brandy and excused himself to obtain another, eager for the slow burn and inevitable numbness of its embrace. Because apparently, no matter where he went, he was haunted by all his choices.

Eleanor was near bursting with excitement. She practically ripped off her cloak, mask and wig the moment she passed the threshold of Lottie's town house in Bloomsbury Square. She'd been forced to hold her news until now, as the prior evening her mother had insisted she attend Lady Bunton's soiree, which had been a wretched bore.

Certainly not as exciting as the night at Vauxhall. Not the time she'd spent with the Earl of Devonington, but the quiet moments stolen in the dark with Charles. Her face went hot at the memory, and she tried to still her pulse-pounding eagerness at the prospect of seeing him again.

Lottie's butler showed her inside and she all but ran into the drawing room where she had spent so many evenings. It was at that moment, when she was anticipating sharing her news with Lottie and Charles, that she realized that for the first time in her life she had friends. True friends whom she trusted.

"I have the most thrilling news to share!"

The words exploded from her before Charles could straighten from his welcoming bow. She clutched the bag of journals to her chest in her excitement.

He stiffened and rose slowly, his jaw locked in a tight grimace. Lottie cast him an odd glance and gave her a confused look.

Goodness, but Charles did look as though he'd put a vinaigrette under his nose. His lips were drawn together and the skin around his eyes was tight.

Perhaps he feared she might mention to Lottie their exchange at Vauxhall. But surely he would know she would keep such things to herself.

"I have the answer," Eleanor said breathlessly.

"Do you?" he asked, in a voice that could only be described as dispassionate. Holding much of the same cold detachment *she* had once been rumored to possess.

Now she understood how unwelcoming that demeanor could be, and why she'd had seven unsuccessful Seasons.

"Yes." She spoke more softly now. "The information we need is only in one journal."

Charles frowned at her from across the room. "What are you referring to?"

Lottie looked between Charles and Eleanor, frowning.

"The journals." Eleanor held up the bag. She'd procured

the remaining five from her father's study, but knew there to be more at their castle in Scotland.

In truth, Charles had been correct—the contents in the journal were not for a lady's eyes. Amid lengthy stories of cracking ancient walls and dusty artifacts were lurid tales of what native women around the world offered by way of pleasure and sex.

One tale had gone into such detail on debauchery she had spent the better part of an evening woolgathering and wondering if such things could even be physically possible. So much so, she'd missed most of the Earl of Devonington's conversation about his new hunting dog while at the soiree.

Not that she'd minded terribly. At least not until she'd gone to bed that evening and the story in the journal had replayed itself in her imagination, and curiosity had caused a warm and hungry hum between her thighs...

The pinched expression on Charles's face relaxed. "The journals. Yes."

It was not only his face which relaxed, but the tension hanging thick between them.

Eleanor went on. "There was a final entry in a hand I did not recognize as your father's or mine. It alluded to another journal—one written only by this author—detailing his research on the whereabouts of the gem in light of growing unrest among them all."

"Yes, my father indicated there being only one we'd need the key for." Charles strode toward her. "Did you bring all the journals with you?"

"I did." Eleanor held out the black bag she'd brought with her. "Well, with the exception of the journals in Scotland, at our castle there."

Lottie peered at the journals, the twist of her lips indicative of her fading excitement. "While these *are* incredibly interesting..." She widened her eyes and looked askance with the exaggeration of a person intentionally lying. "I'll leave you to look them over. But this is the last lesson I give you permission to miss."

She wagged a finger in chastisement at Eleanor, but the threat behind her words were offset by the kindness of her sapphire-blue eyes.

Eleanor nodded obligingly and Lottie excused herself from the room rather than stay and be subjected to something she considered hopelessly dull.

Eleanor dug out the book she'd referenced, and flipped to the last page, where the author had written about the stone.

The door closed behind Lottie, and Charles came nearer. The heady spice of his scent teased at Eleanor and swept her into a stream of memories. His hands on her, his mouth on her, the tug of her evening gown, the touch roaming over her body and coming to rest on her breasts... How she'd fantasized about what she'd read of in the journal transpiring between her and Charles, imagining it in every lurid, sweaty detail until she was dizzy.

She tapped the choppy handwriting with her fingertip, already having taken it upon herself to remove her gloves this time. She was nearly breathless with the hope that Charles would touch her again, kiss her again. "At least now we have the handwriting with which to identify the pages that will be needed to be compared against the key."

"Brilliant." He regarded her with a curious expression. "Is there any other news you intended to share?"

"Did you expect some?"

"Of course not." He chuckled.

The shift in his mood was notably odd.

"I'm assuming you've already sought out this man's handwriting throughout the other journals?"

He had known she would be thorough. The thought

pleased her immensely. "I have," she confirmed. "There are several examples we can review with the key."

Silence blossomed between them, ripe with sizzling memories and wanting.

"I must thank you for coming to my aid in the crowd at Vauxhall."

Eleanor tried to push aside what had happened after his assistance, so she could fully focus on speaking. Only such memories were not so easily swept aside.

"I daresay the Earl was quite upset with my departure."

She almost laughed at how red-faced he'd been the next morning, when he'd called. Even her mother was beginning to grow weary in her championing of him, despite his considerable wealth.

"Indeed?"

Charles studied her face with the intensity of a man who intended to kiss a woman. Was it wanton to wish so desperately that he would? Heat suffused her entire body in a vicious blush.

"In truth, I ought to apologize." He spoke in a quiet, intimate tone, impossible to overhear from the other side of the door. "I should not have kissed you."

Disappointment dragged at her elation. "You regret it?"

He ran a finger down her cheek and she found herself leaning toward him.

"Yes and no."

Her eyes closed, the better to appreciate the sensation of his touch.

"I've been thinking of you far too often…"

Charles's voice sounded gently in her ear, sensual and low.

"How you rob me of my senses…"

His small sigh whispered across her skin like a caress.

"I shouldn't have come tonight. In truth, I should never come again."

Never come again?

Eleanor's eyes flew open. "Charles, don't say such things."

He clenched his jaw and stroked the pad of his thumb over her lower lip. His touch against her mouth brought to mind a curious act described in the salacious tale she'd read, and a small flame kindled the fire.

Curiosity simmered through her.

Did she dare be so bold?

Chapter Seventeen

Charles knew he ought to walk away at that very moment. Leave London with the journals he did have and not return until he was certain Eleanor had been safely wedded and bedded and was forever out of his grasp.

And yet the idea of her marrying Devonington set his blood to boiling.

To imagine her in Devonington's bed...it was more than he could stand. Not that he hadn't imagined her in a bed—only it had been his own, her skin like hot silk under his hands.

She regarded him with a brazen stare, as though she could read his thoughts, as though she meant to entice them. It was getting harder and harder to walk away from the temptation that was Eleanor Murray.

So Charles did not walk away.

He did not even step back to break the inappropriate closeness between them.

He could not bring himself to, no matter how reason played in his mind. His thumb brushed over her full bottom lip once more, reveling in the supple pliancy of her warm skin. Her lips parted—and then she drew in the digit with a hot, gentle suck.

His mouth fell open on a surprised exhalation and his manhood lurched to attention.

She tilted her head upward, releasing his thumb and capturing his gaze instead. "One of the journals proved to be most...edifying."

Charles swallowed around a dry throat. "I think you ought to have taken my advice and not read them."

Eleanor lifted an eyebrow in a show of naughty prowess. "Should I?"

This level of flirtation would make his shaft burst if she continued. Regardless, it did not stop him from speaking—from asking what he should not. "What was it exactly that you read?"

"Of the other things the *ghawazi* do." Her cheeks flushed. "Aside from dancing."

An image of her in swirls of near-transparent silk lodged in Charles's mind, the same image as had done so the last few nights. Ever since they'd looked at that image of the nearly naked woman together. His skin tingled with the nearness of her and his shaft raged against his breeches. Ridiculous, considering she hadn't even touched him. Well, save when she'd sucked on his finger as if...

He shook his head. "You should not have read them. They are not fitting for a lady."

"I have questions."

Walk away, Charles.

But again he did not listen to his own command, and instead found himself pressing deeper into the damning conversation. "What questions?"

She pulled in a deep breath and her bosom swelled against the red silk dress she wore. He thought of her nipples beneath, pink and perfect. His tongue longed to circle the sweet buds, to draw them into the warmth of his mouth and suckle her until the nubs grew taut.

Her lashes had lowered to a languid half-lidded gaze.

"When a woman sucks a man's thumb, is it not in suggestion of her taking into her mouth…?" She paused, bit her lip and looked down to his breeches.

"Eleanor, this conversation is not—"

"Appropriate. Yes, I know." Her blush deepened to an even darker shade of red. "But there is much we have done that is not appropriate. Please answer the question. When a woman sucks on a man's thumb—"

"Yes," he gritted out.

Dear God, this conversation was becoming the greatest torture of the sweetest kind.

She nodded. "And if a man could be pleased thus, could not a woman?"

Sweat prickled on his brow. "A woman can be pleased in many ways."

"So, is it possible to please one another without penetration?"

The woman was going to kill him with such talk. "Yes."

"A man and woman can both be pleased while she continues to remain a virgin?"

Her line of questioning was suddenly apparent.

The room had grown far too warm, her gaze far too bold, and his willpower was far too damned weak. What man could resist such temptation?

Still, he knew he needed to try. "Eleanor, we shouldn't—"

"I know."

She stroked her fingertips over the lapel of his jacket before glancing up at his face. She rose up on her toes and pressed a kiss to his lips. There was no delicate innocence about her. No, this time her affections were those of a woman hot and hungry with need.

Charles ought to have resisted. God knew, he should have gently pushed her away. In truth, he had every intention of doing so—until she boldly sucked his tongue and gave a low, hungry moan. Her body melted against his, a delicious pressure against the strain of desire aching in his groin.

Dear Lord.

He was helpless against the lure of lust. His arms came around her, pulling her even tighter to him. Her hips pressed to his, against the impossible hardness aching here, and she gasped. Her hands slid up his back as she brought them closer still.

They kissed with lips and tongues and the careful grazing of teeth, until their panting breaths tangled with one another. He ran his hands over her body, gliding over the silk as he caressed her narrow waist and cupped the delicious curve of her bottom. She arched her pelvis against his and sent waves of pleasure through him from the hot friction.

She kissed his jaw, then his neck, and ever so delicately nipped the skin just below his ear. Prickles raked down him with an intense thrill. She writhed against him, her dance one of eager desperation.

Charles knew all too well the ravenous need plaguing her. He nudged his knee between hers and she parted her legs. Her skirts rode up to her shapely stocking-clad calves.

She held tight to his shoulders and rolled her hips in the natural rhythm of lovemaking, riding his thigh in a way that made him want her to ride *him*. Her right leg was between his own, and her movements ground against his shaft. He drew down the neckline of her dress with a tug and her breasts popped free, full and firm.

Eleanor's hand moved up to the back of his head. "Yes. Please, Charles."

He bent his head to flick his tongue over her nipple, circling it several times before pulling it between his lips and into his mouth. She gave a quiet cry of pleasure and arched her back.

He moved to the other nipple while he cupped the weight of her silken breast. "Please what?" he ground out.

His mind whirled in a maelstrom of lust and burning hot need. He could barely think to breathe, let alone piece together what it was she asked for.

"Pleasure me." Her voice came out in a whimper.

Hell.

What man could say no to such a request?

Eleanor was so very near to exploding—as though she'd gone too close to the sun and all of her had been set aflame. Heat blazed through her veins and pulsed with such longing it was as if a pounding drum reverberated through her entire body. Her world focused on Charles—on those brilliant blue eyes and the wild passion he aroused in her.

He went still at her request. Would he deny her?

She put her hands to his chest and slid her fingers down his flat stomach, the way the woman in the journal's entry had done, down to where the thick column of his desire rose within his breeches. He choked in a breath.

She grazed the swell rising beneath the placket, tentatively at first. He gave a shuddered exhalation and tensed against her. She fixed her regard on his face and curled her fingers over the bulge. His brows flinched and drew together, as if the pain of his need was as intense as her own. He was hard under her touch, like iron or bone. *This* was the shaft the journal had referred to, engorged and heavy. It was the device from which a man drew his pleasure and gave it in return.

Charles cursed and pulled her touch from his body. Disappointment charged her at the thought of being forever without satiation from such powerful, painful longing. That was until he leaned her back onto the chaise and his hand swept up her calf.

Her breath caught.

She lay back on the smooth velvet as his fingers continued to move higher up her leg, inching up her gown and chemise. Her breath came faster as his touch proceeded, until his fingertips whispered past the edge of her stockings and caressed the nakedness of her thigh. Her core trembled in anticipation.

Yes. Higher. Closer. Almost…

Finally, at long last, he made his way up her entire leg. He eased her hem higher, over her hips, baring her most intimate place to him. She ought to have been embarrassed, but the lust hammering through her was too great. She could scarcely think, let alone feel shame.

He paused, gazed down at her, and brushed the juncture between her legs. A jolt of pleasure shot through her and she gasped at its intensity.

Charles closed his eyes like a man in prayer. "Good God, Eleanor. You are so very wet."

His words were appreciative, which must mean being wet was good. She rubbed her thighs together in anticipation for more.

His chest rose up and down with his ragged breathing and he opened his eyes to watch her again as he drew his finger over her once more. Pleasure, marvelous and perfect, rippled through her.

"More," she whispered. "Please."

He did not disappoint. His finger moved with careful skill, up and down over her, before coming to a stop on a particularly sensitive spot. His stare burned into her as he rolled his digit in slow circles.

Heat spiraled through her. Eleanor covered her mouth to stifle a cry of pleasure and her head fell back. She was unable to focus on anything save the bliss of his stroke between her legs. Right when she felt as though she might explode, he drew his finger away and made the lazy path up and down, up and down over her once more.

Her hips strained toward him and she opened her eyes. "Please, Charles. *Please.*"

He leaned over her and captured her mouth in his, while his fingers found their way back to that delightful spot. His shirt teased against her nipples, his tongue tangled with hers, and his fingers moved and moved and moved, until Eleanor's entire body drew tighter, like a clock being wound to the point of breaking.

And break she did. Into splinters of color and light and heat and everything wonderful. She cried out with the overwhelming euphoria of it and her hips bucked upward. The sounds of her pleasure were muted against Charles's mouth as he continued to kiss her while his fingers worked, until she was too sensitive to stand another moment.

Charles pulled back slightly, his eyes intent on her. "That was beautiful, Eleanor."

This time a blush did heat her cheeks. "That was…incredible." Her voice trembled slightly. "I never knew…"

He gave her a lazy half grin and her heart flipped. "And now you do."

She couldn't help but smile. "And now I do."

The hardness of his manhood rested against her thigh, and called further attention to her curiosity. If his fingers could procure such delight, what might the organ made for pleasure accomplish?

She released her hold on his shirt, where she had apparently crumpled the fine cloth in her fist during the mindlessness of her climax, and let her touch wander toward his shaft.

"No." He spoke through gritted teeth. "Eleanor, do not tempt me."

Oh, but she wanted to tempt him. She wanted him to

be as hopelessly lost in her as she'd been in him only moments before.

"I want to do for you as you've done for me." She continued her path downward. The bulge was hot to the touch.

"Eleanor." He wrapped his fingers around her wrist and pulled her hand away. "I cannot—"

Steps sounded outside the door. Footsteps muted by carpet until they were upon the wooden flooring in their last step before the door.

Eleanor and Charles stiffened as one in surprise, but both were too late even to attempt to move. The doors flew open and Lottie filled the doorway, witness to the full extent of their incredibly compromised position.

Chapter Eighteen

Charles had the presence of mind to shield Eleanor—at least as much as was possible in their precarious position.

Lottie stared in shock, her hand still poised on the door she'd thrown open. Her mouth hung agape, and her eyes were wide enough to indicate that she'd seen it all.

With a gasp, she jerked back from the room and slammed the door shut. The echo of the impact rang out for a solid second before either of them could move again.

Charles immediately turned to Eleanor and found her face as red as her brilliant hair. Her eyes caught his, sharp with guilt, before sliding away. He eased off her and reached to help her adjust her gown, but she brushed him aside. She quickly put herself to rights and stared regretfully toward the door. He didn't blame her. He wished to be gone from the room as well.

"Forgive me, Eleanor. I should never—"

He should never have what? Kissed her? Touched her? Wanted her? Were such things even possible to avoid?

"I should never have compromised you," he said at last.

Though she faced him, she kept her emotions masked beneath the sweep of lowered lashes. Her right eyebrow twitched upward. "I encouraged you." She pulled in a shaky breath. "I wanted you to do everything you did. So, you see, there's no transgression to forgive—except perhaps on my account. Forgive me for pressing you so firmly to…" She gave a shuddering exhalation.

He caught her under the chin with the tip of his forefinger. "Eleanor…" He hated seeing her like this, her pride bruised, her face colored high with shame.

"What's worse is that I do not regret what we've done, but only…" When she finally did look up at him, her eyes were wet with a sheen of tears. "Only fear the result of our being caught might mean Lottie will not allow you to meet with me again."

"Eleanor—" Damn, but words were hard to get out.

She lifted her brows.

"You should marry Devonington." He ground the words out as though they were glass splinters passing over his tongue. It was what he should say, he knew. For her sake.

A look of confusion puckered her brow, followed by a veil of emotionless apathy—the shield firmly lodged back in place. The knife in his heart twisted.

"I see." She lifted her chin in the haughty tilt she'd worn when he'd first met her. "You may keep the journals. You've earned them. Farewell, Your Grace."

She nodded her head politely, as was due his station, and opened the door, leaving the room.

Charles watched her departure, as he had most nights, and felt his heart twist under the duress of his shame.

Lottie appeared in the doorway and pushed shut the door behind her. "How dare you?"

Her voice shook and her glare skewered into his soul. She marched toward him and her silken skirt kicked out in angry thrusts.

"How *dare* you, Charles Pemberton?"

Before he could even open his mouth to speak, she pulled back her arm and her fist connected with his cheek.

He swallowed down the assault. It was deserved. His cheek stung.

"That was quite a hit, Lottie. Have you taken up boxing?"

"Do not jest with me." Her eyes flashed with a murderous rage. "How dare you do this to her? I care for her and you've left her ruined."

He reached for her. "You don't understand. I didn't—"

"*You* don't understand," Lottie hissed. "You've made her like me, Charles. You've ruined her life. Such a promising young woman…" She turned away and a sob choked out of her. "You've made her damaged…like me." Her slender back rounded and she cried with all the force of a broken heart.

But her heart was not the only one to break, for Charles's had surely shattered into a thousand pieces at witnessing such hurt in his childhood friend.

One step had him at her side. He put his arms around her and held her, even when she tried to tug away. "She was not compromised," he said insistently. "Our actions were certainly improper, but I assure you her innocence is thoroughly intact."

"Oh, Charles." Lottie turned into him and sobbed against his chest.

He held her in place and patiently waited for her tears to ebb. At last they did, and she accepted the handkerchief he offered.

She dabbed her cheeks and regarded him with tear-spiked lashes. "It's for the best this way…letting her go. You could never marry her."

Charles gritted his teeth, hating how very correct Lottie's cutting words were. If he married Eleanor it would be a destined failure. If she remained in London while he traveled she would be miserable, and if he were made to forgo his travels he would be miserable.

He needed travel like air to his lungs. It pumped in his veins and brought light to his world. The first time he'd stepped off a ship…the first time he'd glimpsed what he had only read about before…the powerful force that made him feel that much closer to his father… It was an exhilaration he could never sacrifice.

A marriage between them could never be right.

Damn Lottie and her valid statement. And damn how much it piqued his ire.

"And how will she be better off with Devonington?"

"She will never love him." Lottie sighed. "So at the very least our sweet Eleanor will not suffer a broken heart."

With that, she left the room, leaving Charles alone with the weight of his own guilt and the echo of the painful truth.

The wait for Eleanor's hackney took the better part of what seemed like a lifetime. She stood stiffly, beneath the protection of her domino, wig and mask, hoping they were enough of a shield to blanket her mortification.

This was the price of wantonness.

Lottie had come to speak with her once Eleanor had disguised herself and begun waiting for her carriage. Their conversation had been brief, yet poignant enough to play out continually through Eleanor's mind.

She had tried to tell Lottie it had been her fault—which indeed it had been, shameful as it was to confess. Lottie had cast aside her admission with the counter that Charles had known well enough what he was doing and ought to have been in control of his person enough to decline her encouragement.

But it was more than just their conversation—it was Lottie's warning which resided in Eleanor's chest with all the comfort of a sharp stone.

Charles will never give up his travels…not even for you.

Eleanor hadn't expected him to give up *anything* for her, or to offer anything other than the pleasure she sought and a reprieve from the marriage mart. In truth, she hadn't even intended him to have to make good on his promise to marry her. And yet Lottie's words had pierced an area Eleanor had not realized was tender.

You should marry Devonington.

Charles's blunt statement echoed in her mind. Her eyes tingled with the threat of emotion, but she pulled deep on the strength she'd always fallen back on. Murrays were strong, after all. They did not give in to hurt.

Somehow the reminder failed to penetrate the haze of pain, where it glowed in her chest with a white-hot intensity.

The footman appeared and led her to her hired coach. She followed numbly, listening and speaking with mindless action. A similar hackney sat parked across the street. Its very presence rankled her nerves with considerable irritation. Was Bloomsbury truly so popular as to have such traffic dawdling upon its rain-slicked streets?

Eleanor turned her gaze from the offensive hackney and directed her attention back to Lottie's town house, where it rose high and obstinate in the shadows. How would Lottie's conversation with Charles go?

The coach pulled away and Eleanor sat back in her seat. Worrying and wondering would do nothing. Considering how Lottie had spoken to her, Eleanor was sure she would not see Charles again—just as she'd feared. And it was her own fault.

Charles was gone forever—the man she'd somehow let in more than she'd thought. She'd hoped to meet another who could instill her with the passion he did, and yet she had been so dazzled by him the rest of the world had fallen into the shadows. Potential suitors included. She had squandered what precious little time she had.

It wasn't until she was safely home and in her room that

she gave way to the crush of disappointment. She put her face in her hands, where her palms were cool against the blazing heat of her face, ready to let free her tears.

A knock sounded at the door—the gentle rap of her mother.

Eleanor snapped her head upright and sucked in a deep, calming breath before bidding her mother enter.

The Countess strode in with a smile. "I come with the most exciting news." Her mother clasped her hands together. "The Earl of Devonington has asked for my blessing."

Eleanor might have staggered under the news if she hadn't been standing beside her dressing table. She put her hand to its flat, steady surface. "I beg your pardon? Your blessing?"

"The Earl of Devonington. He is smitten with you, my dear." Her mother brushed a lock of hair from Eleanor's brow and frowned. "Are you ill? Your face is hot."

"Devonington?"

Eleanor shook her head. The events of the night whirled themselves into a tangle of thoughts and emotions too great to sort out. Charles had told her to marry Devonington. Actually *told* her to. Her stomach churned.

Frustrated desperation knotted at the back of her throat. "Mother, he is old and fat."

The Countess's mouth fell open in horror. "Eleanor Murray, you are not ever to say such things. The Earl is exorbitantly wealthy and his family well-established. With Evander gone…"

"I know."

Eleanor lowered her gaze from the starkness of her mother's stare. The topic of Eleanor's brother had always struck at a raw wound in them both. Her mother didn't need to finish what she'd intended to say. With Evander gone there was no way to increase the remaining funds in her mother's trust, nor to protect Eleanor from Leopold's avarice. And Eleanor's intention to find someone who made her feel like Charles had been terribly foolish and a shameful waste.

"The Season will be over soon," her mother said.

"I know," Eleanor said again, this time in a whisper.

The Countess stared at her daughter and her eyes softened. "I know you don't want to wed him, Eleanor. You're right—he is old and fat. But he is the type of man who will spend his days hunting and his nights engaged in activities which will keep him from your side. You need only see him occasionally, and he will likely die long before you."

"Mother!" It was Eleanor's turn to gape in horror.

The Countess waved dismissively. "Don't be so shocked, Eleanor. I'm being entirely pragmatic. Once he is dead you will be a widow with the bulk of his wealth. You will have freedom to do as you please without the obsessive scrutiny of the *ton*."

Her mother's words were hollow, but they were true.

"And the alternative is far more dismal," the Countess said with great gravity.

Eleanor nodded, unable to speak around the aching tightness in her throat. Her options were an abysmal marriage or a degrading, destitute existence. This was not how it was all supposed to turn out. She was supposed to have found a man who offered her a life of passion, of excitement.

The Countess patted Eleanor's cheek. "We are invited to a ball at Lady Canterbury's tomorrow evening. The Earl of Devonington will ask you to wed him. What will you say?"

Eleanor swallowed. Her heart throbbed with the weight of her burden and her ribs ached with every breath. "I will say yes," she answered dutifully.

It was not happiness or relief which showed on the Countess's comely face, but concern. "I think that is for the best." A smile twitched at her lips, but the display of discontent did not leave her features. And then her mother did a curious thing: she put her slender arms around Eleanor and embraced her.

Despite the chill of her mother's hands at her back, Eleanor leaned into the embrace and put her face to her mother's sharp shoulder.

"I should have done this more," her mother said on a choked whisper. "When you were a girl…before it was so very awkward." She laughed and leaned back. "I'm proud of you, daughter."

She gently kissed the top of Eleanor's head and left the room.

Eleanor stared at the closed door and tried to ignore the dull pang in her chest. So this was her success, her grand victory. After working hard to allow herself to truly feel, to expect a brilliant life, she was now going to have to shove it all down deep within her once more so that she might become the Countess of Devonington.

Chapter Nineteen

Charles was in a devil of a mood when he returned home. So when Kentworth extended an invitation for a night on St. James's Street Charles was all too eager to agree. They started at White's, of course, with several rounds of brandy and a bit of faro. They played for over an hour before Kentworth decided the table's luck had run its course and they retired to one of the many tables to drink.

All night Charles waited with an anxious blend of fear and eagerness for Kentworth to mention Eleanor again. Thus far the conversation had not broached anywhere near women, let alone Eleanor.

Rawley glanced at his pocket watch—a habit he often employed prior to announcing his readiness to depart. Once Rawley departed, Kentworth would have no one to tame his crass commentary. If Charles meant to ask after Eleanor and Devonington, now would be the time to do it.

"Have you heard any further information about Devonington asking Westix's daughter to marry him?" Charles took a sip of brandy to cover up a grimace at his indelicate bluntness.

Rawley's perceptive scrutiny landed on him with too much interest. Kentworth, however, bellowed a laugh and put his drink onto the table. "You interested?"

Charles gulped down more brandy, his thoughts and tongue loose with drink. "I may be."

"In the wedding or the woman?" Kentworth waggled his brows.

Charles looked between Kentworth and Rawley. *Hell.* He'd opened the topic—he might as well see it properly closed. "The woman."

Kentworth chortled. "Would you even stay in London long enough to see her wedded and bedded?"

Irritation jangled Charles's nerves and he didn't bother to offer a reply.

Kentworth narrowed his eyes and his expression turned more serious. "You could do worse than her…" He tilted his head in latent consideration. "Far worse, actually."

"Are you going to ask her before Devonington has a chance?" asked Rawley.

"Always thinking ahead, this one." Kentworth reached across the table and ruffled Rawley's hair.

Rawley waved him off and brushed his hand over the mussed brown strands until they were swept neatly to the right, as he always wore his hair.

"It is merely a consideration." Charles leaned back in his chair.

"Are you considering when you'll ask or if you'll ask?" Kentworth probed.

Charles shrugged. He didn't know himself what he was talking about. He only knew that the idea of Devonington taking Eleanor into his bed made his world darken.

Kentworth barked a laugh and got to his feet. "I need to attend to the call of nature. You gentlemen continue this discussion and I'll be back in a bit."

Rawley tapped a finger on the table as Kentworth strode away. "Do you love her?"

"What?" Charles asked, chuckling at the ridiculousness of the question.

"She won't increase your social standing, and while her family properties are substantial they're nothing compared to what you already hold. In offering to wed her before Devonington does you'd create a lifelong enemy. Why would you marry her for any other reason than love?"

That was a damn good question.

It was because Charles enjoyed her company and appreciated the frankness with which she spoke, and how she didn't make him guess as to her thoughts and desires as other ladies. Because a passion had been lit within her and it made her glow with a sensuality that drew him like the most attentive of moths. Because every time he thought of Devonington taking her as his wife, wearing her like an expensive bauble on his arm, undressing her and bringing her to his bed, it was like a punch in Charles's gut. But love...

Charles scowled and settled back in his seat. The aged leather under him creaked. "By God, Rawley, I daresay I had forgotten how damn insightful you are."

"It's part of my charm," he replied dryly.

Charles shook his head and chuckled at his old friend. More was the pity the chap couldn't find himself a lady he might be happy with. Many men weren't the marrying sort, but Rawley certainly was. Honest, dependable—a good man any way one looked at him.

"Another question." Rawley held a hand up in silent inquiry. "If I may?"

"By all means."

"Would you remain in London?"

Damn. Charles turned his focus to the cut-crystal glass in front of him.

Rawley continued before Charles was forced to answer. "I do not profess to know the hearts or minds of ladies. However, if you did intend to marry Lady Eleanor for love, I would venture to say she would not do well left alone while you seek adventure."

There always had been a gentle, considerate side to Rawley. Charles had forgotten that too. Perhaps it was because he'd been raised primarily by his mother, after his father had died within days of his birth.

Regardless, Rawley had brought up a point Charles already knew well enough. It was why he knew he could never have Eleanor in the first place. Charles's true love was travel—the same as his father. The idea of him even considering marriage was ridiculous.

And yet the idea of Eleanor wed to that pig Devonington coiled in Charles's gut like something cold and ugly.

Rawley tapped the flat of his hand on the table, severing Charles's ruminating, then got to his feet and nodded politely. "It appears Kentworth might have been waylaid by another faro game, and I have much to do in the morning. If you'll excuse me?"

Charles rose and nodded to his good friend as Rawley made his departure, leaving his brandy glass with several sips remaining at the bottom.

Kentworth was indeed at the faro table, where the conversation about Eleanor did not resurface. Once more he soon declared the faro table to be absent of luck, his tone boisterous with drink, and they found themselves in the West End, at a gambling hell of questionable reputation.

A smoky haze filled the room and the lights cast a low glow. Voices cried out in victory and defeat alike as dice rattled, cards snapped on tables and coin clinked from one hand to another.

Kentworth immediately made his way to the hazard table, sitting beside a woman who tossed him a coy glance as he called his bet. Charles stood several paces behind, not inclined at all to participate. He'd never been one to throw his wealth away.

"What's your pleasure, Your Grace?" a woman's voice asked.

Charles turned and found a red-haired woman in a crimson silk gown that had seen better days gazing saucily at him. She had green eyes, only not as green as Eleanor's... more of a moss-green, where Eleanor's were the color of vibrant emeralds or sunlit grass. Eyes that could penetrate the soul.

"I'll fetch you a drink if you like." The woman bit her lip in the obvious way women did when they wanted a man to stare at their mouths. "Or do you have other vices you'd like to see sated?" Her gaze wandered over him with interest.

A proposition. With a woman who looked like Eleanor. Would that quell the desire raging through him or only whet his appetite? Charles's mind was a sloshing jumble. He needed no more spirits.

"What would you do if you knew a lady was to marry a disgusting pig of a man?" Charles asked her abruptly.

The redhead's mouth pursed. "Depends on how you feel about her, I'd imagine." She gave a knowing smile. "Considering you're asking a woman who's all too willing to give you a night you won't forget a question about another woman, I'd wager you rather like her. And if I were in your position I imagine I'd try my damnedest to stop her."

Charles rubbed at a tense muscle along the back of his neck and nodded, considering her words.

She eased closer to him and the edge of one pert breast brushed his arm. There was a dry, powdery scent about her. "I can make you forget about any woman..."

Except he didn't want to forget Eleanor. Even if he should.

The redhead's words echoed through him. *I imagine I'd try my damnedest to stop her.*

Charles cleared his throat. "I think perhaps I should go."

The woman lifted a single shoulder, indicating that his refusal was of little consequence to her. "You know where to find me." She turned away with a suggestive wink.

He made his way from the gaming hell, knowing Kentworth would not notice his absence. Charles's mind was made up. He would speak to the very devil herself the following day and demand that Eleanor not marry Devonington. And while he was at it he would request the journals he knew to be in the Scottish castle. The journals Eleanor had given him that fateful day had yielded nothing of import.

Yes, in the morning, he would call on the Countess of Westix.

Eleanor stared down at the fresh bouquet of red roses on her dressing table. That made a bouquet every day from Devonington since they'd danced at the masquerade ball.

No doubt it was meant to entice her. Yet the delivery served quite the opposite. The bright blooms inspired no affection in her. They didn't even hold a modicum of cheer. Rather they were a symbol of an ominousness that was far too imminent: her engagement.

It was through will alone that she did not give way to the threat of tears. After all, she'd yielded to the luxury of such emotion once she'd gone to bed the prior evening. Her eyes were still gritty with the aftereffects and slightly swollen.

The door to her bedchamber swung open abruptly and startled her into surprise. Amelia quickly closed the door and ran—truly *ran*—to Eleanor.

Amelia's hands fluttered anxiously in front of her. "My lady, he's here. I think to ask for Her Ladyship's blessing."

Eleanor's stomach dropped like a heavy stone. "But I thought I had at least until tonight?"

Amelia shook her head and her mobcap flapped around her narrow face. "Not the Earl of Devonington, my lady. The Duke of Somersville."

Eleanor stared at her maid, sure she'd heard incorrectly. "I beg your pardon?"

"The Duke of Somersville." Amelia bounced up and down in a bundle of excitement. "I think he's here to seek your hand in marriage."

Eleanor's pulse tripped and then wildly scrambled on at an erratic pace. Elation and excitement, pure and undeniable, thrilled through her. But surely he wouldn't truly offer. He had never expressed interest in marriage. As it was, he had needed time to consider her request even when he was not likely to have to honor it.

She shook her head, determined to tamp down the flame of insipid hope. "How do you know that's why he's here?"

Amelia grinned. "Because he's telling the Countess not to allow you to marry Devonington."

Eleanor leapt to her feet, unable to stop the foolish jolt to her heart. If there was a possibility of being with Charles she would not lose it—especially not for the likes of the Earl of Devonington.

"My lady, stop."

Eleanor stopped and turned back to Amelia. "Yes?"

"You shouldn't go."

Eleanor gawked at her maid. "You told me he was here to put an end to this dreadful engagement with Devonington. Why would you stop me?"

"This way if anyone asks you can tell them I told you not to go and not be lying about it." Amelia winked and shooed at Eleanor. "Go on, now."

Eleanor flew from her room and went as quickly as she dared down to the first floor, where she leaned her ear toward the crack between the double doors of the drawing room and strained to listen.

Charles's voice was the first she heard. "Your Ladyship, if you would only give me a chance."

Eleanor's heart soared with recognition. It truly was Charles. He had actually come here to seek her mother's permission to marry her. Just as Amelia had said.

"Your Grace, you demand my daughter not marry another, and yet you have no one else to recommend." The Countess's tone was on the verge of exasperation.

"I do have someone to suggest."

Charles's deep voice rumbled through the doors. Eleanor could scarcely breathe. Would he suggest himself?

The clink of a glass sounded. "By all means," said the Countess with some amusement.

Eleanor held her breath to ensure she would not miss a single word.

"Viscount Rawley."

Had Eleanor not been pressed to the door, she might have toppled over. *Viscount Rawley?*

"Viscount Rawley?" Her mother's incredulity matched Eleanor's own.

"He is responsible, mild-mannered, considerate." Charles rattled off the attributes like one might a list of items to obtain from the market. "He would be a loyal husband, and one with whom I believe Lady Eleanor might find happiness."

"Viscount Rawley has not asked for her hand but the Earl of Devonington has." The pause suggested the Countess was delivering one of her powerful pointed stares. "Will that be all?"

Eleanor closed her eyes to stay the prickle of tears. Charles had not come to ask her to wed him, but to suggest she to wed another. Someone *he* deemed adequate.

A lengthy silence followed. There was something else. She straightened, her curiosity piqued, her pathetic hope reignited with a miserable spark.

"My father had several journals," Charles began. "I believe you may be in possession of some. Possibly within your holdings in Scotland."

Eleanor clenched her fists. Blast him and his dogged determination to get those journals.

"I know nothing of such dreary things." The Countess sighed. "If there is nothing else…?"

There was another clink, more gently set than the other. "Thank you for your time, Your Ladyship. I'll see myself out."

Heavy footsteps sounded toward the door and Eleanor scrambled back to hide beside a large Oriental vase.

Charles had opened the door to a colorful life—one of feeling, of passion. All of that was now slipping through Eleanor's fingers. She would be left with nothing. Nothing but the memory of how life might otherwise be.

Her chest heaved and her mind spun with the beginnings of a desperate plan taking shape.

Charles emerged through the door, looking smart in a pair of polished Hessians with dove-gray breeches, a deep blue waistcoat and a charcoal jacket. She waited for him to walk partway down the hall, near the alcove by the stairs, and then she darted after him. After all, this might be her last chance to avoid marriage to Devonington and to truly live her life—especially when she had the very thing Charles needed: those damned journals.

Chapter Twenty

Charles was so enraged he almost did not hear the whispered call of his name. He turned cautiously, still unsure he'd heard correctly. Eleanor stood under the stairs in a white day dress, her lovely red hair bound back. Something hard thudded in his chest. God, but she was beautiful.

She pulled open a door in the wall beneath the stairs, revealing a narrow room within, and waved him over. A surreptitious scan confirmed that they were alone. For now.

She slipped into the darkness and he followed suit, ducking into the small space so he wouldn't bash his head against the low ceiling. She pulled the door shut behind him, plunging them into a darkness so great he could not see his hand in front of his face.

But he could smell her. Sweet jasmine, enticing femininity and all those memories, both tender and scorching.

"Charles…" she breathed. "I thought I would never see you again."

The familiarity of her voice, soft and intimate, pulled at a place deep within him. He wanted to follow her words, to blindly locate her face. Devil take him, he wanted to do more than touch her soft skin. He wanted to press his mouth to hers, to be rewarded with her gasping cries of pleasure.

"I know you have no desire to marry me." Her tone

pitched slightly and she paused. "You told me to marry Devonington, though clearly you do not wish for that."

His heart squeezed. How much of his conversation with the Countess had she heard?

"I do not wish to marry him either," she said. "And so I have one final proposition for you."

She rushed on before he could speak again, as though she were worried he would stop her.

"Marry me, Charles. Marry me and we will venture to Scotland, to Comlongon Castle, where the remaining journals are. I will give them all to you."

Marry her.

The boldness of this new offer should have shocked him. But it did not. He knew Eleanor far too well for that. She was determined, stoic in her resolve. Such very admirable traits. And yet he could not clear from his mind the thought of Eleanor alone in the vastness of Somersville House, surrounded only by the invisible presence of servants and loneliness.

A memory panged in his heart—one of the boy he'd been and how very enormous Somersville House had seemed when there was no one to fill it.

Could Charles do that to Eleanor? Leave her there, wondering what he was doing, as she stayed in that large, empty space, her imagination spiced with the readings of their fathers' journals. How could he confine her to such an existence?

"Am I truly so undesirable?" Her voice broke.

She bumped into him and the dull thump of her hand frantically patted the wall. Clearly she was seeking a way out. It was all too much—not only for her, but for him. The break in her voice, her desperation to leave. The knowledge that Devonington would have her, that the journals in Scotland could be his. Knowing he'd hurt her. Knowing that although he shouldn't, he *wanted* her.

"Eleanor, wait." He reached out for her in the darkness and sent something hard clattering to the floor.

The frantic sounds of her search for the door ceased. His hand found her shoulder. Using only the power of touch, he swept his fingertips over her fine cotton sleeve to the delicate hollow of her collarbone and up to her smooth cheek.

"I find you immeasurably desirable." He brushed his thumb over her lower lip. "I believe I have proved as much."

Her intake of breath whispered against his thumb. "Why will you not marry me?"

"Because I would make a terrible husband."

Confessing as much out loud made something in his chest give an unexpected wince. He shifted his thumb to stroke the softness of her cheek.

"Worse than Devonington?" she asked with obvious skepticism.

"I intend to travel, Eleanor, the same as our fathers did. First to find the ruby, and then to explore, once I've seen to the duties required of me as Duke. I have never considered myself a man to sacrifice the world for a family."

"You will have to marry eventually," she said softly. "As part of your duty. Why not let it be me?"

Her question squeezed at his chest. Why not, indeed? Perhaps because she was too intelligent. Possibly even too dear to him. Because, as much as he did not wish to admit it to himself, he did care.

More than he would like to.

"And why would you have to sacrifice your adventures?" Eleanor pressed.

He shook his head, though he knew she couldn't see it. He had lived a life without love for so long he did not know if he could ever create it, if he could ever give it. On so many accounts he would be a terrible husband and father.

"I wouldn't be able to live with myself if I abandoned

you while I sought my own way in life. What sort of a husband would I be to leave you constantly? I refuse to do to my family what our fathers did to us." He spoke with quiet sincerity.

"I'm not a woman easily broken or swayed." Her voice was strong, with her usual show of tenacity. "And I can quite well take care of myself."

He chuckled. "Don't I know it?" He hated this darkness, and his inability to witness the determined flash he knew must be in those green eyes. "But I fear you would eventually hate me."

"I believe I would hate you less than my other option."

Her other option. Devonington.

A spike of discomfort shot through Charles.

Damnation, was that jealousy?

If he wed her he would have the rest of the journals. He would have her. Wholly and completely. His wife. In his bed.

It was then that he knew he could never truly have allowed her to marry Rawley.

"Hate me less, you say?" He couldn't help but grin. "Such flattery from an Ice Queen."

He couldn't stop touching her, letting his hands play over her cheeks, her neck, the graceful line of her collarbone. And she did not move to stop him.

"Your mother will be unhappy." He traced the edge of her collarbone. "And if we wed we ought to do so quickly. I could have a license in two days."

He stroked her neck and felt her pulse quicken under his fingertips.

"Then you agree?" Her question was breathless with anxious hope.

He would have her in his bed, the journals would be at his disposal, and part of his ducal agreement fulfilled. How could he say no?

"Yes." He drew her to him, unable to stop himself.

"Will you be attending Lady Canterbury's ball this evening?"

"I have an invitation, but have not yet accepted it."

This earned him a playful tap on the arm. "You ought to respond to your invitations. Preparations must be made for intended guests."

"I've always been bad at such things. Fortunately for me that task will pass to my wife in the future."

"You're hopeless." Laughing joy was evident in her voice. "Attend tonight," she said. "We can announce our betrothal and the banns can be called later this week. We could be married in a month, easily. It will all be proper, which will please my mother, and she will eventually forgive me, I'm sure. After the announcement is made and the banns are called she will not have me beg off our engagement. Not when it would cause a scandal."

It was an underhand plan, but a solid one nonetheless. "Are you certain, Eleanor? Your mother may not forgive such a deception."

"I cannot imagine my life with Devonington."

Nor could he. The very idea of winning her from the buffoon made Charles want to puff out his chest. Instead, he cradled her face and brought his mouth down to meet her lips. Except he met something decidedly not her lips.

Eleanor gave a little laugh. "You've kissed my nose."

He kissed her lower, touching his lips to her warm mouth. However, once he had managed one kiss he knew it would never be enough again. He anticipated the future with something deeper, more passionate—an ignited lust that would not have to stop.

He straightened, pressed his lips chastely to the top of her head, and breathed in the floral scent of her. Soon he would bury himself in that perfume, tangle in it amid tossed sheets and naked limbs.

"I shall see you tonight."

A crack of light showed at the door and he realized she had pushed it open. She hesitated, her face cast in that slice of light, revealing her beauty to him and, more importantly, where her lips were located. He bent over her and gave her a kiss he was sure she would not forget.

He lingered a moment longer than he should, hesitant to leave when he wanted nothing more than to deepen their kiss. "Tonight."

Finally, he slipped into the brilliance of the empty hall, making his regretful departure as he'd promised the Countess he would.

At last, he would have his journals—and he would also have leave to fully taste Eleanor's passion.

It wasn't until Eleanor and her mother were announced at Lady Canterbury's ball that nerves finally got the better of her. Not necessarily because of the public declaration of her engagement to Charles, but her anticipation of declining Devonington's offer.

Lady Canterbury had always possessed an affinity for roses, and red blossoms now adorned every surface. Why, it almost looked like her own home, after all her hothouse deliveries from Devonington.

Suddenly she recalled Lord Canterbury's support of Lord Devonington in parliament, and her blood went cold.

These roses weren't there to reflect Lady Canterbury's predilection for the flower. Good heavens, they were there for Eleanor. For Eleanor and the Earl of Devonington.

No sooner had she thought of the man than he appeared before her. His thinning brown hair was slicked back against his scalp and he had a quizzing glass raised to one eye, so that it appeared three times its size within the lens. Beneath his black evening jacket he wore a red waistcoat.

"Lady Eleanor."

He bowed over her hand, revealing the balding patch at
the back of his head. His mouth pressed to the back of her
glove and she found herself grateful for the barrier between
her skin and his lips. He straightened and openly admired
her, running his gaze down the length of her sapphire gown
overlaid with black lace.

His chest puffed out. "You look stunning."

Eleanor murmured her thanks—a difficult thing to do
around the weight of her guilt. Devonington, while not the
man she'd wanted to wed, had gone to great lengths to make
the evening memorable.

"My Lord." The Countess inclined her head in a generous nod and held out her hand.

Eleanor waited for the Earl to bend over her mother before her gaze swept the room for Charles and met only disappointment. He had not yet arrived.

She glanced to the entrance, where Lord and Lady Canterbury were still receiving their guests, but did not find
him there either. The music would begin soon. Surely he
would want to be there for the opening set?

The Earl of Devonington grinned down at her. "Lady
Eleanor, would you do me the honor of allowing me to lead
you out for the first set of the evening?"

It was on the tip of her tongue to decline, or at the very
least offer some form of an excuse that might afford her
some time to allow Charles to arrive. But the Earl's smile
wavered and she realized she was taking too long to reply.

"How very flattering of you to consider me," Eleanor
said, as genuinely as she could muster. "I would be happy
to."

All too soon Lady Canterbury was asked to declare the
first set. She cast her sly consideration upon Devonington
and announced that it would be the waltz.

The Earl offered his arm to Eleanor, who had no choice
but to accept. Her glance around the room turned desper-

ate, but all she found were the same familiar faces of the attendees and too many blasted roses. *Where was Charles?*

"This time have a care not to miss your steps as you did when last we danced," Devonington said under his breath to Eleanor.

"I beg your pardon?" she asked, distracted.

"Your dancing could use some improvement, and as you are dancing with me I want to ensure you perform perfectly." He touched her shoulders. "Straighten your back more."

The pressure of guilt in her chest lessened—especially as he'd nearly crippled her last time with his oafish steps. But if nothing else, the dance would help pass the time.

However, it was also a revelation in her understanding that she could never have gone through with a marriage to him. From the closeness of his overwarm body to the unending stories of his hunting dogs and having her feet crushed again and again, she knew she could never have a life with him. Not a happy one.

Finally the dance finished and he escorted her back to her mother while Eleanor searched the sea of faces. Without success.

No sooner had they arrived at her mother's side than the Earl grinned down at Eleanor. Fine red veins crossed like embroidery thread over the tip of his bulbous nose. "I'd like to dance the next set with you as well, Lady Eleanor."

Eleanor turned sharply to her mother, who simply nodded. Suddenly the air seemed too thin to breathe and all the blood in her body rushed to her head.

"But a second set would imply..." Eleanor's mouth went dry.

Devonington smirked and wriggled his shoulders, very much like a cat about to pounce atop a poor unsuspecting mouse. Except that Eleanor did suspect.

He took her hand in his. "Lady Eleanor, I'd be honored

if you would join me in the next set, and be by my side as the Countess of Devonington."

"P-pardon me?" Eleanor stammered, though she'd heard him quite well enough.

"Don't stammer—it sounds common." Devonington's eyes were hard when he spoke. "I want to marry you."

Eleanor's search around the room became frantic—a drowning victim seeking a rope. But Charles was not there. Why had he not shown? He should have been here to save her from having to reject Devonington. Had he changed his mind?

"You do not want to wed this woman."

A masculine voice spoke up. While familiar, she knew at once the man was not Charles.

Eleanor turned in surprise and found Hugh standing before Devonington.

"Ledsey, what the devil are you going on about?" The Earl puffed up, seeming to draw the girth of his prominent belly into the expanse of his chest. "You had your chance at her. Leave her to your betters, boy."

"This has nothing to do with me." Hugh gave a smug grin. "And everything to do with the courtesan who has been training her each night."

Chapter Twenty-One

Eleanor stared in horror at Hugh. Had he truly said aloud that she had been visiting a courtesan at night for training?

Her stomach sank as she remembered seeing him in the hackney by her house. Had it been him in the hired carriage near Lottie's house as well? Eleanor had been so distraught when she'd left that night, so preoccupied with having been caught with Charles, she had not given the threat the attention it was due.

Now she would pay the price for her careless folly.

Devonington took a threatening step toward Hugh. "That is quite the accusation you make against the woman I intend to have as my wife."

Hugh regarded her, his nose wrinkled with distaste. "I'm sure she'll make for a *wicked* wife…based on the lessons she has been given."

"This is a preposterous accusation," the Countess said, her tone sharp.

"I assure you it is no accusation," Lord Ledsey said with a smirk. "I saw her leave your town house wearing a blonde wig after you had departed for Almack's. I followed her to Russell Square and waited while she was in the town house of a courtesan known as Lottie. I didn't think it was Lady Eleanor at first, but then I questioned the servants and I got the whole story about how Lady Eleanor has been instructed by Lottie these last few weeks in 'special lessons.'"

It *had* been him. Heavens!

Eleanor's stomach swam with something vile and her mouth filled with water, as if she might be sick. To have her secrets bared thus was almost more than she could stand.

"Did you know?" Hugh tilted his head toward the Countess and tapped his chin in mock contemplation. "Or were you blissfully unaware of your daughter's misdeeds."

The color leached from the Countess's face. Eleanor would be ruined no matter how the conversation turned. Too many had been witness to the accusation. Too many were still listening.

The Countess opened her mouth, but Eleanor stepped forward. "She didn't know. I didn't tell her as I feared it might give her an apoplexy. Look now at her face—at the shock you've given her."

Eleanor's mother shook her head, her face falling with disappointment, though only Eleanor knew the truth behind the breaking of the Countess's composure.

"*You* told everyone how cold I was," Eleanor said to Lord Ledsey. "Do you have any idea how difficult it is to attract new suitors while saddled with the moniker Ice Queen? I wanted to learn how to be kinder, sweeter, more likeable— the way your lovely Lady Alice has always been."

A sad, despairing part of Eleanor bade her skim the room for Charles once more. But truly she did not need to confirm what her heart already knew. He had not come. He had abandoned her to this fate.

It would appear she had been too aggressive in their conversation earlier that day. She had badgered him into agreeing to marry her.

The Earl of Devonington turned to Eleanor, the quizzing glass firmly lodged against his owlish eye. "Are you saying this is true, Lady Eleanor?"

How could she deny it?

The attention of all attendees fell on Eleanor. "It is true," she whispered.

Hugh folded his arms over his chest, satisfied with her answer.

Lady Canterbury strode forward and placed herself between Eleanor and Devonington. "Your Ladyship, kindly escort your daughter from my home. She is no longer welcome here."

Eleanor's mother opened her mouth and shook her head. "It was—"

"Forgive me, Mother," Eleanor rushed in. "I should have told you."

Her mother gave a small nod and reached for her with a trembling hand. Eleanor took it and pulled her mother close. Together they slipped behind their societal shields, their faces devoid of all emotion despite the torrents driving through them.

The music had stopped and the silence of so many people lent a surreal presence to the room. A wall of jewel-toned gowns and waistcoats parted to make way for Eleanor and the Countess as they made their shameful departure from the rose-laden ball.

Their last ball. And not just for this Season.

Charles had not come and now even the possibility of wedding Devonington was gone. Eleanor had lost her prospects and damned them to a life of poverty, all in one awful evening.

The Murray women were completely and utterly ruined.

Charles's head ached like the very devil himself. He groaned, and even the rasping growl in his throat set off a pain in his brain so deep the sound might as well be a sharpened weapon plunging through his skull.

Good God, what had he drunk to leave him so ill?

He hadn't been this stale drunk since his university days. Well, aside from perhaps that one evening with the bottle of absinthe, after a French import had been impounded on the coast of Africa.

"Thomas…" The valet's name came out in a slur.

Regardless, Thomas appeared beside the bed. "How are you feeling, Your Grace?"

"Like I've gone for a jaunt on the Thames and then been stampeded by a herd of elephants."

Thomas tsked to himself and helped Charles sit upright.

The room spun and the sun streaming in through one window seared into Charles's eyes.

Thomas pushed a glass of something murky and foul-smelling toward him. "Drink this. It'll help."

Charles grunted. "Isn't it drinking which has got me to where I am presently?"

Thomas smirked in that obnoxiously optimistic, affable way of his. "One would assume so…though I find it odd that only one drink would cause you such misery."

"Only one drink?" Charles slugged the bitter mixture down. It was thicker than he had expected and stuck in the back of his throat, no matter how many times he swallowed.

Thomas, angel that he was, passed Charles a cup of tea. He gave his servant a grateful look and let the hot liquid scald away the remnants of the foul concoction. His tongue prickled with the effects of a righteous burn, but it was a far cry better than that awful unpleasantness.

"You had a glass once you returned from the Countess of Westix, Your Grace." Thomas took the empty tea cup. "More?"

Eleanor's mother.

Charles's mind snagged on a troubling thought. Why had he gone to see that devil of a woman?

The single thought tugged and the rest came tumbling

back in a great rush. He had finally agreed to wed Eleanor. He would have her *and* the journals. Their engagement was to be announced that night.

"Reply to Lady Canterbury, if you will, Thomas." Charles sagged back against his bed. "Inform her that I will be attending the ball tonight."

"Forgive me, Your Grace, but the ball was yesterday."

Charles jerked upright. "Yesterday?"

Thomas nodded. "You fell asleep in your study after having called upon the Countess of Westix. I left you sleeping as I found you for two hours, then finally brought you to your bed. You slept on through the night." Thomas frowned. "I don't understand it. The bottle only appeared to have one measure taken from it."

The blood drained from Charles's face and left him cold. They were not yet married and already he had left her abandoned.

"Eleanor. The ball. I have to go to her."

Charles swung his legs over the bed. When he rose his legs did not seem steady enough to support him, and he had to catch himself on the mattress to keep from falling.

"Not like this." Thomas shook his head. "Whatever was in that bottle did not agree with you."

"Damn it—what bottle?" Charles growled.

"In your study. The one you received as a gift. I thought you knew who had sent it?"

The memory swam up in Charles's mind now. The fine bottle of brandy…the note welcoming him home and signed with the stamped gold Adventure Club insignia of a compass. He'd thought it a lark—a jest from Eleanor.

Unease blared through the fog in his mind.

Something wasn't right.

In fact, something was very, very wrong.

He staggered to the edge of the bed and held onto the bedpost for support.

"Please, Your Grace." Thomas rushed to his side. "You are not well."

"I daresay I was drugged, Thomas." Charles staggered to the door and burst through it. "I have to go to my study."

Thomas was immediately beside him and he slid Charles's arm over his steady shoulders. They made their way thus to the study, where everything appeared as Charles had left it. He pulled his arm from Thomas, steadier now that the valet's brew had begun to take effect. The liquid had been dreadful, but it apparently worked miracles.

His study was perfect. Too neat. Especially his desk, which all the servants knew better than to touch, even for cleaning.

The five journals strewn haphazardly over Charles's desk were missing. Only the bottle Thomas had mentioned remained.

Charles's stomach plunged to his toes, for the journals were not the only items missing. So too was the key.

Charles gave a groan of despair and sank to the floor.

"Your Grace…" Thomas tried to pull him from where he'd fallen to his knees.

"The journals…the key. All of it." Charles stared dismally at the desk. "Gone."

Thomas regarded the expanse of empty desk. "The key… You don't mean that bit of metal with holes in it, do you?"

Charles dropped his head to his chest. "Yes. It is the only way I'll ever know where the location of the stone might be." Thomas snorted a choked laugh and Charles glared up at him. "What's so damnably funny?"

The valet's face immediately smoothed. "Forgive me. Only it was stuck to your face when I pulled you up to stand. I tried to peel it off and had quite a time extracting it from where it was plastered to your cheek." His mouth twitched and went straight, then twitched again. "You had dots all about your face where the holes had settled for so long they'd left marks."

His face contorted into an exaggerated frown before curling up into a smile, and he covered a laugh with a very unconvincing cough. As he described it, the scene did sound rather humorous. But the most important fact of all from the story was that the key was still in Thomas's possession.

"Do you have it?" Charles asked. "Were the journals gone when you found me?"

Thomas helped him to his feet. "The journals were not there, but I do have the key." He pulled open one of the drawers and withdrew the flat bit of metal. "Here it is, Your Grace."

He approached the desk, lifted the bottle and sniffed.

He scowled. "Laudanum."

"Are you sure?" Charles asked.

"My mother was stuck to the stuff when I was a boy. I'd know the smell of it anywhere." He grimaced toward the bottle. "This was no accident."

Accident or not, Charles had failed Eleanor when it was most important that he be at her side. His heart slithered into his roiling stomach.

"An investigation will have to wait for later," Charles said grimly. "Get me dressed—and quickly. I must go to Lady Eleanor."

"Your Grace, you need rest."

But Charles would not listen to protests. Not when Eleanor no doubt assumed he'd thoroughly failed her.

Chapter Twenty-Two

By the time Charles made his way to Westix Place it was long past an acceptable hour for morning calls. In fact the ladies were most likely readying themselves for their constitutional in Hyde Park. He could recall Eleanor so vividly from those times they'd walked together, with the outdoors making her green eyes sparkle and her cheeks rosy…

He waited in the foyer for the butler to announce him, despite the servant's discernible disapproval. After a worrisome length of time had passed the butler reappeared.

"Forgive me, Your Grace. I have been told to advise you that Lady Eleanor will not be taking callers."

Charles's stomach knotted. She was home, then. "I understand," he said at last.

But, damn it, he did not. He couldn't bear the idea of Eleanor being there and his being unable to see her. He had abandoned her, and now he was without the opportunity to offer an explanation.

By God, he would *not* let this be the end of everything they'd pursued together.

The butler held open the door for Charles to leave. But Charles did not leave. Instead he dashed through the foyer to where the stairs arced up to the second level.

The butler was amazingly fast for his age, and sprinted ahead of Charles to block the stairs.

"I don't wish to fight you," Charles said between gritted teeth.

"And I won't have you harming the ladies of this house." The butler did not move.

Charles tried to force his way around the older man—to no avail. *Damn.* But there was another way around the older man.

"Forgive me." Charles pushed the servant to the right, careful not to hurt him. The butler staggered through an open door, which Charles swung closed, twisting the key and pulling it free. The butler began banging on the door, but Charles did not wait to see if it drew attention and instead quickly dashed up the stairs.

"Eleanor?"

He shoved through the first door to find a water closet. Empty, thank God, for that might truly have been an unforgivable offense. He tried a second door and found a room filled with trunks strewn about, bursting with colorful gowns and simple day dresses.

Eleanor's maid appeared, screamed, and threw the slipper she was holding at him. The red satin dancing slipper bounced ineffectually off his chest and landed soundlessly on the carpet.

"Please," he begged, ignoring the inept assault. "Lady Eleanor. Where can I find her?"

The woman gaped at him. "Your Grace, you most certainly—"

"I have to see her. *Please.*"

Desperation scrabbled over him. For all he knew the Watch had been notified of his forcible entry. He might have only minutes to plead his case.

"I was drugged last night. Robbed. I couldn't come.

I only woke up an hour ago. I fear… I fear I have let her down."

The maid's face lost its harsh resentment and she pressed her palms to her heart.

"I have most certainly let her down," Charles muttered, more to himself than the woman.

"You have indeed disappointed me."

Eleanor spoke from behind him. He whirled around to find her standing in the doorway of what seemed to be her dressing room. The mass of her gorgeous red hair was bound in a simple knot atop her head, with several loose ringlets spilling over her shoulders like fine silk.

"Your presence here is unwelcome and highly inappropriate." She pointed to the open door to her chamber. "I'm asking you to leave."

Charles didn't bother to move. He wouldn't—at least not until he'd said his piece. "I had to see you, Eleanor. I was drugged last night." He shook his head. "Yesterday afternoon. Before I was to prepare for the ball. For seeing you."

Eleanor folded her arms over her chest, her stubborn chin set decisively.

"I thought *you'd* sent me the brandy," he rushed on. He looked toward the door, expecting a small army of footmen to appear and haul him away. "It was a gift and it had the Adventure Club's compass on the card. I thought… I thought it was from you." He grimaced, knowing his story made him sound mad. "When I awoke only an hour ago the journals were gone."

She straightened. "Gone?"

"Stolen," he amended grimly. "And I've the devil of a headache. Apparently the brandy was laced with a heavy dose of laudanum. I don't remember much after arriving home from here yesterday afternoon. It's all hazy."

Her shoulders relaxed somewhat. "What about the key?"

"It was hidden, and thus was not taken." Hidden under

his face, that was, but he was not about to share as much. "They most likely didn't know to look for it."

He drew the stiff metal key from his jacket pocket and looked around the room once more, really noticing its state of disarray for the first time. The drawers of her dressing table were pulled out and the trunk beside it half full of various bottles and pots. Gowns and shoes were laid out over the blue silk coverlet on the bed, arranged in neat order beside yet another trunk.

"We won't be staying in London." Eleanor's tone was solemn. "Charles, we're ruined."

"I beg your pardon?"

"Lord Ledsey saw me going into Lottie's and warned the Earl of Devonington away from me during the ball. Everyone heard, of course." A pained look creased her face. "We were asked to leave."

Charles winced. He had not been there to protect her from what had to be the worst night of her life.

She strode to the bed and let her fingertips sweep over the delicate beadwork along the sleeves of one of the gowns. "We're going to Westix Manor, where we will most likely remain. This was to be my last Season anyway. Most likely this is my last day in London."

She was leaving? Everything in Charles went on high alert. Damn it, he had not come all this way to see her slip through his fingers.

"Eleanor, this does not change anything for me."

"I am a pariah, Charles. There will be no grand wedding at St. George's, nor banns read." She shook her head. "This was all just…ridiculous."

Her voice caught and she turned away from him.

This was all his fault. If he had been there he could have protected her somehow. He had to make it right.

He gritted his teeth. "It was not all ridiculous, Eleanor. Not to me." Charles closed the distance between them and

drew her toward him. "We can leave on our own. Now.
We can go to Gretna Green. No one there will give a fig
about Lady Canterbury's ball or the damned gossip." He
stroked a hand over her face and reveled in how her green
eyes softened when they met his. "You need not be ruined."

Eleanor cast him a chagrined expression. A lock of red
hair had slipped from the loose knot and now fell becom-
ingly over her forehead. "Gretna Green... Of course. Because it is near the castle."

"The castle?"

"Comlongon Castle." She lifted an eyebrow. "Where
the journals are. The entire reason you even came here.
They're the only thing you ever think of."

Yes. Of course. The journals. Though the thought came
as a surprise, for it suddenly struck him that in all his panic
over having abandoned Eleanor he had not once thought
of those journals in Scotland. Yet again, he had thought
only of her.

Was Eleanor mad? Was she truly trying to dissuade
the Duke from continuing with their agreement? Marrying Charles was the only option she had, aside from being
ruined.

Charles watched her with a curious expression, one set
somewhere between concern and—dared she think it?—
tenderness.

"I was not there to protect you," he said. "Let me make
this right."

"It's not your responsibility to make it right, Your Grace."

Though even as she said the words her voice faltered.
What was it about this man that drew out her emotions?
They rushed through her veins unbidden and left her
thoughts scattered. This man who had promised so much
and made her experience life with more color, more vivacity than she had known possible.

She put a hand to her brow to still the chaos churning within. "Charles. Please…"

He stepped toward her and tentatively reached for her hand. She looked up at him, reminded again of how very tall he was. And how terribly appealing, with his brilliantly blue eyes. The tenderness there was unmistakable now, far outweighing the concern, and it threatened to undo her.

If she were a smart woman she would offer to sell him the journals at an exorbitant price. And yet here, held in his gaze, she found she could not properly speak. Nor did she pull her hand away when his fingers met hers, glove-less and naked. His touch sent a tingle of warmth up her arm where it radiated outward.

"Marry me, Eleanor. Not to save yourself from ruin but for our mutual compatibility." He slid a side glance at where Amelia stood, clutching her hands over her chest in rapt attention. "In all things," he added with discreet intimacy.

Eleanor's breath quickened. How could she deny the passion between them, and the candor they'd shared? And yet could she live with the riot of feelings he set loose within her? He would leave often, as her father had done. She would have to expect it and ward off any swaying toward love. To protect herself. She had previously assumed love to be something of stories. She knew now its existence as well as its danger.

"Yes, Charles," she answered in a quiet voice.

Amelia gave a little squeak.

Charles glanced to the side once more, this time with mild irritation at their spectator, who was now fanning her glossy eyes.

"But we will have to leave now," Eleanor said. "Before Mother learns of it. Amelia, please pack a bag for me."

"And quickly," Charles added. "I believe your butler may have sent the Watch for me, if he does not appear himself, armed with a pistol."

Eleanor turned from where she was pointing to several garments for Amelia to pack. "What happened with Edmonds?"

"I locked him a room," Charles answered. "The library, I believe. It was not my intention, but the man fought like the devil to keep me from entering."

Eleanor held up one hand and pinched the bridge of her nose with the other, belatedly realizing it was an action her father had done many times. "You locked Edmonds in the library?"

Charles grimaced. "To see *you*. I will compensate him for his troubles and beg his forgiveness."

The very thought of Edmonds battling Charles to protect her endeared her to the overly formal servant. It had been valiant. She would be personally thanking him as well. Once they returned.

A giddy bubble of excitement tickled up within her, despite her attempts to tamp it down. For when next she returned to London she would be a duchess.

"I expect no less." She only hoped Charles's efforts would be enough for Edmonds after what he'd been through, the poor man. "It was quite brave of him. Please ensure you provide restitution."

The doorway remained thankfully clear during the short time it took to get a simple trunk packed and compose a hasty note to her mother. Within several minutes Eleanor and Charles were racing down the servants' stairs to avoid being seen.

Soon they would be wed. And finally, after all the frustration and pain of their precarious situation, Eleanor and her mother's troubles would be over.

Chapter Twenty-Three

After Charles had packed his own trunk at Somersville House, they had only one stop to make: Lottie's town house.

"We needed a second witness," he said, in reply to Eleanor's confused expression. "Aside from Thomas. I trust you approve?"

She beamed up at him and accepted his proffered arm. "Most assuredly."

Charles and Eleanor were shown into the drawing room, where Lottie rose to greet them. The neckline of her red gown was a bit low-cut for Charles's taste. Well, perhaps a *lot* low-cut for his taste. Her hair fell in a heavy curtain of glossy curls down one shoulder and she'd applied a thin layer of kohl to her eyes, giving her a dramatic, seductive appearance.

Charles did not much care for that either.

She ran to Eleanor and embraced her in a heartfelt hug. "Lady Eleanor, I am terribly distraught over what happened at Lady Canterbury's ball."

Lottie did indeed appear distraught. The dark smudges under her kohl-lined eyes indicated a lack of proper sleep. And, now that he looked at her, the flush to her cheeks appeared to have been put there by cosmetics rather than good health.

It was no wonder Lottie took Eleanor's distress so personally. He knew Lottie saw her lessons as a personal failure. However, it also meant she would need to return to the life she'd led before her attempt at educating the daughters of London society.

Lottie looked from Eleanor to Charles and her eyes narrowed. "Is there a reason the two of you have arrived together, without a chaperon?"

"We require a witness." He lifted his brow. "For our marriage."

"Well." Lottie's face remained blank for a moment, before she gave an overzealous clap and beamed a mite too brightly at them. "I am overjoyed for you both. Felicitations on your upcoming nuptials."

"We will leave as soon as you pack a trunk," Charles replied. "We need an additional witness when we get to Gretna Green."

"Please, say yes," Eleanor implored. "We will stay for a few days at Comlongon Castle, which is nearby. It will be such a delightful break from all the wagging tongues."

Lottie folded her hands in front of her. "Charles, may I speak with you a moment in the library?"

Charles glanced at Eleanor, who nodded. "Go on," she said. "Though if you still have those kittens, Lottie, I'd very much love to see them."

"I am certain they would very much love to see you as well," Lottie said. "Once they're a bit older you may choose one to keep as your own. As a wedding present."

She rang for one of the footmen to fetch the kittens and motioned Charles to follow her. She did not speak until the door to the library was closed behind them.

"Tell me this is not all in the pursuit of those damned journals." She glanced to the closed door, as if she could see Eleanor through it. "That young lady has been through so much already. The rumors of what happened last night are dreadful. I am ashamed that her association with me has left her so besmirched. I cannot in good conscience allow you to further use her."

"Lottie, I…" He ran a hand through his hair. "Yes, we had made an agreement for the journals, I confess."

An enraged snarl sounded from Lottie's throat.

"However," he rushed on, "when I missed the ball where I intended to announce our agreed-upon arrangement I was in a frenzy to see her, to explain. It was only when she brought up the journals herself that I realized…" He shook his head at his own confused thoughts. "I realized I hadn't even considered them. I had only been thinking of her."

Lottie's frown melted into a slow smile. "Very well. I will come. Only I have one request." She curled a length of dark hair around her finger. "I wonder…is it possible to leave tomorrow?"

"Do you need so much time to pack?"

She was silent long enough for concern to scrape at the back of Charles's mind.

"What is it, Lottie?"

"I have an…engagement this evening," she said softly.

The confession hit him like a slap. Charles swallowed around a suddenly dry throat. "A lesson?" he asked with hope.

Lottie's stare slid from his. "No."

Hot anger flashed through him. "Lottie, you said you were done."

"I said I was trying a new venture." Tears filled her eyes. "It didn't work."

"Let me give you money to live on. Eleanor will understand. In fact, she'll encourage it."

Lottie put up her hand. "Stop. Please. You know I won't accept your charity."

It wasn't charity. Charles bit back the argument, knowing it would do no good. "We must go now," he said instead. "The Countess is unaware of her daughter's departure— or perhaps she is aware now. At any rate, we cannot risk being stopped."

Lottie gave a deep sigh. "Very well. I will send my regrets and hope we can meet once I return."

Charles didn't move, overwhelmed at his own self-hatred for having abandoned her all those years ago, when she'd needed him most. "I despise that you're doing this."

"And yet you love me enough to understand I must live my own life." She regarded him in silent search of confirmation.

His shoulders sagged. "Yes."

Lottie rose on her tiptoes and kissed his cheek. "Give me a moment to pack."

"You were more of a success with Eleanor than you realize," he said, before she could turn away. "You brought a light to her world she never would have had without you."

Lottie's smile touched her eyes. "And that is enough for me."

Charles nodded and left her to pack. For now he had everything he needed. Even though Lottie was forgoing a potential protector—at least for the time being. Eleanor's reputation would be salvaged once they were wed, and he would be getting the remainder of the journals. Thomas would even stop haranguing him about his ducal duty to wed.

For the first time since his return to London everything was going exactly right.

In all, the exceedingly bumpy trip took the better part of six days—primarily due to Eleanor insisting on several occasions that they stop at an inn for the night, to sleep in a real bed rather than endure another stiff slumber on the narrow seats of the coach.

It was a curious thing to reconcile herself in those six days to the idea of having a husband. After seven failed seasons and a botched courting only two months prior, Eleanor had become resigned to a spinster's future. Never had she thought she would be on her way to Gretna Green to wed an incredibly handsome duke.

During those days she sat beside the man who would be her husband, very aware of every part of him. His intoxicating scent and the heat of his thigh touching hers. In truth, all of him was impossible to ignore. He gazed at her often, in a manner she believed he thought discreet, and glanced away each time she met his stare, perhaps accepting the idea of marriage to her very much the same way she was doing with him.

Late into the afternoon of the seventh day, they arrived at the small inn near the blacksmith's at Gretna Green where many clandestine marriages took place. As with all their prior stops, Charles got them each their own room, which were well-appointed and comfortable.

Regardless, Eleanor lay awake, her body and her mind on fire with curiosity and anticipation for what the next day would bring, when they were wed.

When the sun had finally risen high enough to deem the day worthy of waking, Eleanor was more than ready.

Lottie helped her dress in a white gown of Brussels lace and silver beadwork that twinkled at her sleeves and hem when she moved.

Lottie herself wore a pale blue gown of a much more demure fashion than any other garment Eleanor had ever seen her wear previously. The clothing made her even more beautiful, with her silky black hair and those large blue eyes.

It was Charles, however, who took Eleanor's breath away. She saw him first when she began to descend the stairs of their quaint inn. He stood on the first floor, waiting for her, wearing champagne-colored silk breeches, white stockings and a blue waistcoat Eleanor had never seen him wear before, in a deep blue brocade set against a paler background. All of this was quite nicely complemented by his navy jacket.

He stopped his conversation with his valet as if he'd sensed her approach, and looked up the short flight of stairs to where she remained in observation of him. His gaze moved slowly over her, devouring her like a delectable treat. He did not wait for her to descend to him, and instead climbed the stairs to be at her side.

"You are stunning." Charles offered Eleanor his arm.

"And you're the most handsome man I've ever seen."

And he was. His face was clean-shaven, his dark hair swept smoothly back, and the brilliance of those blue, blue eyes was shining as it rested on her.

"Are you ready to become my wife?" he asked.

"I daresay I would not have engaged in such a journey if I were not."

Charles chuckled. "I'm inclined to agree with you. I'm eager for a few days' escape in Scotland." He led her down the stairs and spoke in a low and intimate voice. "Alone. With you."

The breathlessness came rushing back, and the decadent torment of hot temptation. *The journals*, she reminded herself. Despite what he said, she knew what they meant to him. She would do well to keep that at the forefront of her mind.

He led her outside to where an endless sky spread over the lush, rolling green hills. Eleanor closed her eyes and breathed it all in—the sweetness of the sun-warmed grass, the moisture in the air suggesting it might later rain, and the wonderful spice of Charles's scent. Then together they walked to the squat white building where the infamous anvil awaited them.

With Lottie and Thomas behind them, Eleanor and Charles strode through the wooden door of the simple blacksmith's. The whitewashed walls were pocked and smeared with soot, and various odds and ends of the trade hung from pegs.

A large man tottered into the room. Sweat dotted his brow and stained the leather apron he wore. His head seemed screwed down into the bulk of his neck and he eyed them for a considerable length of time.

"Could you direct us to Joseph Paisley?" Charles asked.

The man nodded. "'S me. Ye are here to get married, then?"

A prickle of alarm washed over Eleanor. The man didn't look like he'd bathed in some time, and there was a sickly pallor beneath the layer of sweat glistening on his skin.

Joseph Paisley scoffed before Charles could answer. "Of course ye are, or ye wouldna be here. Let me make the necessary preparations."

Eleanor took the moment of his absence to look to Charles, who must have seen evidence of her concern for he nodded to her in silent comfort.

Joseph Paisley staggered back into the room and grabbed a book off a nearby shelf. The odor of stale alcohol hit her and his lurching gait suddenly made sense.

Joseph Paisley, the man who would see them wed, was entirely sotted.

Chapter Twenty-Four

It was indeed fortunate that Charles held his bride in such high esteem, for truly the venue for their marriage was abysmal. Mr. Paisley leaned to the right and then to the left before swaying back to the center. For a tenuous moment Charles thought he might be forced to catch the man.

A younger man appeared, thin, and wearing a dark jacket of some elegance. He approached them immediately and waved Mr. Paisley away. "Ye've been unwell. Have ye a rest. I'll take care of these two."

Lottie stepped forward and gave an encouraging nod. "If he's unwell, perhaps that might be best."

"I'm fine," Mr. Paisley said firmly. "Stay to help if ye like, but I'll wed them."

Content, the young man clasped his hands at his back and stood resolutely at Mr. Paisley's side.

Eleanor tensed against Charles's arm.

Mr. Paisley drew in a deep breath and braced his stance wide, his belly thrust out like a barrel. "We are now gathered here in order that I may solemnize your marriage in the presence…"

He did not look down at his book as he read, and his words slurred together, thick with drink and bored memory.

"Before ye…" He pointed at Charles.

Charles stared back blankly, unsure what the man intended.

"Please state yer name, sir," said the younger man.

"Charles Christopher Pemberton." Charles nodded to the younger man in appreciation.

"And ye…" Mr. Paisley pointed this time to Eleanor.

Eleanor, having the great benefit of learning from Charles's folly, replied promptly, "Eleanor Susan Murray."

Charles looked down at his soon-to-be wife. He hadn't known her full name before, and it pleased him to know it now.

Mr. Paisley cleared his throat and waggled a finger between the two of them. "Before ye're both joined in marriage, it is my duty to remind ye—"

The man's face suddenly went bright red and he bent over with a hacking cough.

Charles's arm shot out to pull Eleanor back at a safer distance from the ailing man—for all the good it might do. "Good God, man. Are you unwell?"

Mr. Paisley continued to cough, his face having gone nearly purple.

The younger man led him to a bed set near the back wall, which Charles hadn't noticed until that exact moment. Mr. Paisley continued to cough in great racking waves while the younger man tucked him into the bed with soothing tones.

Eleanor glanced up at Charles, her brows lifted with concern. He was beginning to share her apprehension. As distasteful as London had become, they could at least have been wed there without fearing the spread of disease.

"This is preposterous," Charles conceded.

His mouth twitched in a tickle of laughter and Eleanor's did the same.

"Truly disastrous." Then the humor in her eyes shadowed. "Are you quite sure this union will be considered valid?"

"Very." He looked to where Mr. Paisley was being fed a posset of some kind by the younger man.

"I now require that ye make a declaration!" Mr. Paisley bellowed from across the room. From his bed.

Truly, it was shocking.

He waved them over and they obliged, walking closer.

The man eased himself into a sitting position and breathed heavily with the effort. "I would ask that everyone present please be upstanding," Mr. Paisley continued. He indicated them each in turn. "Charles Christopher Pemberton and Eleanor Susan Murray. Before ye're joined in marriage, it is my duty to remind ye…"

Mr. Paisley's voice rattled on and on, reciting words he had clearly spent a lifetime saying.

Charles's attention, however, was on Eleanor—the woman who would become his wife, the daughter of his father's greatest enemy. There was a twinge in his chest as he regarded her, a sharp affection that had crept up on him through their lessons with Lottie, on those promenades through Hyde Park, in the quiet, intimate moments shared between them.

"Charles Christopher Pemberton!" Mr. Paisley called. "Will ye take Eleanor Susan Murray's right hand in yers?"

Charles took Eleanor's small, delicate hand in his and stared down into the eyes of the woman he was giving his name to, sharing his title and his life with. "I, Charles Christopher Pemberton, am taking Eleanor Susan Murray's hand."

The young man quietly rushed over, took their joined hands and carefully pulled them in slow shuffling steps until they were directly over the anvil. He nodded, then dashed back to his place beside Mr. Paisley's bed once more.

Mr. Paisley proceeded to shout out the most important words of Charles's life—the vows which would bind him to Eleanor and have him see her forever cared for. It was a series of "wilt thee" and "wilt thou" Charles could barely understand with the man's slurred and shouted speech.

"I will," Charles replied when the man stopped talking.

Mr. Paisley asked the same of Eleanor. The mirth quieted in her eyes and turned into something warm and affectionate. "I will," she answered with reverence.

"The ring?" Mr. Paisley barked from where he sat.

The younger man ran over with his hand outstretched. Charles pulled from his jacket pocket the emerald ring he'd taken from the safe at Somersville House—his mother's. It was the one his father had given her on their wedding day. The green stone glittered against the fashionable gold setting, almost a perfect match to Eleanor's eyes.

The younger man took it to Mr. Paisley, who muttered over it a moment.

"We won't have to kneel, will we?" Eleanor asked in a quiet whisper, with a grimace toward the dirty floor.

Charles had only time to shake his head before the younger man brought back the ring and he was advised to present it to Eleanor. Complying, Charles slid the ring on her finger and smiled as it fit perfectly.

"Oh, Charles, it's perfect," she whispered, and stroked the emerald with her thumb.

Mr. Paisley hiccupped and then continued with the ceremony, until at last he uttered the final words they had all been waiting to hear. "I now pronounce ye man and wife."

The young man rushed over with his quiet steps once more, hefted a hammer and struck the anvil with a resounding smack. He grinned up at them. "Felicitations on your union."

Felicitations, indeed.

Charles pulled close his lovely bride and kissed her full on the lips for all to see. It was a slow kiss, with the parting of mouths and the tantalizing skim of tongues—

a tease for what would certainly come soon. Very, very soon. Thank God.

His body roared with an eagerness to fulfill his wedding vows. Eleanor melted against him with matched expectation.

A male voice splintered through the moment.

"Are you Joseph Paisley?"

Charles broke off the kiss and regarded a young couple, standing anxiously at one another's side.

"I believe our time is up." Charles led Eleanor from the building with Lottie following them. Thomas remained behind a moment longer to collect the marriage lines.

No sooner had Charles stepped into the freshness of clean air, away from the prevailing heat and sickness in the building, Lottie threw up her hands in exasperation. "What the devil was *that*?"

Eleanor threaded her bare fingers through Charles's and laughed. "The most outrageous wedding of all time."

Charles reveled in the silky warmth of her palm resting comfortably against his. Eleanor was now the Duchess of Somersville. His wife.

The poignancy of that moment was not lost on him, and suddenly he found himself possessive of her, and eternally glad to have her at *his* side and not that of Devonington, or even Rawley.

She was his.

The celebration of their union was a quiet affair, and one that ended quickly—much to Eleanor's delight. Or rather to her delight, excitement, anticipation, nervousness, and everything else that loomed in her expectation of impending intimacy.

Charles led her to his room at the inn by a gentle hand, his gaze locked on hers as he opened the door. Though he had been there only one night, his wonderful scent of rich, foreign spices lingered in a room identical to her own. He closed the door and plunged the room into total silence.

Her breathing came fast and her body buzzed with heady anticipation as he approached her.

"My wife." His mouth lifted in a charming half smile. "Do you have any idea how long I have wanted you?"

Her heart leapt at such words. "I believe I do have an idea."

He grinned and pulled her to him. His mouth lowered to hers in a slow, sensual kiss that told her they had all the time in the world, and that he planned to savor every second of it. His fingers skimmed down her gown and began to work at the delicate line of buttons going down her back.

"As beautiful as you are with this on, I imagine you are far lovelier with it off."

A soft sound of longing hummed from the back of her throat as each button fell open in turn under his subtle touch and widened her gown further and further. He watched as he undressed her…as the fabric began to loosen and gape.

Wanton though it might be, there was a part of Eleanor that *wanted* him to disrobe her, to leave the hot tension of her skin exposed to the open air. And, if she were being entirely honest, a wickeder part of her longed to see him as well.

At last the gown slipped off one shoulder and Charles eased it carefully down to the ground, so she stood in only her unmentionables. Her heart pounded in her chest with an intoxicating blend of expectation and excitement.

Charles paused for a long, slow breath and then pulled free the tie holding her petticoat in place. It shifted from her waist and puddled on the floor. He immediately set to work drawing the bow from her corset, where it was laced up at the front, one loop at a time. Within mere seconds the strings hung limp at her sides and Charles swept his hands over her shoulders, caressing her as he pushed the corset from her body.

"Your chemise," he said in a deep, smooth voice. "Take it off."

Eleanor paused then. For it was one thing to have her husband undress her, and entirely another to do it herself as he watched. Heat singed her cheeks and the warmth in other places grew hotter still.

She took the smooth fabric between her fingertips, carefully pulling it up her body and over her head. She let it float to the floor and stood before him wearing only pale silk stockings tied at her thighs. He took his time taking her in, lifting his steady stare up her legs to her breasts, then settling on the thatch of red hair between her legs.

"Stunning," he said. "It would appear I was right. As lovely as you were in your gown, you're far lovelier out of it."

He closed the distance between them and delicately ran a finger from her shoulder down the side of her breast, along the curve of her hip to her thigh.

Her breathing grew faster and her skin burned where he'd touched her. The pleasant throbbing between her thighs increased its tempo in eagerness to experience more of the pleasure they'd shared.

His hand curled around the swell of her bottom, feather-light, and he caught her lips with his own. The kiss was tender at first, until his tongue touched hers and the embers were fanned to flames. Eleanor lifted her arms to his shoulders and tilted her face toward his, her own tongue seeking and stroking.

His delicate touch at her bottom became more inquisitive, more restless, roaming up to her waist, up to her breasts, where he teased at her sensitive nipples, and then down, down, down to where he'd stroked her before.

At the first sweep of his finger over the source of her

need Eleanor's knees buckled. She pushed at his jacket, shoving it from his shoulders so it fell unceremoniously to the floor.

"I want to see you, too." Her voice was husky with lust.

She moved to the buttons of his waistcoat. Her fingers trembled, fumbling in her impatience to have him as naked before her as she was to him.

"Relinquish your stockings," he said against her mouth. "And I'll remove my waistcoat."

She obliged, rolling her stockings down her legs. Her skin was alight with intense sensitivity, so that even her own touch along her thighs left her flesh prickling with pleasure.

Charles unbuttoned his waistcoat with expertise. And he did not stop there. He next removed the collar from his shirt, revealing a hint of curling black hair, before tugging the cloth over his head. Lines of muscle showed along his stomach in tight bands, and the power of his chest swelled beneath a smattering of black hair.

Eleanor drew in a soft breath.

He pulled off his boots and stockings while the strength of his arms flexed and bunched in the most fascinating of ways, powerful muscle working under firm flesh with each movement. He worked at the buttons of his breeches, where the thick column of his shaft showed under the fine fabric.

She made a little sound in her throat before she could stop herself. She'd thought of this for far longer than any respectable girl ought to have. The memory of what his fingers could do mingled with the lurid tales from the journal, swirling into hot lust in her mind.

He pulled the loosened breeches from his narrow hips and stood before her in his full, powerful glory, the proof of his need jutting toward her.

No sooner had she begun to admire him than he drew

her into his arms, his warm skin on hers and his shaft pressed hot against her belly. The hair on his chest scratched pleasantly against her nipples and Eleanor's pulse fluttered with erratic, wild beats.

For this time there was no innocence to protect, no barriers to keep them apart. There would be no stopping until all her curiosities had been thoroughly sated.

Chapter Twenty-Five

Charles held his wife against him, skin to skin, pounding heart to pounding heart, and knew there was no place in all the world he'd rather be. Every inch of Eleanor was wonderfully silky and supple, and her mouth was eager beneath his.

Her legs parted around his thigh and he knew all too well what it was that she wanted. He skimmed his fingers over her inner thighs and reveled in the eager intake of her breath. He found the wet heat between her legs and slid the pad of his middle finger over her core until he reached the little bud. Her hips twitched upward reflexively and she gave a sigh of pleasure.

Charles bit back a groan and his shaft flexed against her. At this point the greatest feat of his life would be remaining in control and not throwing himself upon her as he so desperately wanted to.

He continued to stroke, teasing the little knot of her desire. He carefully dipped his finger inside her, fearful of causing her discomfort. She was impossibly tight, slick with wet heat and promise. Charles gave a long, low groan of anticipation.

Eleanor gave a breathless cry and swayed slightly. "Yes…" she whispered. "Please. More of that."

His manhood lurched. There was not much more that Charles could take. He needed her on the mattress, spread before him. He wanted to touch her, tease her, ready her. Taste her.

He caught her parted legs and spread them over his waist, lifting her in order to carry her to the bed. She moaned and ground her body against his. The heat of her rubbed over the length of his shaft and the decadence of such temptation was so much that he damn near dropped her.

He clutched her to him, carrying her the few feet to the four-poster, where he lay her down on the firm mattress and bent over her. She did not uncurl her legs from his waist. She locked her heels against his buttocks and continued to grind against him with a frustrated craving that readily echoed in the ache of his tight balls.

God, but she was a sweet enticement. It would be so easy to shift his shaft against her and glide in. The very idea made his nerves jangle with insistence.

But when he did finally take her there would be a virgin's pain. He had to be gentle, careful. Slow.

She panted against his mouth and let her touch wander over him with abandon, hot hands making an exploration that damn near drove him mad. Over his naked back, across his chest, raking over his nipples before driving down his stomach.

He'd managed to kiss her throat on his path to her nipple, when her fingers curled around his shaft. His world stopped and his mind plunged into utter blankness, forgoing any thought but the excruciating pleasure radiating through him.

"Will you teach me?" she asked, her voice low. "To pleasure you? To take you in my mouth?"

She sat up slightly and regarded him. Her carefully crafted coiffure had become mussed and several long tendrils spilled down her shoulders.

She pursed her reddened lips. "Like in the journals. It seemed to bring the author great pleasure. And if it brings you pleasure I'd like to try."

Charles swallowed. "Eleanor…"

She slid out from underneath him and off the bed, so she stood at its side. Charles turned to watch her, still too damn stunned to come up with a polite answer.

She was his wife.

And yet the idea of her hot mouth surrounding his shaft…

With careful precision she pulled the pins from her hair and let them plop to the thick carpet one by one, until the glory of her red hair spilled down her shoulders and breasts like she was some mythical mermaid. She bent over him and kissed him, her tongue expertly finding his. Her breasts arched to his chest and she whimpered against his lips.

His body lit with wanting immediately, insistent and demanding. Her fingers brushed over the head of his shaft and a groan tore from his throat. She explored him, touching, stroking, cupping. His world was pinpointed on the the sheer pleasure of it all, where it radiated out from his shaft and coursed through him.

"Teach me to take you in my mouth."

She looked up at him with an expression both sultry and imploring. To hear his wife speak so intimately, and with such base words, drove him absolutely mad with wanting.

"You'll need to get on your knees," he heard himself say.

She gracefully obeyed, and gazed at him for further instruction. Her attention shifted to his shaft and she licked her lips.

"Take me in your hand and guide me into your mouth…" Charles somehow managed to get the words out.

Her fingers curled around the base and her lips parted just over the head, the most sensitive part. His shaft disappeared several inches into her mouth.

"Close your lips," Charles instructed. "And suck."

Her mouth closed around him, hot and wet, and she drew him in with an obedient suck. Charles's balls tightened and he knew he would not be able to take much of this before she unmanned him. Sweat gathered along his brow and his entire body trembled with the effort to stave off his climax.

"Move your head. Up and down. Over…" God, he could barely talk.

Eleanor slid the suckling warmth of her mouth toward the head and then sank back down again, halfway down his shaft. She did this three more times, bobbing her head over him until he was near bursting.

"Enough." It came out as a growl. On his honor, he truly could take no more.

Eleanor released him with a startled expression. "Have I hurt you?"

He swept her onto the bed and braced himself over her. "I've been ravenous for you for too long without having you, Eleanor. I cannot take much more before…" He smiled. "It's your turn."

"My turn?"

He was already kissing a path down to her breasts, where he paused to flick his tongue over her nipples before descending to her slender stomach.

"I'd be willing to wager this wasn't in that journal."

Before she could offer any protest he kissed his way down to the fiery curls between her legs and ran the tip of his tongue over her glistening center.

Eleanor's awareness blazed with pure bliss.

Charles watched her and traced his tongue over her sex.

Pleasure tingled through her and prickled at the tips of her nipples. A soft cry escaped her mouth and she was only mildly aware of Charles spreading her thighs further apart.

He flicked his tongue where his fingers had been before, sliding it over her, circling the part of her that made everything quiver, plunging it inside her. The hunger and the longing all knotted together, and wound her into a deliciously tight ball of glorious feelings.

Something entered her, long and deep, while the caress of his tongue twirled over the little nub that brought such breathtaking euphoria. Eleanor cried out at the sheer exquisiteness of the blended sensations, and glanced down at him to find his finger thrusting into her while he continued to lick and tease.

Her body wound in on itself, tighter and tighter. So close, so close, so close…

But then, just as she was fully prepared to career over, Charles withdrew his attentions and rose over her. Those brilliant blue eyes of his found hers, unfocused and heavy-lidded with lust. His body was hot and hard against hers, and the length she'd so eagerly loved with her mouth now pressed with heavy insistence against her inner thigh.

Eleanor arched her hips upward, eager for Charles to satisfy the maddening, thundering want raging through her.

He braced himself so his weight did not crush her. His powerful body flexed with the effort, and she could not stop herself from stroking his beautifully corded body.

He remained locked in place, unmoving.

Her hips rolled of their own volition, undulating in a primal dance she hadn't needed to be taught. "Please, Charles…"

He kissed her, long and sweet. But Eleanor didn't want sweet. Sweet wouldn't quell her ferocious craving.

"Please, Charles…" she panted again.

He rested his damp forehead against hers and clenched his eyes shut, as if he were in pain. "I don't want to hurt you," he said raggedly.

She knew there would be pain. She'd overheard the conversation of recently married ladies.

"You won't," Eleanor ground out. "Please. You must do this or I'll go mad with wanting."

He opened his eyes and flexed his brows in consideration. Finally his shaft shifted from her inner thigh to the throbbing ache of her need. He pushed into her gingerly.

More. She needed more.

She spread her legs wider and he pressed forward, until the very entrance of her stretched around the girth of him.

He clenched his jaw. "Are you ready?"

Eleanor nodded, and opened her mouth to speak just as he thrust into her. A flash of pain burst through the haze of her lust.

Charles froze where he remained, still buried in her depths. He was large within her, slightly uncomfortable, and the feeling was foreign and awkward.

He touched her face. "I've hurt you…"

She shook her head, unable to speak. Her body would adjust, and then there would be gratification.

He pulled out and a ripple of pleasure went through her. She drew her legs around him and rocked her hips with the same natural motion as before. He followed the slow pace she set, slowly easing deeper inside, and deeper still. His breath came fast against their shared kisses.

Just as Eleanor had known would happen, her sex became accustomed to him—not only accustomed to the invasion of her intimate place, but welcoming it with slick, wet heat. His hand moved between them and found the spot where he would drive her to the edge of ecstasy. He circled it with his thumb in time with his thrusts, until Eleanor's body tensed with impending release.

"Yes…" he breathed against her ear. "Yes, come for me."

He didn't need to ask. She couldn't stop it even if she tried. Her body clenched until she feared she would begin to tremble, and then the pleasure exploded around her like the flashing fireworks of Vauxhall Gardens in the night sky.

The spasming of her core gripped around Charles's length repeatedly, further heightening their bliss and prolonging their satisfaction. Charles pushed firmly inside her and gave a tight grunt. He twitched within her depths and a delicious wave shuddered through her.

Unwilling and unable to move, they remained in their joined position for a long moment, both gasping to catch their frantic breath.

Eleanor's heart raced harder and faster than it ever had before, frenzied with the excitement of their intimacy. And as her breath began to calm, a quiet contentment swept over her, bringing total and complete satiation.

Charles slowly pulled away from her and motioned her to remain where she was while he strode across the room in all his nude glory. She watched his form appreciatively, enjoying the play of light and shadows over the powerful planes of his back.

When he returned he carried a wet cloth and gently cleaned her. Though the heat and pain of his initial intrusion had ebbed, the coolness of the cloth against her sensitive area was most welcome.

He regarded her tenderly. "Are you all right, love?"

Love. Her lips curled into a dreamy smile. "It was beyond words, Charles. Truly, in every brilliant way."

Eleanor stretched back onto the bed and Charles pulled her into his arms.

She could lie there forever at his side, she thought. Listening to his heartbeat, wrapped in his embrace and trying not to fall in love.

Chapter Twenty-Six

The following day Eleanor found herself in the confines of a carriage once more—but this time she hardly minded. It was only for a short time, while they made their way to Comlongon Castle, and she was with her new husband. The one who had kept her up the better part of the night with another round of teasing and satiating and loving.

Her body hummed with the languid warmth still thrumming in the slight tenderness between her thighs.

As if he were considering similar thoughts to her own, a soft smile touched Charles's lips where he sat across from her in the private carriage they'd taken. Once more they were blissfully alone, with Thomas and Lottie having remained to see to their effects at the inn so Eleanor and Charles could arrive at Comlongon together.

Charles's brilliant blue eyes were fixed on Eleanor's. It would be hard not to love a man who looked at her so, and yet she knew it best to guard her heart.

"You look radiant, my Duchess." He settled back in his seat with a contented grin. "I am the luckiest man in all of Christendom."

"To have had so fine a wedding?"

Together they laughed over the episode at Gretna Green.

It was the kind of shared joke they would tell in the years to come.

The trees cleared away around them to reveal a large span of lush green grass with the powerful form of Comlongon Castle rising at its center. It wasn't so much the sight of it that robbed Eleanor of her speech, but the memories which crashed into her with such alarming clarity it rendered her quite overwhelmed.

For many summers her mother had taken her and Evander to Scotland. To familiarize them with their roots, she'd said. To learn to be strong Murrays, her father had clarified.

Either way, when they'd been in Scotland, beyond the watchful gaze of their father, who'd used the time to travel abroad, her mother had released the control she'd held over her children.

Together, Eleanor and Evander had run free about the castle and its grounds. They had been two scamps, romping and playing like hellions every one of those summers, until Evander had been sent away to school. He didn't return home often, and when he did, they both treated one another civilly, coolly, with all the love and laughter stripped out of them.

Pain squeezed at Eleanor's heart. For *she* had been the cause of his abrupt departure. She had been too excitable, her father had said, too desperate for affection. It was low-born and improper. When once she had tried to stop her father from leaving on yet another trip, and had dared to shed tears, the Earl had shown his disappointment with blows and with the most crushing punishment: sending Evander away.

While she'd never regarded her childhood after that with fondness, she *had* cherished the years before. She'd tucked them somewhere private within her, and locked away the pleasant memories of those summer days with Evander.

They rose up within her now, sharp as a familiar scent, and tore through her with bittersweet joy.

Evander had possessed a high-pitched laugh when he was a boy—an unfortunate attribute he'd luckily outgrown as an adult—and he'd been quite a sight as a youth, or "a lad," as they'd called him in Scotland, with his shock of red hair and his silly laughter.

And, oh, they'd had such times for him to laugh. Such as the afternoon they'd set a frog loose in the kitchen and it had propped itself on Cook's large rump for the better part of an hour before she'd even noticed. Or the summer they'd released all the foxes caught by the hunt to liberate them from their terrible fate. Or the time—

Charles sat forward. "Eleanor? Are you crying?"

Was she?

She touched her fingers to her cheek and pulled it away to see they were indeed wet. "It would appear I am."

Concern showed in his eyes. "What is it?"

The carriage bounced along, carrying them past the woods Eleanor had run through with Evander, and past the lake where she'd swum on days when the weather had been warm enough to make the loch only slightly less than freezing.

"I came here with my brother when I was a girl." She shook her head. "I haven't thought of those memories in years. I haven't thought of…him."

"Loss is never easy."

He shifted in his seat and she recalled his own father's recent death.

"I'm very sorry you've had your own loss as well," Eleanor said gently.

His gaze was fixed on the gray face of the castle, growing larger as they made their way closer.

"It doesn't seem real, does it? As if by not acknowledging it, somehow that might result in it never having happened. Which is foolish."

"No, it's not."

The closer they got, the more Eleanor's heart ached. For the young brother she'd played with and loved, for the serious grown man he'd become and the cold rift set between them. For his absence without reconciliation.

"I believe my mother feels similarly," Eleanor said. "She seldom discusses Evander. Though I think we both expect…" She shook her head. "I cannot even say it."

The carriage drew to a stop before Comlongon Castle and a ball of dread tightened in Eleanor's stomach at the thought of the ghosts which might linger in those ancient halls. Not of Murrays long dead, but of the Murray too long missing. Perhaps it had been a poor decision to suggest the castle.

"We will heal with time, my dear Eleanor," said Charles, and exited the carriage and waited to help her down.

Eleanor stepped down onto the familiar crunch of gravel. Her heart pounded in her throat and there was a headiness inside her which made her feel quite faint.

She hadn't been honest when she'd told Charles she hadn't ever had a confidant. When she was a girl, it had been Evander. And, although the years and their father's demands had spread a gap of silence and maturity between them, Evander had gone off to reclaim the family fortune, to save her and her mother from ruin, and it had most likely cost him his life.

Eleanor clasped her hand tightly on Charles's arm to keep her trembling legs from pitching her to the ground.

Charles knocked on the door and waited.

A butler appeared and lifted his bushy gray brows. "May I help you?"

"I am the Duke of Somersville and this is my new bride, formerly Lady Eleanor Murray." Charles smiled down at her before continuing to address the butler. "We are here to spend several days in Scotland and to celebrate our marriage prior to returning to London."

The butler bowed. "A moment, if you please, Your Grace. I must notify the Earl."

The Earl? Eleanor's mouth fell open in outrage as he showed them inside, where they were left momentarily blinded by the absence of sunlight behind the block of thick castle walls.

The butler disappeared before she could offer protest.

"Charles, someone is masquerading as Evander!" she hissed.

"I'll see to this. Don't concern yourself."

The butler appeared once more. "If you'll follow me, the Earl of Westix will see you now."

Eleanor had to force her steps to the pace of a well-bred lady, for all she wanted to do was run to the room at the end of the hall, push her way through the doors and demand to know what scoundrel would dare impersonate her lost brother for his own personal gain.

She would let Charles kill him in a duel and not lose a wink of sleep. No, she would kill him herself. With her very own hands. Her body blazed with the fire of her rage and her jaw ached from clenching it so ferociously.

The butler opened the door and saw them in. Eleanor looked at the tall figure standing beside the fireplace and only just managed to smother her cry behind the press of her fingertips.

For there, looking as handsomely young and strong as he had when he'd left for his expedition, was her long-missing brother: Evander Murray, the rightful Earl of Westix.

Chapter Twenty-Seven

Eleanor couldn't take her eyes off her brother, standing so casually before her. As if he hadn't been missing for years. As if they hadn't all assumed him to be dead. And then he smiled. *Smiled!*

Eleanor's hand was pressed to her mouth and her eyes filled with tears. "Evander…" She pulled free from Charles and staggered toward her brother. "Is it truly you?"

"Eleanor." He strode to her. "My butler has informed me you are a new bride. Felicitations on your marriage." His gaze slid toward Charles, all emotion masked.

"We thought you were dead!" She fell then, pitching toward the ground.

Evander caught her and gently held her upright. "Why ever would you think that?"

The weakness in Eleanor's legs strengthened with the force of her ire. "Why would we think *that*?" she demanded. "Because you have been missing all these years without any word of where you were or when you would be home or even—" Her voice broke. "Or even if you were alive."

He frowned. "I confess I did not write as often as I should have, but there have been at least two letters sent."

"Two?" she gasped. "In four years?"

"I gather they did not make it to you."

Evander had the good sense to cast his eyes downward at her admonishment.

"Have you been here in Comlongon the entire time?" Eleanor drew herself away from him, fully able to stand on her own once more. "While we have feared the worst?"

Evander shook his head. "No."

It was then that she finally noticed the room, crowded with many items—relics and tomes and crates. In truth, it was cluttered with such mess it looked not at all like a proper receiving room, but rather one meant for storage.

"I do not wish to betray our family troubles to you, sister."

He cast a glance toward Charles. Which meant he did not wish to discuss such matters in front of Charles. She looked between the two. Did they recognize one another? Did they know each other to be the son of their father's enemy?

Neither one's expression gave any indication.

"You mean our dire financial situation?" Eleanor pressed. "It was the reason you left."

While Charles hadn't been offered the details, it was apparent that he had already worked out the finer points on his own—or at least was playing the part of knowing admirably.

Evander narrowed his eyes at Charles with a flash of distrust. Maybe they were acquainted after all.

"Yes, well…what I anticipated only taking several months took several years." He gave a mirthless chuckle. "It would appear that our fathers told rather grandiose tales of their travels without recounting the liberties they took when obtaining their treasures."

Charles lifted a brow.

"What do you mean?" Eleanor asked.

"They were not moral," Evander scoffed. "Were I as unscrupulous, my task would have been over in six months' time and I would have been home with those I love."

He nodded to Eleanor before claiming a glass of amber liquid from a nearby table.

Eleanor shook her head, not comprehending. "But if you were here—" Her throat tightened around her words and cut them off.

"I have only recently returned, Eleanor. I confess that I was so focused on selling the goods I had accumulated to rebuild our wealth that I did not wish interruption. And I did not send correspondence until I had reestablished our wealth. I assumed the letters I sent were enough to allay your concerns. I realize now how very wrong I was."

Confusion and anger and...yes, hurt—mostly hurt—blazed like a glowing coal in her chest. "Why did you not come to London to sell the items?"

Evander took a sip of his drink. "We all know how gossip spreads through London like fire. As no one visits Comlongon anymore I expected it to be safe to come here without rattling hope and inciting rumor. I did this to protect you and Mother." He lifted his glass to Charles. "Would you like one?"

"Dear God, yes," Charles replied promptly.

Eleanor followed her brother to the small table of cut-crystal decanters. "I think I would like one as well."

She wrestled with the power of her emotions as he poured two glasses, handing one first to Eleanor and then to Charles.

Eleanor cradled the cool glass against her palms and took a shuddering breath. "Evander, we thought..." Her throat clenched tight around the words. "We thought you were dead. Do you think we value fortune over love?"

"*Everyone* values fortune over love," Evander said simply.

Was that what he thought? That she and her mother

were so keen on an abundant fortune that they would rather wealth than him?

"That isn't true," she protested. "We would rather have had you with us in London. Mother is overwrought at your loss, and I…" Tears blurred the room and a sob choked from her throat. "I tried to push aside my memories of you, but when we arrived here, when I recalled all those summers when we played together—Evander, you have broken my heart."

And it was true. He had indeed left her heart broken.

"Eleanor…"

There was a catch to Evander's voice, and it snagged at a deep, wounded part of her. Without saying more he rushed to her, his arms open, and pulled her into a solid embrace. It was the way he'd done when they were children and she was upset. Before he'd gone to school—before the emotion had been strapped out of them all.

She curled into the embrace and let the truth of it all wash over her. Evander was alive. He had tried to let them know he was safe. He had tried and he had done all this for *them*. The tears came in a flood: relief that he was alive, happiness to be having this incredible reunion, and sorrow for the years they had lost.

"I only wanted to help…" Evander's voice rumbled around her. "I never expected it to be like this."

Eleanor took a shuddering breath. Evander smelled different. When he was a boy, he had smelled of wet grass and sweat—now, as an adult, he smelled of shaving soap and Scotch.

"Will you forgive me, Eleanor?" he asked softly.

She looked up, gazing into a face she had often thought never to see again. How could she not, after all he had done for her and Mother?

"Yes, of course," Eleanor replied, and tightened her grip on him, never wanting to let him go again.

* * *

Charles had slipped from the room to give Eleanor and the Earl of Westix privacy in order to discuss whatever it was siblings discussed after a reunion in which one had been presumed dead. He didn't imagine it would be an easy conversation to have, let alone in the presence of one's enemy.

Except he did not consider the new Earl of Westix an enemy—not in the way he once would have. If Charles had had a sister, wouldn't he have done something similar to see her well cared-for?

He took a long draught of Scotch. It was good-quality, and the burn in his stomach was smooth and pleasant.

Westix being alive added complications—and Charles could not help but consider the impact of such a change.

He now understood that Eleanor's reason for offering her original request had been financial necessity. Now, with Westix returned, with their fortune restored, she had no need of this marriage.

Except it had already been consummated. There could be no annulment.

Then there were the journals. They were no longer Eleanor's to give, and Charles doubted Westix would willingly offer them to his enemy.

He regretted not having brought the key with him to Scotland. He'd left it behind for two reasons. The first being to prove to Eleanor and to Lottie that this marriage meant something to him. The second because he had been worried that if he did find the answer he sought with the key he would be chomping at the bit to leave immediately. He knew several day's difference would not matter on his departure to find the stone, but that these few days at Comlongon would matter to his new wife.

If he'd had it with him now, however, he and Eleanor

could have searched for the journals and used the key without Evander being the wiser. *Damn.*

The butler strode down the hall, cast him a curious look, then pushed through the door of the room where Westix and Eleanor were.

"Forgive the interruption, My Lord, but it appears there are two more in their party who have only just arrived."

"Show them in," the Earl replied.

That must mean that Lottie and Thomas had arrived. Charles waited for the butler to bring them in and then followed them into the room.

Eleanor's eyes were red-rimmed but dry, her tears having ceased. She removed herself from her brother's side and approached Charles. For one tense moment he did not know how she would react to him now that she truly did not need him any longer.

He put his arm around her shoulder and was awash with relief when she melted against him.

"This is charming," Lottie said in the affected manner she'd always possessed.

She looked around at the stacks of wooden crates and ancient artifacts before her eyes fell on the new Earl of Westix. The smile drained from her lips, along with all the color from her face.

And it was not only Lottie looking at Westix, for he was staring as intently at her, his face equally pale.

"Lottie?" Charles asked, from where he stood holding Eleanor's shoulders.

Westix opened his mouth and closed it, then opened and closed it again.

Lottie was not so indecisive. She marched forward, drew her hand back and slapped him across the face.

Westix touched his cheek. "Lottie, I'm so sorry…"

Lottie. Charles was rankled. The Earl was uncomfortably familiar with her.

"You lied to me," Lottie said sharply. "You swore to come back for me and you never did. I waited—" Her voice cracked.

Realization slammed into Charles with the suddenness of an unexpected punch to the gut. He recalled Lottie's refusal to discuss the man who had ruined her, the insistence she'd placed on helping Eleanor. And now here was Westix, standing there, saying Lottie's given name when he hadn't been in London in four years.

Good God.

Westix was Lottie's lover.

Charles's hands rolled into fists, ready to exact vengeance for the woman whose life had been ruined—whose good prospects had been dashed by the Earl's lust.

Without so much as a passing thought Charles released Eleanor. He lunged with his arm cocked back and let his fist slam into Westix's face.

Eleanor and Lottie screamed in unison.

It was Eleanor, though, who grabbed Charles's coat in an effort to draw him away. "Charles, explain yourself."

He let himself to be pulled away—for Eleanor's and Lottie's sakes. Certainly not for the piece of rubbish standing before him with a reddened cheek on one side of his face and a blackening eye on the other.

"He ruined Lottie, Eleanor!" Charles snarled. "She was a vicar's daughter—a woman with many prospects. Your brother seduced her and abandoned her. If he hadn't robbed her of her virtue when her father died she wouldn't have had to—"

"Charles." Lottie put a hand on his tense arm. "I believe this is a conversation I ought to have with the Earl myself, rather than see my scandal aired so publicly."

Charles's anger clenched into a searing knot in his gut. "Very well."

"You and your wife ought to be shown to your rooms."

Lottie's smile didn't reach any part of her face but her lips. "You and I can leave this discussion for later. For now, I would like a moment alone with the Earl of Westix."

Thomas indicated the closed door. "Shall I summon the butler to show you to your rooms?"

Charles glanced behind him to find Eleanor's cheeks had gone quite red. She gave a subtle nod, and he realized she was agreeing with Lottie and Thomas. The door to the room clicked open and Thomas disappeared.

Westix bowed to Charles. "If you'll excuse me, Your Grace? I would very much like to speak to Lottie alone."

Charles gritted his teeth. "If you hurt her, I'll kill you."

Westix did not so much as blink at the threat. "If I hurt her in such a way again, I'll kill myself."

"Evander!" Eleanor gasped in horror.

Her brother shook his head. "I have committed many egregious wrongs, sister. And for all of them I'm heartily sorry."

The Comlongon Castle butler entered the room and politely asked Charles and Eleanor to follow him.

This time Eleanor did not protest, and neither did Charles. They obligingly followed the butler from the drawing room, leaving Westix with Lottie and the ugly truth about what his abandonment had cost her.

Eleanor was unsurprised to find they were shown to her girlhood room at Comlongon Castle, with its billowing white curtains framing a cherrywood four-poster bed.

"We have several maids who can see to your unpacking," the butler said in a drawl of regal nonchalance, and nodded to the small pile of their effects.

"Perhaps later." Charles nodded his thanks and the butler took his leave.

Then Charles turned toward her, his gaze full of concern. "Eleanor…"

The way he said her name was tender, and weighted with all the sorrow of what had transpired. Laughter bubbled up in Eleanor's throat. Or was it a sob? By her word, it was impossible to tell at this point.

Evander was alive, in Scotland, at Comlongon Castle. And he had tried to send letters. If they had got through, how many years of heartache might have been avoided?

Her throat grew tight.

"Eleanor…" Charles said her name again and strode toward her, his arms open.

She needed no further encouragement and ran into his embrace. His body was strong, protective.

Once she'd confessed to Evander why she'd married Charles he had offered to allow her to stay there in Scotland. It would be so easy to set herself free of the entire mess of it. Even the scandal they'd caused in London would soon be buried beneath something more salacious. Fortune, after all, did have a way of encouraging acceptance.

Except that her marriage to Charles could not be annulled.

It would be safer for her to stay in Scotland—for her heart at least. This last day with Charles had pressed upon her with more difficulty than she'd imagined. How could she be with him and not fall in love? And if she lost her heart in her attempt to live a true life would that be a worthy sacrifice? Or would it only bring a greater misery?

Her head ached at the torrent of thoughts smashing around in her skull.

"The journals are no longer mine to give you." She was grateful her face was buried in Charles's chest, so she did not have to see his face when she spoke the horrible truth.

"I'm well aware." Charles rubbed a gentle circle over her back.

"My side of our arrangement is woefully short." She

squeezed her eyes shut, as if she could as easily close off her hurt.

"I still needed a duchess," Charles replied. "I am glad to have you as my wife."

A wife he would soon leave in pursuit of the ruby. For she knew he would never abandon it. No doubt he would approach Evander about the journals the first chance he got.

The ache in Eleanor's chest became palpable.

"I want you," Charles said softly. "As a confidante, to continue our candid discussions, as a beautiful woman on my arm, and to share my bed and explore the passion we share."

Eleanor's breath caught and her body immediately reacted with a low, warm pulse between her thighs. She drew her arms around the back of his neck, eager to give in to the pull of passion and liberate herself from the chaos in her mind. For right here, right now, she would allow herself the luxury of unfettered longing and the beauty of being sated.

And for this one blissful spot in time she would allow herself to be swept into the sweet oblivion of his embrace, where she didn't have to think of the challenges ahead—including the very precarious state of her heart.

Chapter Twenty-Eight

Eleanor's fine warm glow cooled as she descended the stairs for an early dinner. Evander and Lottie awaited them.

It had been all too easy to put her brother from her mind when she was upstairs with Charles. Evander. But not only was he alive, he was the scoundrel who had destroyed Lottie's future.

The very thought settled as an ache in Eleanor's chest.

As if sensing her unease, Charles put his hand to her lower back and carefully guided her down the stairs. The touch was intimate and surprisingly reassuring. She looked up at her husband and hated the tightening of her chest and what it meant.

She'd seen those blue eyes alight with passion. She'd kissed those lips and experienced the pleasure they could bring. And it was because of this knowledge that the most handsome man she'd ever seen was suddenly all the more so. Dangerously more so.

They reached the bottom of the stairs and Charles leaned in close. "All will be well, my Duchess."

Together, they approached the dining room, where Lottie and Evander sat at the long, familiar table with the blue runner down its middle. Their voices were impassioned with a loud whispering that went silent when Eleanor and Charles entered.

Evander rose immediately in welcome. At least he had not lost his manners.

Lottie got to her feet as well, her cheeks stained with a deep flush. "Excuse me. I find I am without an appetite this evening."

She did not give anyone a chance to reply and all but ran from the room.

"What did you say to so offend her?" Charles asked Evander, with an edge.

"The offense was given long ago."

Evander pushed a hand through his hair and a tuft of it jutted out over his right temple. That particular bit of hair had always been stubborn, even when he was a boy. It was a stabbing reminder of the young brother Eleanor had loved, and it endeared him to her, in a deep place in her heart, where her affection for that young boy could never be uprooted.

Evander sighed and motioned for them to sit. A muscle worked in his jaw. "It is an offense for which I will never be able to make amends," he said. "And I believe the cost is no more than I deserve."

Charles scoffed and then helped Eleanor into her seat before taking his own.

The footman came forward and presented them with a delicate savory soup.

Evander stared into the distance, forgoing his soup in favor of the wine at his side. A crease showed on his brow, similar to the one their father had often had when he was disappointed.

"Will you tell us of your adventures?" Eleanor asked. "The journals make everything seem so very fascinating."

Charles stiffened at her side at the mention of the journals.

Evander turned his gaze in her direction. "You have read them?"

She lifted her chin. "I have."

"Elly…"

He said his childhood nickname for her in a sad, slow tone. There was a tired look about him that made her want to coddle him.

"Those aren't appropriate for you. There's so much in them…"

"I am well aware." Eleanor slid the spoon into her soup. "I am no longer a child."

"But you are still a lady."

"We have more journals here, do we not?" She kept her gaze from gliding toward Charles. He had accepted her without the journals, but she knew what they meant to him regardless.

Evander settled back in his chair, with no interest in the food before him. "Our fathers were men without honor."

"Not both of our fathers were," Charles replied evenly.

"Both of our fathers." Evander steepled his fingers and touched his forefingers to his lips in contemplation before speaking. "They stole their treasures. They looted the wealth of poor countries without any means to stop them. Reaping treasures from religious and holy sites. One of the other members of the Adventure Club was apparently exceptional at discovering artifacts in a way they were not. They stole from him as well."

Charles slapped the table and set the wine glasses trembling. "Ridiculous!"

Eleanor stared in shock at her new husband. After some of the hideous entries she'd read in the journals she possessed, Evander's claims did not seem unlikely. Unfortunately…

Evander regarded Charles. "I assure you it is not ridiculous. I followed the path detailed in one of the journals

I had with me. There were many villages with starving people whose temples had been plundered."

Charles simply stared at Evander.

"You know the truth of it even if you don't want to accept it." Eleanor's brother gave a wry twist of his lips. "I was trying to rebuild my family's fortune, but I could not bring myself to take what belongs to others. I dealt primarily in the purchase of spices and silks—a task made difficult with the war, which appears to have finally ended now that I've established enough wealth."

"My father was honorable. A man determined to bring ancient cultures to London for all to experience," Charles countered. "He was admired for his relics...for the care he took with them."

Eleanor knew that Charles had also admired his father, and held him in the highest esteem. Therefore she also realized it was not rage behind his words, but fear.

And with good reason.

From what she'd read in their own hand, their fathers had *not* been good men.

If Evander had other journals here, and if he gave them to Charles, Eleanor had a strong suspicion that in getting exactly what he most wanted Charles would also be learning exactly what he most feared.

Charles no longer had an appetite. Who could with such dinner conversation?

Westix pushed away from the table and rose, giving up all pretense of attempting to find interest in his own food.

"I know you don't want to hear this, Somersville, but our fathers spent more money on acquiring their treasures through bribery than any profit they might have generated. Tell me, did you not encounter the situations of which I speak in your own travels?"

He pulled his glass from the table by its rim and strode

toward the window to stare out into a field of vibrant green.

Charles knew the Earl was giving him a moment to contemplate what he'd said. It was true, there had been great poverty in the foreign countries where Charles had traveled. And there had been rumors of treasures taken from those countries. But those had been by thieves—not English gentlemen. And certainly not Charles's father, whose acclaim had grown with each unique discovery.

Charles himself had acquired treasures on his travels, all accumulated through morally correct avenues. Indeed, there had been the opportunity to bribe, but Charles had not permitted himself to be drawn into such temptation. He'd assumed his father would never have engaged in such immoral actions.

"I have something to show you," said Westix.

He opened a drawer in a large chest near the window and withdrew a journal. Its battered binding was of similar appearance to the ones Eleanor had given him in London.

She sat higher at Charles's side. "You *do* have them here…" she breathed in wonder.

His heart smacked his ribs. Damn him for not having brought the key.

Westix tossed the book unceremoniously on the table beside Charles. "Look for yourself."

He turned and requested the footman bring more wine.

Charles picked up the journal. The script within was choppy, written in the same hurried hand as the one Eleanor had shown him.

"That's the handwriting we need," Eleanor whispered. "Get the key."

"I don't have it," Charles muttered.

"Read it." Westix nodded to him.

Charles ignored Eleanor's questioning look and read aloud. "'Avarice has pervaded the Adventure Club, rendering it rife with treachery and perfidy. What was once a group of morally sound men has descended into a group of men committing the sins of debauchery, bribery and blatant theft. The taking is done without regard to the owners, or to the deficit such losses will press upon the cultures they have plundered. It is ironic that the greatest offenders are none other than the esteemed men of good breeding who conspired to instigate the club's institution—a certain earl and duke whose names I will not put to paper.'"

Charles stopped, unable to bring himself to read more. The author did not have to put such names to paper—not when Charles already knew.

His father had been a thief. A great man brought down by the force of his own greed.

The soup churned in Charles's stomach.

The footman placed a glass of wine before him. Charles reached blindly for it and drained it in one gulp. The alcohol burned a path down his chest and pooled in his unsettled stomach, assuaging the need to retch.

If only the pain in his chest could be so easily quelled.

The foundations of Charles's life—the greatness of his father and the accolades surrounding his incredible findings—had all been built on a lie.

Chapter Twenty-Nine

Charles grappled with what he'd read in the journal. In fact, with what he'd read in several more journals. All of which Evander had gladly turned over to him.

Dinner had gone largely uneaten and they had all retired immediately afterward, overwrought with the events of the day.

Now Charles made his way to the room he shared with Eleanor, weighted with the burden of newfound knowledge. No, with the confirmed knowledge of what he hadn't allowed himself to consider previously. It settled like a rock on his chest, rough-hewn and heavy.

Eleanor didn't say a word until they were in the privacy of their room. Then she turned to him, held out her arms and drew him into a tender embrace. "I'm sorry for what you have learned of your father."

Charles let himself be cradled against her perfumed warmth, breathing in that lovely jasmine smell of her. "I'm sorry about your father as well."

Eleanor released him and shook her head. "My father was never held high in my esteem. He was not…not kind."

Charles bristled. "Not kind?" he repeated.

"He did not like what he could not control, and that meant me and my emotions." Eleanor slid her gaze away and walked toward the vanity, where she sat and began to pull the pins from her hair, her back ramrod-straight as she spoke. "He did not like us to show emotion of any kind. Not happiness, for it made us too excited, and certainly not rage or fear, for that made us weak. Except I did feel, and it was a visceral ache when he left so often."

Charles approached Eleanor and helped pull the small pins from her beautiful hair.

"I missed my father when he was gone," she said quietly.

Something in Charles's chest went tight. He would need to be gone soon too, the way her father had been gone. This was the truth he had not wanted to face—the reality of the critical issue of their marriage. He would need to leave, to put the calamitous piece of his soul to rest with travel, while she remained in London, alone. He slid a pin free and gently uncoiled the length of red hair it had held in place.

"Once I asked my father to stay. The thought of him leaving again was too great." Eleanor dropped her hands from her hair and clasped them together in her lap. "He ignored me and I started crying. I begged him and he…he…"

"He what?" Charles tensed, knowing innately he would not like the answer.

"He struck me." Eleanor lowered her head. "It happened so fast…and he was so strong… Evander was sent away soon after that. The soft affection I'd once been afforded went hard and I was given a rigorous education in its place."

"He struck you?" Charles growled. If her father were still alive, Charles would strike *him*—repeatedly. Stand up for the girl who had not been able to stand up for herself.

Eleanor pressed her lips together before speaking again. "He did not have the extensive lineage my mother had, and he'd always overcompensated for his new acceptance into the nobility. He wanted us to be iron, emotionless, strong."

Charles clenched his jaw with restrained rage. He reiterated in his mind, if the former Earl of Westix were still alive Charles would kill him. To think of Eleanor being so helpless against the power of a grown man...

"The loss of love was far more painful." She turned her face up to him. "And all for treasure."

Charles's heart flinched.

"Charles..." She met his gaze in the mirror.

His stomach sank. Would she ask him to forgo his travel? "Yes?"

"What if the only way for you to get the ruby you seek is to employ the tactics they used?" Her brows pinched together. "Would you still reclaim the stone?"

He didn't respond. He couldn't. His final promise to his father had to be fulfilled. Experience had taught him that not all treasure could be legally acquired. In the past Charles had let it be—it was unnecessary to bring everything back. But the Coeur de Feu...

It was the one thing he knew he could do in his life that would have made his father proud.

"I shall endeavor to keep my morals intact," he replied slowly, diplomatically.

"And if they cannot be kept intact?" she pressed. "How great is your desire to possess the stone?"

Again, he hesitated, hating this part of himself, hating the burden of his father's dying wish.

"Did you ask Evander if you could use the key on the journal?" She resumed the task of pulling pins from her hair and unraveling her long, glossy hair.

"I didn't bring the key with me."

The pin in Eleanor's hand pinged onto the table.

"This trip was about our wedding." He put his hand to her shoulder.

"We ought to return to London soon, then." She gave him a cool glance over her shoulder. "So that you might get the key and have your journey underway. And Mother will want to know Evander is safe."

Charles said nothing. How could he when a fire burned in the pit of his stomach? Eleanor had not asked him not to leave, and yet he knew she did not want him to go. It would be on him to make the decision to stay in London, and he could not do that. Not when he was so close to redeeming himself with his father.

Except he would have to do it knowing that in making good on his father's dying wish he would be hurting the woman he cared about more than any other.

It was not only the aggravated silence between Lottie and Evander that was growing in the carriage upon their drive back to London—there was a length of silence between Eleanor and Charles as well.

Eleanor knew it to be of her own making. After all, when she'd agreed to marry him she'd known he would be going after the Coeur de Feu, no matter the cost.

Why, then, did she feel so hollow inside when she thought of him leaving?

It was more than just the possibility that he might have to employ immoral practices to get the stone. It was the idea of being left alone. *Again.* Every man in her life had left her to experience the world. She had subsisted as they'd *lived.*

And it would be happening again with Charles.

She'd anticipated that the empty feeling would dissipate, but it had only grown like a festering wound inside her, hot and red and raw with powerful emotion.

And while Eleanor had tried to convince herself that she could keep her heart guarded, its pathetic leap every time her eyes lit on his handsome face suggested otherwise. Which was why it was better to cut her emotions to the quick and rely on older, safer habits—the habits that protected her from feeling.

Finally, after a tense and interminable ride back to London, and dropping Lottie at her town house, they returned to Westix Place so that Eleanor and Charles could offer their apologies to her mother. And witness Evander's homecoming.

By the time they made their way up the steps Edmonds was already pulling the door open. He looked first in surprise at Eleanor, then glowered at Charles. But when his gaze caught on Evander his mouth fell open, and the older man could only stare before stammering out an acceptable welcome.

No sooner had they crowded into the receiving room than the Countess approached, fanning herself to ward off an apparent flash of heat. "Eleanor Susan Murray, you—"

Her mother stopped, and the fan fell from her hand and dropped to the marble floor with an audible smack. Her fingers trembled where they hung in midair before coming to rest on her partially opened mouth.

"Dear God… Evander." She blinked, and a tear rolled down her cheek. "My son."

She reached for a small table near the wall to brace herself and missed.

Evander caught her before she could fall. "Forgive me my prolonged absence, Mother."

She gave a choked sound, as if it had been wrenched from the depths of her soul, and then touched his face, her fingers shaking. "It's you. It's truly you, my sweet boy. You've come home. You're…safe."

She turned away abruptly and the room was filled with the soft gasps of her weeping.

Evander put his arm around their mother's slender shoulders. "I won't be going away again. I've accumulated enough wealth—we shall not have to worry for generations to come."

"I don't care about the fortune. My children…both of whom I'd thought lost forever…have returned."

The Countess looked to Eleanor and held one arm out to her daughter. Eleanor took her mother's hand and found herself pulled into the extremely rare embrace of her family.

She smiled at Eleanor through her tears. "I am not pleased with your decision." Her mother jabbed a glare at Charles. "But I am pleased to have you home."

Pain twisted at Eleanor's heart. Was she herself glad for her decision? Or would she come to regret it in a wash of loneliness and hurt?

The Countess pressed a kiss to each of her children's foreheads, going on tiptoe for Evander, and then pulled away. She swept at her cheeks and smoothed her immaculate blue day dress.

"Yes, well…" She sniffed. "Excuse me a moment. I must freshen up. And then we will all take tea."

Eleanor sat silent and stiff through tea, letting her mother and Evander do the talking. Charles remained at her side, equally quiet, his constant glances at her the only indication that he suspected something might be wrong.

She should tell him, and yet she could not quite work out the best way to say the words.

How could she possibly ask him to forgo the stone and stay with her in London?

Chapter Thirty

Charles was not so foolish as not to know something was amiss with Eleanor. Nor was he daft enough to wonder at the cause, when she had said it so plainly herself prior to their departure from Comlongon.

The loss of love was far more painful. And all for treasure.

He knew he should not go on his journey, and yet how could he forgo his opportunity to find peace with his father? How could he sacrifice the excitement of the world to simply stay in dreary, dull London for the rest of his life?

And love… What was love? It was not what he had felt for his father—that had been respect. Nor was it what his father had felt for him—that had been obligation. Perhaps it was what he felt for Lottie—but surely even that was sisterly affection?

He knew he enjoyed Eleanor's laughter and her smiles, that they made his heart swell when he elicited them. He knew he'd never once hesitated at the thought of traveling until he'd known her. And he knew he was frightened that he might somehow lose her.

Later, upon their arrival at Somersville House, and after a brief introduction of Eleanor to the household staff, she immediately went up to her rooms with her maid. It was then that Grimms informed Charles that Lottie had sent over a letter, in the short time he had been at Westix Place. He expected to read of Lottie's heartache, considering what had transpired between her and Westix.

Charles made his way to the library, where he firstly extracted the key from the safe and then opened Lottie's note. His heartbeat quickened with delight as he read.

It seemed Lottie had received a considerable amount of mail in the short time of their travel—all of it from mothers, and even some fathers, with daughters in the *ton* who might benefit from her instruction. She would no longer need a protector.

Smiling, he set the letter on his desk beside a bottle and pile of unopened letters.

Bottle? The smile faded from his lips.

Why the devil was there a bottle on his desk when he hadn't been home long enough to have put anything there? The last one had been thrown out with the rubbish. He'd seen to that.

But there it was, with a card dangling from its thin neck, glinting with the imprint of a compass.

This bottle was full—new. Which meant that whoever had put it there had been in the house—and most likely very recently. A shiver of warning went up Charles's spine and he felt an immediate and sudden need to ensure Eleanor was safe.

For in his gut he feared she was in danger.

Eleanor had not expected such grand rooms—though, considering the vastness of Somersville House, she ought to have known the Duchess's chambers would be glorious.

Amelia had agreed to come to Somersville House to ready the rooms when Eleanor had left for Scotland with Charles. Now she fluttered about like an excited child while she detailed every feature of her new residence.

"And the best part, if you don't mind my saying, Your Grace…" Amelia pushed at the wall. A quiet click sounded and a portion of the wall popped out to reveal a hidden door. "It leads to the Duke's chambers."

Eleanor pulled at the hidden door. It slid easily toward her on silent hinges. She looked at Amelia, who grinned and nodded toward the passage.

"Go on," Amelia said. "I believe your Duke said he'll be joining you soon."

"He did…"

Eleanor kept the trepidation from her voice. She had known that the closer they had drawn to London, the sooner Charles would be leaving. It was unfair to ask him not to go, and yet… And yet it had been impossible not to soften her heart to him even in her ire. How could she possibly do it while they lived together? Shared a bed together?

She slipped through the hidden door, which immediately clicked closed behind her. The chamber she stepped into was powerfully masculine, with heavy mahogany furniture and artifacts used in its decoration throughout. The familiar exotic spice of Charles's scent filled the room and set her pulse pounding.

A creak sounded behind her. Eleanor was startled from her thoughts and spun around.

At first she saw nothing, and then she noted where the wall had parted to reveal yet another hidden door across the room. Not the one she'd entered through.

She swallowed down a prickle of fear. Surely Charles hid behind it, in an attempt to surprise her? She pulled it open and found the passage empty. A chill crept up her spine. She frowned to herself at her childish fears and closed the door firmly.

The chill did not abate. In fact, her skin practically crawled with primal apprehension. Not silly, nor foolish, but a true and persistent warning.

She turned slowly—and choked back a scream. A man stood not more than ten feet in front of her. Not Charles, but a man she recognized nonetheless.

The Earl of Ledsey.

"Hugh...?" she managed.

He curled his lip. "I heard he'd married you. The servants talk, you know." A muscle worked in his jaw, where he clenched his teeth. "*I* could've married you."

"You have Lady Alice." She backed away from him.

"Everyone wanted her. How could I resist?" Hugh smirked. "But then you came in as an Ice Queen at the masquerade ball...and you were magnificent."

He stepped closer and Eleanor realized she had no way to back up further.

"And then *he* began sniffing around you and I *knew* you had them still."

Her mind reeled. *Had them still?* The Earl had lost his mind. She edged to the side and he followed her step in a mocking, macabre dance.

"Did you like my tulips?" he asked. "You never once even looked outside to see me there, watching you. Imagine my surprise, though, when you went to that whore's house." Hugh laughed—a scoffing, snort of a sound.

"Don't you dare call Lottie that!" Eleanor concentrated all her fear and her anger into grabbing a statue of a gold elephant and hurling it at him. The thing was heavier than she'd anticipated and veered wildly off course, before landing with a muted *thunk* on the carpet several inches from his feet.

Hugh tilted his head at this inept attack. "A whore is exactly what she is. And you're no better—married or not."

Eleanor spun on her heel and darted away from him. She'd only taken a few steps when she felt a sharp rip of pain at her scalp, and found herself wrenched backward by her hair. She gave a surprised scream and was thrown to the floor.

Hugh stood over her and placed the sole of one immaculately polished Hessian on her chest. "This will all be over soon and I'll finally have what I have needed from you since the beginning—the journals."

He drew a pistol from his jacket, then lowered it and aimed it directly at her face.

Chapter Thirty-One

Charles took the stairs two at a time and broke into a sprint on the landing, racing toward Eleanor's rooms, where he bolted through the door.

Her maid shrieked and dropped the ivory-handled brush she held. At least she hadn't thrown it.

"Did you hear that?" Charles asked. "A heavy thud."

The maid shook her head.

"Where is she?" he demanded.

"N-next door, in your room."

Charles ran back into the hall and found his own door locked from within.

His heart was sucked into his throat.

He darted back into Eleanor's room, not stopping until he was at the concealed door.

Amelia followed behind him. "Your Grace...?"

He threw open Eleanor's secret door, then his, and stopped.

Lord Ledsey stood on the opposite side of the large bed, looking down at something Charles could not see.

What the devil was Ledsey doing in his chambers? The Lord's attention snapped to Charles. "Come any closer and I'll kill her."

Her.

Eleanor.

Dear God, no.

The maid's gasp sounded behind him, followed by the pattering of her footsteps over thick carpet. She had evidently made the same assumption as him, and would surely be going for help.

Ledsey nodded at Charles. "Close the door and lock it behind you."

Charles hesitated. He didn't want to close the door, or lock it. He wanted to spring across the room like a savage lion so he could tear the blackguard's throat out and ensure Eleanor was safe.

But he was no lion. He was only a man, helplessly standing too damned far away to protect her.

"Do not test my patience, *Your Grace*." Ledsey sneered out the title. "Close the door."

Charles pushed the secret door closed, but did not lock it, and hoped Ledsey would not notice. Charles put his hands up in surrender and moved deeper into the room.

"What is the meaning of this, Ledsey?"

He was nearly around the bed when his gaze fell on the splash of vibrant red hair against the blue carpet and the glint of the pistol held in Ledsey's grip.

Anger erupted through Charles with brilliant intensity. "Let her go."

He stalked around the bed and drew to an abrupt halt when he came to Eleanor, lying with her back against the thick carpet, rigid and stiff.

Eleanor. His wife.

A panicked jolt shot through his heart. He could not lose her. He *would not* lose her.

"I want the journals. And the key." Ledsey's stare flicked to Eleanor, but he did not appear nervous, merely watchful.

Charles had opened his mouth to reply when Eleanor spoke.

"You couldn't have known about the journals…or the key…unless…" She gasped.

The realization slammed into Charles at exactly the same moment. "It was you who drugged me that night. You took the journals. You put that bottle—"

Ledsey smirked. "Yes, it was me. The previous Duke made it so easy, with all these passages and hidden rooms. I was able to wait for you to fall asleep, then I crept in and took them. Clever of you, though, hiding the key."

"How do you even *know* about the journals?" Eleanor's voice was sharp with demand—certainly not the voice of a woman being held at gunpoint.

"How do I know about them?" Ledsey stared incredulously down at her. "My father was in the Adventure Club. He's the one who found most of the artifacts. Your fathers took them from him. They basked in public adoration while he was relegated to the shadows."

His upper lip curled back in disgust.

"Who do you think wrote about their misdeeds? He told me about the journals, about the Coeur de Feu, but I didn't know about the key." His face twisted wryly. "He must have written the journals and made the key on his last trip to India, just before he died."

Charles didn't answer. In truth, the names of the members of the Adventure Club were kept anonymous, with the exception of his and Eleanor's fathers. The other members hadn't been as wealthy, as famous or as influential, and clearly their names had faded, leaving no connection to the acquired accomplishments.

"The Duchess and I have recently learned the sordid details of those discoveries," Charles answered. "But sinking to this level, where you are threatening a woman, will never elevate your standing with anyone. Least of all me."

"I want the Coeur de Feu." Sweat was beginning to bead on Ledsey's brow.

"You can have it."

Charles reached into his jacket to claim the key without

thought. Damn the journal, damn the key, and damn his promise to his father. Eleanor. She was all that mattered. His wife. The woman he loved.

"No!" Eleanor said sharply. She kicked her foot out at Ledsey, catching him in the shin. The blow sufficed to knock him back half a step.

Ledsey grunted in pain and again pointed the gun down at Eleanor. "It would appear I need to ensure I'm taken more seriously."

His arm tensed and the gun went off.

An extreme pressure slammed into Eleanor's arm and she was vaguely aware of a salty taste in her mouth. An acrid odor hung in the air, stinging her eyes. Her ears rang with the explosion and Charles's voice bellowed in the distance—outraged, horrified, undecipherable.

She pushed up and nearly fell to her right. Her arm seemed somehow inoperable. The room swirled around her. She looked down to where an ache blazed with insistent pain. Blood bloomed like a violent flower over the pale pink of her sleeve and spattered the rest of her gown.

Blood?

Her mind reeled with confusion at the dark, bloody hole in her upper arm.

When did that happen?

Her heartbeat throbbed too fast. Her breath was too shallow. Her lips tingled.

Charles lunged forward, moving as if very slowly, but before he could reach her, a heavy object landed by her feet. A pistol, with a stream of smoke still curling up from its barrel.

And yet hard metal jabbed into Eleanor's temple, shoving her head savagely to the right.

"If you come any closer I'll shoot her in the head this time."

Hugh's voice.

Suddenly it all rushed back to her and dislodged the addled freeze of her brain. Hugh was holding her hostage, demanding the journals and key, claiming them to be his father's. And he'd shot her.

He'd *shot* her.

Her mouth was dry. She tried to swallow and found her throat stuck against itself rather than finding relief.

Blood soaked through her dress, intensely opaque and red against the gentle pink. The agony of it rushed through her arm, blazing.

Charles stared at her, his eyes wide, his face completely white as if he'd been shot as well.

"Good thing I loaded a second gun," Hugh said in a mocking tone.

Pain mingled with the metallic taste of fear and left her stomach whirling with nausea. The barrel of the pistol dug into her scalp, forcing her to crane her neck. Emotion clogged her throat, but she kept herself from crying out.

"Give me the journals and the key," Hugh demanded.

"Don't hurt her." There was pleading in the strength of Charles's voice. "I swear to God if you hurt her, I will kill you."

"The journals and the key," Hugh repeated.

Charles set the key on the ground and withdrew the journals from the trunk he'd had in Scotland.

A ball of frustration welled in the back of Eleanor's throat. She knew what those journals meant to Charles. He was sacrificing them, sacrificing the fulfillment of his father's wish—*everything*—for her.

The dam in her heart holding back her emotion broke then, and overwhelmed her with the very truth she'd been trying to ignore for far too long.

No matter how desperately she tried to deny it, or to

shield herself from the truth, she loved Charles. She loved him with every nook and cranny of her heart.

Charles shoved the stack of books toward Hugh. "Let her go."

Hugh didn't reach for the journals. Instead he pushed the pistol barrel harder into her head.

A cry rasped from Eleanor's throat despite her attempt to maintain her composure.

"Do you truly think I'd let you both live after this?"

Hugh's feet were so close to Eleanor they pressed against her thigh where she sat in a daze on the floor. Panic raced through her. They couldn't die. Not now. Not like this.

She put the hand of her good arm to her brow, as if mopping the layer of sweat there, then drove her elbow down with all the strength she could muster.

It connected sharply with the side of Hugh's knee, exactly where she'd intended to strike. Her aim had been true and Hugh's legs folded against themselves as he fell to the ground with a shout.

Charles did not hesitate. He ran at Hugh and kicked him square in the face. The sound was hollow and wet, like a melon breaking against a hard surface. Then Charles bent and retrieved the gun before dropping to Eleanor's side.

He gathered her in his arms and the pulse of pain splintered into mindless agony. The world swam in a wavering light in front of her, threatening to pull her under.

"Eleanor..." There was alarm in his voice, a quivering pitch she'd thought never to hear from a man as brave and strong as Charles.

She was of a mind to answer him, to tell him she was fine and cry out at what he'd sacrificed to save her. And she wanted to tell him that she loved him, more than life itself.

But her voice did not correspond with her mouth any longer. An intense fatigue washed over her and left her with a thick and lazy sensation.

"Eleanor." Charles caught her face in his palms and stared down at her with wild eyes. "Please. I love you."

I love you.

The words floated above her pain and smoothed over her heart like a balm.

"Don't leave me." Charles stroked her face, his eyes red-rimmed.

Tears leaked from her eyes at his admission, and her heart gave a weak flutter. The room began to fade.

"Please," he begged. "Focus."

Yes, focus.

She squinted her eyes at him and did exactly as he bade. Her thoughts centered on watching him, on resisting the urge to succumb to the sweet lure of oblivion, on wanting him to say he loved her again and again and again.

A shadow rose over them and Charles's head snapped to the side. He collapsed to the ground the way a marionette might do if its cords had been cut. Eleanor fell to the ground too, and pain shone bright anew.

Helpless, she could only watch as Hugh bent over Charles and grabbed the gun. Charles did not stir. The darkness pressed around Eleanor. She tried to blink it away. She had to do something. She had to help.

There came a loud crack at the opposite side of the room. Still Charles did not move.

"Halt!" The voice was authoritative, coming from where Eleanor could not see. "Put the gun down, my lord, or we will have no option but to use force."

In answer, Hugh raised the gun, pointing it at Charles's face.

The fog of exhaustion dissipated for a brief moment.

No. Not Charles.

Eleanor struggled to stand, drawing from a waning well of strength. Black dots swam in her vision and her body went limp. She fell to the ground, only vaguely aware of the agony in her arm when the hurt in her heart was so great. Too weak to even save Charles.

The pounding of footsteps thundered for only a scant second before the popping of gunfire filled Eleanor's ears and she could no longer fight the pull of darkness.

Chapter Thirty-Two

Charles's head throbbed with pain and his ears shrilled with a high-pitched whine.

A sharp scent hung in the air—thick and unpleasant and redolent of gunfire. He tried to turn his face from the odor, but his scalp screamed in protest. He blinked his eyes open and found Ledsey lying on the ground beside him, holding something wet with blood, his face twisted in agony.

Footsteps and shouts came from nearby, distorted as if Charles were listening underwater. Men appeared around and over him. One in particular pointed next to Charles's head.

"You've got the angels on your side, Your Grace," the man said. "That bullet was meant for your head."

Despite the pain of doing so, Charles turned his head and found a scorched hole in the carpet, directly in front of his face.

"Come along, my lord."

Another voice spoke this time, followed by an anguished scream from Ledsey.

Charles looked up in time to see Hugh being led from the room, with a mangled hand clutched against his chest. Only when he was gone did Charles see Eleanor, lying on the ground.

The whole world faded away, leaving only the horrific sight of his wife in a pool of blood.

A man appeared in front of him, reaching down to help him to his feet. Charles leapt up on his own and ignored the way the world tilted. He had to make his way to Eleanor, to confirm she was not…

He couldn't even think the word. Not when it made his insides blaze with incomprehensible loss.

Eleanor, his beautiful wife, with all her boldness of character, so passionate and vivid in his life and in his heart. He couldn't lose her.

He staggered to her and dropped to the floor at her side.

She lay unmoving, her face pale.

"Eleanor?" Her name caught in the tightness of his throat.

She wouldn't answer him—he knew that in his soul. The massive puddle of blood welling under her told him all he needed to know, all he hated to acknowledge: she had lost far too much blood. Surely one couldn't lose so much blood and…?

But she couldn't be…

Surely she wasn't truly…?

He couldn't even think properly.

It wasn't possible. Not when they had just started their lives together. Not when he loved her.

The well of agony burst in his chest and became so damn unbearable his vision blurred.

"Eleanor…" he said again, unable to stop himself.

Only this time when she did not answer he felt a visceral crack as his heart broke.

A man bent over her and attempted to gather her in his arms.

"Stop." Charles glared at the man. "I will have your skin if you touch her again."

The man gave an efficient nod. "Forgive me, Your

Grace. But I'm an officer, aye? You must understand we need to make her comfortable. The physician was summoned when we were called and he needs to see to her."

Charles stared at him dumbly. "I…" He cleared the knot from his throat. "I beg your pardon?"

"Your Grace, please."

"You mean, she's…?"

The man nodded. "Alive. Please, Your Grace."

Charles backed away quickly and nodded, nearly choking on his relief. He would do anything in his power to ensure Eleanor lived. Anything.

The man lifted her easily, minding to hold her arm over her chest, so it did not dangle and cause further injury. Charles tried to get to his feet once more and stumbled, his legs too weak to support him. But he had to follow Eleanor. He had to make sure she would truly be all right.

Eleanor—his Eleanor. His love.

Thomas appeared at Charles's side. "Let me help you, Your Grace." He clasped Charles at his elbow and pulled an arm over his shoulder.

Charles managed to stand upright, albeit a bit wobbly. The world swirled in a dizzy rush around him, but Thomas's hold did not relax and he managed to keep him solidly in place.

"Give it a moment, Your Grace. You took quite a knock to your head."

"Eleanor—" Charles gritted out.

"The physician is seeing to her." Thomas guided Charles to a chair beside the fire.

Charles pushed against his valet's hold, forcing them both to move back to the secret door connecting the rooms. "I must go to her."

Thomas shifted direction once more. "After you sit for a moment. Please, Your Grace."

The room swirled and Charles's knees buckled, nearly

sending him to the floor. "Very well, but for a moment only."

He sank into the chair and sat until the room ceased its spinning and his breath was sufficiently restored. Until he could take the waiting no longer.

Charles pushed to his feet and walked on his own across the room, with Thomas hovering like an anxious hen at his side.

Amelia appeared in the doorway, her face drawn. She twisted a hand in her skirts. "You can't come in, Your Grace. The physician is with her. Thank Heavens the servants summoned him at the same time they went for the Watch when I told them. Or else..." Her eyes welled with tears.

"By God, I *will* see my wife." It took all he had in him not to roar at poor Amelia, who already appeared quite ready to drop.

She chewed on her lower lip.

"I want only to be with my wife." Charles spoke with a gentleness the urgency raking through him did not warrant. By God, he wanted to see Eleanor, and no man or woman would stop him. "Please. I love her."

Amelia's face softened and she put her hands over her chest. "I'm sure the physician would not complain if you remain quietly to the side."

She stepped back and allowed Charles to enter the room. The door clicked closed behind him, shut by either Amelia or Thomas, and Charles was left in the silent room, where a physician bent over the bed against the opposite wall.

"I assumed I'd be seeing you." The older man's voice grated out.

Charles approached the bed where Eleanor lay, unmoving and pale. His heart sank lower than it had ever fallen.

He had expected...what? That she would be awake? Speaking?

"The bullet passed straight through." The physician spoke as he wound cloth carefully around Eleanor's arm, where the fabric of her sleeve had been cut away. "We are fortunate for that."

"And she will recover?" Charles's throat was so tight he could barely force the words out.

The aging man looked at him from behind wire-rimmed spectacles. "Her Grace will need rest, but she will recover. I recommend broth to strengthen her and laudanum for the pain." He indicated a clear bottle on the bedside table. "The healing will be more uncomfortable than a lady can bear."

"I think you underestimate my wife," Charles said.

After all, Eleanor was no ordinary lady. In the face of danger she'd first kicked Ledsey, in an attempt to keep the journals from him, and then had knocked him to the ground when he'd rounded on Charles to shoot him.

Had she not been given to such bravery Charles might very well be dead. Certainly the officers would have been seconds too late to see him saved. No, Eleanor was not an ordinary woman at all.

Her eyes blinked open and met his. The corners of her lips drew up in a soft smile and his heart soared with relief.

The concern on the doctor's face faded and his wrinkles pulled back in an affable expression. "I think she will recover quite nicely, Your Grace."

With that, he gave a bow and left the room, leaving Eleanor and Charles alone.

"Charles…" She opened her eyes fully and pushed against the bedcovers, as if trying to sit further upright.

"Please stay where you are." He rushed to her side and stopped short.

Her skin almost perfectly matched the white sheets of the bed, but the sharp brilliance in her eyes remained. Even tired and battered, she was the loveliest sight he'd ever seen.

An ache returned in the back of Charles's throat. "Eleanor."

Her gaze went glossy. "Charles. I thought he'd killed you." A tear slid down her cheek. "I thought I'd lost you."

"I thought I'd lost you, too, Eleanor." He knelt at her bedside and took the hand of her uninjured arm. "My God, woman, I love you."

She drew in a sharp breath and squeezed his hand.

"I do." He kissed her knuckles. "For your bravery and your warmth and your incredible passion."

"I love you, too," she whispered. "I thought I'd lost you, that I'd never see you again or have you in my life."

"You have me." Charles eased up onto the bed. "It is why I've made the decision I have."

He took a deep breath and said the words he knew had to be said. For the sake of keeping her, of loving her.

"I will not be going after the Coeur de Feu. Never again will I do anything that means I might lose you."

Eleanor jerked as though she'd been struck. For surely she had. After everything Charles had done to get the journals—everything he'd sacrificed in the pursuit of his father's dying wish—no, he could not give it up. Not for her.

"Charles, no."

He shook his head, his face lined with concern. "I cannot risk losing you again. I do not want to be separated from you for months, sometimes years at a time, any more than I want to abandon you the way our fathers did us."

"Perhaps there is a way you can fulfill your promise and have me at your side." She smiled coyly up at him.

His brow furrowed and then smoothed as understanding dawned on him. "Surely you don't mean—"

"That I join you?" Her heart raced a little faster at her own bold decision. "Of course I do."

He frowned and opened his mouth, but she began speaking again before he could protest.

"I have read the journals, Charles. And in them I found a taste of a life I've never known. Excitement and adventure unlike anything London can provide. I confess I loathed the idea of being here by myself while you traveled, but I realized that was because I envied you the opportunity to see the world."

Charles leaned closer and the bed creaked beneath them. "It isn't always safe, Eleanor, nor clean or hospitable."

"I'm a Murray who has married a Pemberton." She lifted her head with pride. "Adventure surely runs in my veins."

"You certainly can hold your own. You never told me you were an accomplished bruiser."

He smiled and his eyes crinkled at the corners in that way she loved.

His gaze flicked toward her bandaged arm. "Will you agree to wait until your arm is healed?"

"Of course."

She kept her voice even, but her pulse thrummed wildly in her veins at the prospect. Imagine! Witnessing the world herself, sampling its cuisines, meeting its people. And, though she knew she shouldn't care, she couldn't help but wonder if her father would have been proud.

"Though I will demand a higher moral integrity than our fathers had," she said resolutely.

Charles nodded. "I would never do anything to compromise us the way our fathers did. Even for the stone." He searched her face with his beautiful blue gaze. "I've learned there is so much more to life than treasure."

Tears tingled in Eleanor's eyes. He truly did love her. She blinked her emotion away. "We cannot go anywhere if we do not know where we're going." She grinned up at him.

"Shall we examine the journals with the key?" Charles asked with a twinkle in his eye.

"Yes!" It came out far louder than she'd anticipated.

"It's driving you mad, is it?" He laughed, the rapscallion, and then called for Thomas to bring them the journals and key. "I confess I'm eager to know as well."

Eleanor wriggled in her bed to sit higher up, for a better position to view the journals, and tried to ignore the sharpness of discomfort in her arm.

Thomas did not leave them waiting long, and brought the three remaining battered books to the bedside. He passed them crisply to Charles and left them alone in the room once more.

Charles took the flat piece of metal and opened the first page of the first journal. It held no information. The second journal, however, revealed squares that fit neatly in spaces with no writing. This appeared several times until about the seventh page, when the holes matched perfectly over a series of letters.

Eleanor held her breath and tensed. Those letters formed words.

DECCAN PLATEAU CLIFFSIDE ON R

Charles drew the key up and turned the page.

"Do you know where that is?" Eleanor asked.

"I do. It's in India. I've even been there once." He put the key to the second page.

IVER WAGHUR WHERE THERE IS A U

Charles shifted the key to the opposing page. Again and again he did this, until the entire message had been spelled out.

*Deccan Plateau cliffside on River Waghur
Where there is a U-shaped gorge*

A door will open to a large room
Seek the hollow stone

Eleanor's heart raced faster and pulsed in the injury of her arm. "Charles, this is it."

"It might be. There has been much speculation for years on what became of the stone. This is one of many assumptions."

But even as he spoke with such skepticism, his eyes were alight with the joy of their discovery.

"We've deciphered the code! Charles, we did it." She flushed with their accomplishment.

"Indeed we have." He folded the key into the journal. "And it couldn't have been done without us working together. I think we make a fine Adventure Club on our own."

A pleased blush warmed Eleanor's cheeks at his praise. "That we do. Do we leave soon?"

His brows rose. "When you're well."

"I could heal on the boat while we journey." She beamed up at him in the way she knew he liked.

He chuckled and shook his head. "You truly were born an adventurer, my Duchess."

Epilogue

Deccan Plateau, ten months later

A trickle of sweat ran down Eleanor's back and the heavy fabric of her skirt continued to catch at the brush. The oppressive heat was ubiquitous, pressing and suffocating. Loose tendrils slipped from the knot of her hair and were left to curl about her damp face.

Mad though it might seem, never had Eleanor been happier than when she was hiking through the wilds of India with Charles at her side while they followed their guide. The young boy was named Sahil, and he had a mop of dark hair perpetually falling into his soulful brown eyes.

Every day took them on a new adventure. Even if they had not yet discovered the Coeur de Feu, she was happy to continue to search every inch of India to find it.

At present they were staying in the opulent rooms of an Indian inn decorated with lights that shone through cut sheets of fashioned metal. They ate food spiced with flavors that tingled on Eleanor's tongue, and they slept and loved on a bed heaped with pillows and felt decadently colored silks against their bare skin.

Charles's hand found hers and he threaded his fingers between her own. He moved through the mass of twisting vines and overgrown trees without pause, his confidence evident in the ease of his stride. This was the element in which her husband thrived.

He smiled at her, his teeth a flash of white against his tanned skin, which had become all the more golden in these past two months of their searching.

"Why are you grinning at me like that?" she asked, smiling in return in spite of herself.

"Because you're lovely."

Eleanor self-consciously brushed at the sweat-slick curls plastered to her face. She was quite sure she was *not* lovely, with her cheeks flushed beneath a new smattering of freckles and spots of perspiration darkening her dress.

"I fear you may have touched some poisonous plant." She slid him a glance. "You're delusional."

Charles chuckled. "It's no poison, my Duchess. You are the most beautiful woman in this entire jungle."

Eleanor laughed at that—a clear, bright sound that carried unabashedly around them. And she didn't give a fig that it wasn't a bit ladylike. "I believe I am the *only* woman in this jungle at present."

"Yes, but you're the loveliest woman no matter where we go." He stopped and gave her an appreciative glance over. "By God, you make me a happy man, Eleanor."

Sahil appeared behind them suddenly and began speaking rapidly. Eleanor had only just begun to learn the exotic language but managed to recognize the words for *cave* and *near*.

He pulled at Charles's sleeve and then ran forward into a deeper portion of the jungle.

Charles glanced back at Eleanor and his blue eyes flashed. "I think this is it."

Together they followed the boy, their pace fast despite the thickness of growth.

Sahil gave an excited squeal and leapt into the air. *"Ya-haan."* He pointed vigorously. *"Yahaan."*

Here.

Charles moved forward and pulled at the vines covering the bulk in front of them. They fell away to reveal a wall of rough-hewn stone. Eleanor's pulse quickened. Perhaps this truly was it.

Charles pulled a flat metal bar from his pack, slid it into a crack at the side of the stone and pulled with all his strength. It gave with a grinding, popping sound and slowly slid open. The sound echoed within, indicating a large, empty depth.

"It's a chamber," Charles said excitedly, and stuck his head inside. The air whooshed out from his lungs as he pulled Eleanor to his side.

She stared into the vast darkness with awe. There, lit by a sliver of sunlight, was a vast room lined with columns along either side and a massive structure toward the back. Clumps of color showed on the columns.

"Go in," Charles encouraged. "I'll ready the torch."

Eleanor shook her head. "We go in together."

He smiled proudly at her and captured her hand in his. "I've never been so eager to see a discovery in all my life."

"It is the Coeur de Feu," Eleanor said with a lift of her brows.

He shook his head and stared down at her in wonder. "No, it's you. It's us. I've never had someone to share this with before. You give this experience a power and excitement it never before possessed."

Eleanor found herself blushing "Shall we?" she asked.

Together they entered, and bore witness to the remnants of colorful paintings along the columns, where colors were still recognizable as gold and russet and white and blue. The ceiling arched high overhead and echoed their scraping footsteps back at them.

An intense feeling of reverence fell over Eleanor. For what care must have been placed in creating such a structure, what love and time spent on each carefully sculptured and painted bit of wall.

Charles gazed at the splendor before them. "Our fathers would have wanted to break this room into pieces and transport it back to London."

Eleanor regarded him and his thoughtful expression. "And what will *we* do?"

"My father wanted the stone, not the chamber." Charles took her hand in his and kissed her knuckles. "And I believe this is where true adventure lies. To know of its existence, to experience it, and to leave it for future generations to enjoy in its entirety. I think our fathers never understood as much."

"I am grateful that we do."

"As am I, my love. As am I."

He tilted her head upward for a kiss. His lips were salty and warm and completely enjoyable. A low pulse of longing hummed between her legs and she found herself looking forward to their return to their room.

He must have been of the same mind, for his tongue dipped into her mouth and brushed hers.

Eleanor pulled away slightly. "If you continue to kiss me thus I do not know that I can wait for our return to the hotel," she whispered, even though she knew Sahil did not speak English.

"That may result in bug bites in unfortunate locations." Charles grimaced comically and began rapping on the stone, in search of the Coeur de Feu's hidden location.

Eleanor chuckled and knocked on a piece of stonework herself. They all worked thus, including Sahil, gently thumping at every sound piece within the room. Until at long last Eleanor's raw knuckles struck against a particular square of stone behind one of the many columns. Its hollow sound echoed within and rang out against the high ceiling.

"Charles." Before she had even completely got his name out he was beside her, kneeling and studying the piece. "Do you think this is it?" she breathed.

Sahil appeared with the torch, his large dark eyes fixed with fascinated wonder on the square.

"We can but hope."

He put the edge of a pick to the stone and gently tapped it with the hammer. A crack showed immediately. He hit it a second time and a corner crumbled inward. A third careful blow created a fist-sized hole.

Charles lowered the tools and reached in, his eyes narrowed in concentration. His face cleared, and a smile stretched over his mouth. He drew his dusty hand from the hole, revealing a massive red stone clutched between his fingers.

The ruby glinted in the torchlight, despite the coating of dust atop it, and sent sparks of color dancing around the walls of the cave.

They had found it. Together. The Coeur de Feu.

"Be careful, Eleanor. Nothing will melt an Ice Queen like the heart of a fire." Charles winked at her.

She closed her hand over his and kissed him. "I think you mean the heart of a duke."

* * * * *